KAITLYN BANKSON

A Man of Silence

First published by Kaitlyn Bankson 2025

Copyright © 2025 by Kaitlyn Bankson

This novel is entirely a work of fiction. The names, characters and incidents portrayed in it are the work of the author's imagination. Any resemblance to actual persons, living or dead, events or localities is entirely coincidental.

Second edition

ISBN (paperback): 979-8-9940905-4-1
ISBN (hardcover): 979-8-9940905-7-2

This book was professionally typeset on Reedsy.
Find out more at reedsy.com

Contents

I

PART ONE

CHAPTER I

Mary held onto the solid oak doors. Chips of old wood fell from them when she gripped her little fingers around the pockmarked edges. She had always been fascinated by the monastery, and now she was peering into its stained glass belly.

Entering the cross-shaped part, she passed under the rood, startled by her own shadow even though she was already eleven and no longer afraid of monsters under her bed. Still, the air was stale in here and the dark limestone walls made the belly so dark.

There were four-foot-tall tapestries of men who fight for the Good. The monastery echoes this cry to be humbled, frightened, and awed by something "other." Mary's soul feels unquiet, as if there was a certain level of anxiety bubbling up from below. She looked up at the Mother Mary draped in blue and holding onto her child, Jesus. And beneath her is the Man himself hanging from the cross—nails pounded into His flesh. His head crowned in thorns fell over to the right shoulder. Mary watched other people bending down on their knees to release somehow the guilt that they have found gripping their hearts. She felt small and disgusting standing there underneath such depicted sorrows.

For a long while, Mary stood in front of the altar, studying the bleeding wounds of Christ until the fear and agony no longer held her interest. Her taste for the macabre started young when she was first told by the preacher that she was born with the original sin Jesus took away. But before His sacrifice, she was born filthy, destined to mess up in many ways. Mary was told to grovel at the feet of the Lord who saved her from even more suffering upon this earth, even though she was not really sure why she should feel guilty before she had done anything wrong. In fact, life had been good to her, and she was happy. She never felt sinful before. Rather, she felt free. Yet, here in this monastery, she was made to feel ugly for the first time in her life.

Trying to escape the uncomfortable feelings the space brought out, Mary often enjoyed hiding herself among the small cruxes of the monastery, usually where there were little enclaves off the side to pray. Sinking down on the burgundy velvet cushion, Mary kneeled like the other people she had seen, waiting for some kind of sign. But nothing ever came.

She got up with a child's fervor and ran down the south aisle of the interior, her footsteps echoing quite loudly for such a small-framed girl. But Mary came to a halting stop, covering her hand over her mouth to scream when she suddenly came face-to-face with a grotesque-looking gargoyle. It sat atop a column staring straight at her with its lolling tongue and grinning mouth full of sharp teeth and eyes that resembled a cat's. Her nerves twisted even tighter when she breathed in the musty cloud that another person had recently kicked up from the floor.

It was so hard to see through the cloud of dust that Mary felt trapped, trapped in this large place that was so cold and dark it made her heart freeze. Still, to scream out in that place was probably the most embarrassing thing she could imagine doing. No one made a sound in there. Surely, if she screamed at all, she would be beaten by one of the monks.

The monks there all looked the same: they all wore white robes, many of them with a black scapular over their habits; they were all men who were bald or balding; most of them had the palest of skin; and most of them wore glasses. Mary could tell if a monk was approaching simply from the sound of their footsteps, which were always slow and measured. Even the old people visiting the monastery never walked as slowly as these monks.

They were frightening people to young Mary, for they always had a serious look on their faces and wrinkles that formed around their brows from all the contemplating they did here in this tomb.

Someday, maybe when she was older, she would come to understand what it was they were always contemplating. What exactly were they looking for? she wondered. For now, Mary scurried off away from the scary gargoyle to the other side of the nave to look at the rood screen. The screen was made of wood and was intricately carved, so intricate that it must have taken a million years to carve out all of those parts, Mary thought. Her parents told her that in the Middle Ages, the carved wooden screen would separate the altar and choir from the nave. It was the separation between the outside pilgrims wandering around and the inner space of true worship.

The altar where Mary and Jesus hung was the most sacred place in the monastery. Oh, how Mary longed to reach up and touch Jesus's wounded foot to see if some of the magic would rub off on her. But those items were too high for her to reach, plus she knew a monk would catch her in the act in an instant, so to compensate, she turned to touch the pews, the cushions, and the pillars of the monastery instead.

She pretended that the armchair-carved animals were her pets and that the portraits could hear her when she spoke to them. The monastery began to feel like a living, breathing thing. To Mary, the most gorgeous part of the place was the stained glass rose window at the center of it all. The circular eye illuminated the inside of the otherwise dark stone walls brilliantly with its red and blues. The limestone pillars absorbed the light that came from every sunrise and sunset. Every new day brought with it a rainbow of colors for the monks to glorify. Living here must make it easy to find beauty in every corner, thought Mary, as she turned back around to figure out where her parents went.

She turned down another aisle in the nave and stopped before completely passing by another image of Jesus crying, memorialized by stained glass, with His ribs sticking out of His sallow flesh. Beside him were Mary and Joseph crying for their sacrificed son as all the others gazed up into the Heavens for Jesus's salvation. The gold paint and stained glass relate to the other stories of the Bible and all of them say, "You, child, are dirty." Mary's own bones told her that.

She had experienced this feeling before after attending church one day. Her parents went to a Protestant church where its congregation only went Sundays, sang some songs, greeted one another with their "peace be with yous," and then forgot about godliness until the next Sunday morning. But even in this looser world of religion, there was the art and the songs and the sermons that told Mary she was dirty. Songs hit her especially hard because the melody opened her heart up while the words gutted her. One day after church, Mary remembered going to take a bath and trying to scrub her own skin off with her mother's loofah. Unfortunately, it only irritated her skin, and she did not deglove any of it as planned.

That day in the tub, Mary looked at her own skin in a new light. She did not have sickly, yellow skin like the Man depicted on all the walls. She could not discover what caused her to shiver when the blood of Christ fell on her from the sky above. Her flesh was innocent and new, but Christ's was not. Churchgoing was growing into more of a burden for Mary as she grew older and began to understand the words of the songs she was singing and the prayers she was miming.

How many of the people in her church were true believers? How many were sincere? The questions remained in her head even now as she walked around the hall of this enormous monastery. Mary's parents were here visiting with their church community to see if they could assist in their apple orchards and gardens over the spring. Her parents always thought that community was the best part of being with a church.

Pushing the imposing oak doors open, Mary found her parents outside, talking with a group of monks and other church members. They all smiled and laughed in the sunlight. The grass never looked so green after emerging from that dark abyss of the monastery. If I was a monk, I'd live outside all day, Mary thought, skipping down the stairs and running toward her family.

"Hey, there darlin'," said one of the church members. He rubbed her head too roughly and Mary ducked down to avoid his hand. One of the monks saw the aversion and said, "You must respect your elders, you know."

Mary wanted to defend herself, but the monks all seemed so imposing that she decided against saying anything at all. Only a slight pout of the lip would do.

The outside of the monastery commanded praise for its height alone. How could people have made such an intricate and heavenly building? Did the power of religion give them superhuman abilities? Mary squinted, trying to look up to see the pinnacles of the tower, but the sun would not let her. The furthest up she could see was where the rose window was in its multi-colored glory. A bit below the window stood the entrance doorway with an elaborate Creation scene carved into the limestone edges. The lower columns surrounding the entrance adorned two gargoyles which appeared much less intimidating in direct sunlight. Still, Mary found them cruel and devious creatures, to which she felt the need to stick her tongue out at them in protest.

As soon as her tongue popped out of her head, a monk appeared in front of her.

"Children of God do not make vulgar faces to match the gargoyles. Besides, gargoyles are often misunderstood creatures. They are there to ward off any evil spirits from the church while also serving the practical purpose of directing rainwater away from the church. You see, the French word for gargoyle is actually *gargouille* meaning "throat." They are downspouts where the rain comes out through their throats. See? Now, do you think they deserve your disdain, little one?"

Mary had never been given a history lesson while being scolded before. She was so in shock and embarrassed that she turned and hid behind her mother like a child, never answering the monk in return.

"I am so sorry. I will make sure my daughter never does

something like that again. She knows better than that and I have no idea where her tongue went now," said Mary's mother.

"Perhaps she swallowed it," laughed her father.

"Children of God are quick learners, I think she realized the wrong she has done," answered one of the other older monks.

"Let's go back to the gardening, shall we?" said one of the church members. She was a little old lady with the permed white hair that every old woman seemed to don. Her back bent over like a candy cane and Mary was unsure how she could do anything to help with the monastery's garden.

The adults continued their idle chatter while Mary wandered off again. She found herself constantly waiting, bored stiff, by the church community. She should have known better than to believe that this meeting would only take an hour. Before the adults knew it, the sun would set without even having figured out a schedule to meet for the gardening work.

With a deep sigh, Mary walked away, trying not to bring down any more monks on her head. She decided to see the monastery's garden for herself. It must be around here somewhere..., she thought. Walking all the way around the building, right by its side, was a stairway that descended slightly into the magnificent garden.

Upon descending the stairs, the very first thing that Mary saw was a bamboo gate separating her from the rest of the garden. She pushed it open with ease and saw a koi pond tucked away to her left. The little fish swam vigorously without ruining the silence of the brilliant garden. She watched their vibrant orange bodies dart underneath the very surface of the water, their little mouths gaping and closing in unison. Coming closer, she squatted down on the stones surrounding the little pond and formed a shadow over the water, scaring all the koi fish away.

"Oh, sorry, little ones, I didn't mean to scare you," Mary said, quickly backing away from the stone ledge. The fish resumed swimming where her once black shadow had been moments ago.

"That was very kind of you," said a voice behind Mary. Mary swiveled around on her feet at the sound that cut through the silence. It was one of them—a monk. But he looked young and had his hair and did not have glasses. In fact, Mary may have even thought he was handsome for being a monk.

"I really didn't mean to scare them. I just wanted a closer look. It's not every day that you get to see fish," Mary said, feeling silly as she said it. She backed up a little in order to resume her exploration through the garden and end whatever conversation this may turn into between herself and this monk.

She turned right, away from the monk who stood looking at the fish, and walked down a little path of stepping stones that were surrounded by moss. They led her past a beautiful row of trees and she could see in the distance a rose garden laid out next to the kitchen garden and other herbs being grown further away. Mary decided she would get to those after she distanced herself from the monk.

The stones led her directly to what looked like a little hut. Even though she was eleven, Mary still pretended that the stones beneath her feet were the only safe spots while the rest of the ground was hot lava that she had to avoid. So, she jumped from stone to stone rather ungracefully and, in an irreligious fashion, pulled open the door to the hut.

Inside was nearly empty. There were these beige mats on the floor, a couple of small tables, and a biblical quote hanging on the wall. Why was there an empty hut here off to the right side of the garden? Mary walked back outside and found a plaque hanging by the door that she had missed earlier. It said, "In Memory of Father Dominic, 1849-1923. Thank you for your service to the Lord and for glorifying Him with this Tearoom."

So, this was a bit of the Eastern flavor mixed in with the Western tradition, Mary thought, how strange. Mary went back inside searching for a teapot and cups, but everything must have been locked up in the chest that sat there in the room. A naturally curious person, she decided to go over and see if the chest was actually locked. To her surprise, the lid opened and a beautiful cast iron teapot sat there surrounded by four little cups without handles. She dove right in to pick up one of the cups, but before she could even touch it that blasted monk from the pond said, "Please don't touch that. The tearoom is only used at a certain time of the day and everything must remain pure for the ceremony. We rinse everything with fresh well water before we even begin such a sacred ritual."

Mary stood there horrified that she had been caught doing something dirty, naughty, daring. She had tried to touch something that was not hers. She felt the same knot in her stomach that she felt in the monastery when she watched Christ crying for us all. A red, irritating, burning sensation rose to her cheeks as she carefully lowered down the lid to the chest, keeping her back caved in and her face away from the open door until she could calm her reddened face back down to its normal hue.

"I'm sorry I am bothering you again, but I can tell that you have an impish spirit. You must be visiting here today, I presume?"

Mary really started to find this man irritating. Who did he think he was? Just because he was a monk, he was still a man underneath the title, Mary thought. He was *just* a man. There was nothing to be afraid of, she kept reminding herself as she answered him in the affirmative: "Yes, my parents are part of the local Protestant church here and they wanted to help you in the garden this spring. So, I wanted to see what the garden looked like for myself."

"Ah, I see. That is very thoughtful of them to do the Lord's work of tending to the garden. You know, getting your hands dirty again like when you were a child brings you closer to God and immerses you in the beauty of His creation. It is wonderful work for the soul. That's why I love to spend my days out here in the garden whenever I can, contemplating God's words, while I work with my body to prune the flowers or pluck the weeds to water the garden or feed the fish. Anything the Lord calls me to do that day, I follow His commands."

Mary did not want to sit through another sermon today, so she walked around the monk and jumped from stepping stone to stepping stone, making her way toward the roses. They were gorgeous even in their bud phase since winter was just starting to close its eyes for another season. The monk was left again, looking at the interior of the tearoom, seemingly in no hurry to continue his conversation with Mary.

He must know by now that I do not want to talk to him, Mary thought, as she made her way closer to the roses. She could see their prickly thorns easily since much of the garden was still frostbitten and bare. But the growing going on in the garden was palpable. It flowed through her veins, and she was growing still along with nature. Maybe there was something to what the monk said about being in God's beautiful creation. Mary loved noticing all the life, all the movement commencing in the silent garden. There was no human voice or commotion, yet there was an overwhelming buzz of movement as the flowers grew and the fish swam and the birds came back to roost.

The flowers in the garden made Mary feel much better as opposed to the gargoyles and wounded Christ figures strewn around the monastery's interior. Outside, the flowers could not make her feel guilty; all they could do was grow and face their leaves toward the sun. They had one sole job which was to survive. But for the images inside the monastery...what were their jobs? Mary wondered. Were they meant to cause pain and guilt? Were they meant to force people down on their knees? Were they there to bring money to the religious community or else to make people beg for forgiveness to atone for their sins? Mary could not shake the sense of something being wrong with the inside of that building and being outside right now made it clearer.

Taking in a deep, refreshing breath, Mary stuck her nose right into one of the beautiful wildflowers. The name on the stake in the ground said they were "*Baptisia australis*" flowers, also known as the "wild indigo" plant.

"Huh, maybe that's where my name came from," Mary mumbled to herself.

"That is a very pretty name," said a familiar voice behind her. It was him again. The very persistent monk.

Mary did not turn around this time, saying, "Yes, my name's Mary Baptisia. I guess I didn't realize that there was a plant by that name too."

"My name is Brother John Abelard, but most of the monks just call me Brother John. Although Abelard probably came from Peter Abelard, who was a medieval French theologian, among other things. Do you know the story of Abelard and Heloise? It's a tragic medieval love story that was actually real."

Brother John's blue eyes burned brighter with each word. They were all very carefully mouthed and clearly thought about over and over again in his own mind before he spoke. How many times had he told the story of Abelard and Heloise to someone? Mary thought. Still, on the cusp of childhood, Mary was innocent enough to not feel the need to shy away from his engaging eyes. They seemed to bore right into the core of her being, but she did not flinch.

Mary's friends always said that she had the green eyes of a snake. Could Brother John trust her? Mary let him search her eyes for any deception and, in true childhood fashion, they came to a mutual understanding of trust.

"No, I have never heard the story," said Mary.

"Well, for children I always tell the story this way: Heloise's uncle found her a teacher to fulfill her intellectual curiosity, but soon the teacher and his student become inseparable and fall in love with each other. However, once the uncle finds this out, he attacks Abelard and separates the lovers. The two realize they cannot be together in this lifetime, so Abelard becomes a monk and Heloise becomes a nun until the two shall meet again in Heaven. That's a very truncated version of the story, but someday you can read their letters and learn more about it for yourself."

"I thought it was a sin to even think about sex," Mary said, gently touching the wild indigo petals in front of her.

Brother John looked startled for a moment, clearing his throat before saying, "I did not use that word when telling the story, you know. And yes, we are celibate in every way. But

I believe that love in its purest form can be felt without the need to have sex."

The image came to Mary of when she would hide in her mother's arms when she was afraid of something—the feeling of a warm chest against her cheeks and two arms protecting her from the world—that was true love. It seemed you could love without sex.

"Do you ever miss home?" Mary asked.

Brother John nodded slowly and solemnly. "I do miss my brothers and my parents now and then, but I also remember that this is the life I chose. I *want* to be here."

"Did you ever fall in love before coming here?" Mary asked, hoping that this question was not too personal, as she bent forward a bit more to pet a sleepy bumblebee on its furry back.

The monk stayed quiet for a moment too long. A minute passed, then two, when she glanced back behind her and could see the monk's set face, lost in thought. He was carefully crafting what he wanted to say. His face was pale from being in the monastery walls most of his days, trapped in there with his nose in the Bible. His full lips twitched and his brows furrowed as he actively thought about how to reveal a vulnerable piece of himself to this strange young girl.

"Yes. I loved a woman once in the purest way. She is still my one and only love, my soul mate. But, like Abelard, I cannot be with her if I am to find any semblance of peace on this earth. I want to be happy, though she is certainly my deepest regret and pain…"

Now, this monk was becoming interesting, Mary thought. He was here voluntarily, but he had a life before this one…a normal life with a woman, and maybe he could have even had a family one day.

CHAPTER II

"What happened?" Mary asked, assuming that if she got this far with him, then maybe he would reveal even more.

"I did not want children. I wanted to live a life of contemplation, a life of hard work, and a life of pursuing the Truth. The rituals I have built up at this monastery have guided me on a path to happiness." Brother John only sounded half-convinced to Mary's ears, but when she looked at him, she could tell that he had confirmed this with himself every single day since he had made the decision to leave.

"Maybe I'm too young to understand, but I think I would feel awfully lonely and unhappy if I had to live under that roof every day," Mary said, pointing toward the gloomy monastery.

Brother John chuckled. "I suppose the mood fits me well. Though, I agree, the monastic life is not for every soul."

"I mean, I do feel spiritual here, but my gut feels better outside with nature and other people than in there worshiping statues and tapestries from long ago. Do you know what I mean?" Mary asked, quite earnestly, as it had been a topic on her mind all day. Why did her gut tell her that something was deeply wrong in there?

Brother John watched a bird bringing a delicate bundle

of twigs over to a new nest, to help strengthen it against predators. The bird's beak stuck right through the side of the nest with the bundle and when he pulled his beak out again, he left the sticks behind. Somehow, magically, the little bird knew how to make his own shelter.

With a mysterious air of confidence, Brother John only said: "When you form rituals, you focus less on the objects around you and more on the inner life, which is teeming with spirituality. So, it becomes easy to forget the tapestries and the statues when life becomes the daily practice of internal contemplation."

"I suppose it is like when my parents buy a new piece of furniture which everyone avoids for a while because they don't want to mess it up, but eventually they stop seeing it as new and shiny. They start to sit on it regularly and enjoy it for its utility and not so much for its looks or newness anymore. Is it like that?" Mary asked.

"Yes, very similar to that feeling. You are only visiting here today, Mary. All the opulence and awe brought by the power of art strike the fear of the Lord in you. It can make anyone uncomfortable, but if you lived here, you would not feel the same way."

"Well, I can't say I'd want to be a monk, not just because I'm a girl, but I don't think thinking all day is all that fun and exciting. Plus, a nunnery sounds even stricter than a monastery does."

A burst of robust laughter pealed from the monk's mouth to the point of being almost jolly. What did she say that was so funny? Being a nun does sound soul-sucking and scary, Mary thought.

Brother John wiped his teary eyes with his robe sleeve and then made a head nod for her to walk with him up to the kitchen garden area.

Mary followed obediently. This monk was a real person; he seemed as down-to-earth as she was in many ways. He was not like the other monks.

Stepping over some sticks, much too big for a bird's beak, Mary ducked under a bush, believing that the monk may follow her there. Would God see them in a more secretive space of the garden? Maybe Brother John could reveal more of his thoughts to her, away from God's eyes and ears. She kept moving further in when she came across the bones of a bird, all of them still perfectly in order from when the bird exhaled its last breath.

"Oh!" Mary said, spooked. She averted her eyes just as suddenly as when she discovered the bones belonged to a bird. But her own morbid curiosity made her look over again and take in more of the scene. How did a bird get here? she wondered. Perhaps the bird knew it was sick and wanted to die in peace, away from the commotion in the trees and the open ground. Mary thought, I could understand wanting to be hidden when I am at my most vulnerable. Poor bird, its world ended when it closed its eyes, and no one probably even noticed it here until me.

"What are you doing down there?" asked the monk.

"I found a dead bird. Poor thing," said Mary.

Shocked, Mary heard the monk kneel and scurry underneath the bushes to where she was cooped up, keeping his eyes open for the bird. She had to remind herself that he was not old enough yet to be unable to bend down and crawl on the ground still. In fact, he was rather quite athletic and graceful in the way he approached.

"See? There the poor bird lay, all alone, until I found him,"

Mary said.

"Ah, yes. When we monks are outside weeding, we often find birds that have died in secrecy like this," said the monk.

"Why do they seem to hide?"

"Why do most animals hide when they are wounded? It is to stay away from predators while they try to recover or pass on."

"That does not sound very religious of you."

Brother John smirked but said nothing.

Mary was starting to rethink bringing them both here out of God's prying eyes. "I think we should probably leave the bird here in peace. Or do you think we should bury it?"

The monk looked at the bird intensely and for too long before agreeing to leave it behind the way they had found it.

"Goodbye, Mister Bird. I hope someday we meet again," Mary said, only after saying it aloud did she realize how childish she sounded. But her heart meant the well-wishes.

The two moved on to actually looking at the herbs in the kitchen garden. The monks grew their own organic basil, rosemary, mint, and thyme. Mary kneeled to smell the leaves and the fresh fragrances they each produced. "It is truly amazing that this world can provide us with so many wonderful varieties. How could anyone ever tire of living?" Mary said.

"I know that I certainly will never tire of it. But I think you are special in that you, as a young person, can already savor the small things. It takes true contemplation to put a microscope to life and appreciate it for all of its divine details. I always loved science for that reason. Science allows Man to examine things on a minute level to understand truly how they function. And once we figure it out, then its existence is all the more awe-inspiring. Looking closely at everything takes a lifetime and understanding it all takes an eternity. I will never know the answer to everything...and it may sound silly to you, but that makes me sad. I wish I could know and understand it all." Brother John wiped his teary eyes, which were no longer teary from laughter but sadness. His entire mood had changed.

No longer was there a man full of life beside Mary but the shell of a man trying to find answers. His frame reflected the shells of the other monks Mary saw walking around the monastery. So that is why they looked so sad and solemn... maybe they just wanted more and more knowledge that they could never have on this earth. Why, that could make anyone sad...to never accomplish their dreams while still alive. That seems awful, thought Mary.

"Brother John, may I ask how long you have been here and where you are going? You seem very young still," Mary asked.

The monk's eyes sparkled once more, thinking about his future. "Well, Mary, I am pretty new here. I am twenty-seven and only joined the monastery nearly half a year ago. At first, I began as a Candidate, meaning that I spent several weeks joining the monks for choir and working beside them in the garden and such. But I was made to sleep in the guest house, apart from the other monks. It was a lonely time for me and there were many interviews with the abbot and other senior monks about my intentions.

"After six weeks, I was finally asked to participate as an Observer, which is where I am now, though my time is almost over before I can ask to become a Postulant. As an Observer, I am taught all about the history and spirituality of monastic life and I take part in the day-to-day life of the community.

So now I can basically eat, sleep, and work beside my fellow brothers.

"This is my sixth month of being an Observer, and by the end of this month, I will ask to become a Postulant, then after at least another six months a Novice, then after two years a Professed Monk until death."

"You mean you want to stay here doing the same things until death?" Mary asked, her mouth agog at the level of commitment he was prepared to make. "Why? What about wanting to travel and see the world?"

"In my old life, I saw enough of the world and its people to know that I no longer want to be a part of it. I do not want to be distracted and constantly running around without aim or purpose in my life. I chose to come here for the silence that the monastic life brings. Did you know we cannot even go back home for funerals? We have cast off our old lives entirely and opted for new ones. I have escaped the rut of normal life and exchanged it for one shrouded in silent contemplation about how the entire universe functions. I have no need for global travel," said Brother John. His face was set and cold as he said this. It was a topic that he had no doubt engaged with on many occasions inside his own head and he was, again, quite sure of himself.

"You are certainly different from other people," was all that Mary could get out, as she was feeling particularly foolish for thinking that travel was something everyone wanted. But did she even really want it? This conversation was starting to make her second-guess everything she thought was universal.

The pair walked together through the ancient boxwoods and hollies, past the main sundial and various birdbaths, past a wayside cross, and up to the center of the entire garden.

Brother John said: "This is a medieval baptismal font and the small garden surrounding it is called the Hortulus, or 'little garden.' There are circular beds surrounding the font and they are planted with the same types of herbs that the medieval monks grew, like tarragon and sage. The top is marble, and the pedestal is made from limestone, much like the material that our monastery is made from. I come here often to contemplate and watch the water inside the font ripple when it rains."

"It is beautiful. May I touch the font?" Mary asked, already sticking her hand out to feel its gritty sides.

"You may. I am sure that God won't mind." Brother John smiled as he, too, touched the sides of the large baptismal font.

"It's funny, but I always thought my last name was more from the word baptism anyhow than a plant type," said Mary.

"It could still very well be," added the monk.

"Maybe I fit in here more than I initially thought." Mary and Brother John laughed a big, hearty laugh before they felt a heavier, more uncomfortable silence fall between them.

Mary piped up first: "Well, perhaps I should go back to find my parents. I'm surprised they are still yapping and not taking in the sights of this magnificent garden."

"Yes, they will learn more about themselves here than amongst themselves. I am happy that you came out to see it in all its glory today," said the monk.

"I may see you again soon when summer starts and I can join my parents working out here in the garden. Right? Are you allowed to have pen pals?" Mary naively asked.

"Unfortunately, we cannot communicate with the outside world, as I mentioned before, even in letter form. But yes, I am sure to see you if you work in the garden this summer," Brother John said, smiling as he did so.

"That is a bummer. I don't have very many friends, but I will be sure to look for you in the garden. Anyway, it was nice meeting you, Brother John." Mary awkwardly curtsied as she was unsure whether he could touch another human hand, and she turned around to exit the garden the way she came—up through the bamboo gate, ascending the stone steps, and walking around the side of the monastery back to the front entrance where her parents were still chatting.

Mary crept up beside her father, but the move was moot since her parents barely even noticed her absence. The group was still contemplating how they would schedule out their days in the garden with the monks. Everyone had their phones pulled out and were absorbed in their calendar list of things to do.

I hope that my life will never look that busy, thought Mary. All they do is run from appointment to appointment or from errand to errand. I will *never* be an adult if I have to live that way. I would rather weed the garden or read all day or walk around the monastery for miles. Mary got lost in her own thoughts until her mother tapped her on the shoulder and told her it was time to leave.

Following her parents back to the car, she got in and noticed that Brother John was watching her leave from the parking lot. She looked back, wondering if he noticed her watching him until he was just a little speck in the background.

***

Brother John sighed. He was left alone again to battle with his own thoughts. He turned around once he could no longer see his new friend's car. But she was an outsider, a sinner, stuck in the world out there of chaos and failure. He wished to save her, but she still seemed to find joy out there in the

23

loud world and a true worshiper must approach the religious lifestyle voluntarily.

He imagined Mary in a nun's robe and veil. She looked so peaceful and whole, kneeling there in front of an altar of Christ and reading His Good Book. Mary would make bread, the body of Christ, in the kiln with her sisters, laughing and talking about how grateful they all were to be here, apart from the world outside. When she sat down to write letters to the only man she knew, her Husband, she would tell Him all about her day and pray for another one that was just as good. The surrounding community all wished her well and she would appear more youthful as she aged. Brother John wanted her to stay as holy as she appeared today before him, but he knew that the longer she lived on the outside, the more cynical and wizened she would become, like the other women who were part of the chaos. His heart ached.

If she left behind her world at the end of her teenage life, then she could work on saving her childish self. The child was closer to perfection than an adult will ever be, thought the monk. And although nunneries were open to reforming even the worst of our kind, like prostitutes or criminals, Brother John never wanted Mary to fall that low. She had a pure soul. I could sense it, he thought.

He closed his eyes as he took in a deep breath, allowing the breeze to move the tiny hairs on his face to and fro. Tears formed wells in his eyes that found nowhere to travel but down. The rivers ran down his face as he envisioned her beauty as she took up painting in a nunnery. She could learn so quickly with her intelligence that learning to paint would take her but a season, and she could make Michelangelo cry with her images of Jesus and His followers. Mary's brushes would be cared for with the softest touch to avoid distorting the bristles made from the finest horsehair. And she would never let her paints go dry, always ensuring to wipe the lids off old paint and securing them on tightly. Her works would only be known inside the nunnery, never to be exposed to the outside world because they could not understand or appreciate her holy work. It belonged in the most sacred of spaces.

Brother John had felt this way before. He frequently felt this way about his previous love. He would never speak her name again because he no longer deserved to speak that name. But she was also childlike in her nature, pure of spirit, full of soul, and dangerous in her intellect. Much like Heloise, her alabaster skin and beautiful face did not cure her of her constant yearning to learn. She always desired more as did I, thought the monk, and yet, she could not rid herself of the sensual. Her need for touch was too great, too tremendous to put her in a nunnery, where she told me she would wilt and die. She knew herself well enough to know that all of her creativity flowed from touch and living amongst virtuous people. She could not rip herself from the chaotic world of movement and life to force herself into a kind of silent vacuum.

But is this really a vacuum, love? wondered Brother John. Is this not really a place for you to hone your skills and share them within a community that actually cares? Is this not a place for you to become the best version of yourself? He had not noticed until now that his fingernails left deep marks on the insides of his palms as he squeezed them in anger and frustration. Women are weak, he thought. They must be if they would wilt without breeding and creating new life and desiring the warmth of another human body every night which is nothing but temporary sinew and future dust on this earth. Women are too much of this earth. They are not capable of going beyond and exploring the very edges of their own personality and fragility. Women are too soft to understand that the mind is her most powerful tool, not her body.

Brother John shook his head, hoping to banish the thoughts he had about his former lover and young Mary. They were both lost causes due to their very nature, and no thought should be wasted on them in divine contemplation.

Enough time had passed now that Brother John was assured that Mary would not be coming back before he turned around in the garden and continued pruning the rose bushes, muttering curses under his breath, which he promised to confess about tomorrow.

***

The hand pruners Brother John used to cut the dead branches and deadhead the spent blooms helped the plant to regrow faster and stronger. Although he found the red rubber grips an obnoxious color and opposed to his contemplation, he covered up most of the handles with his gardening gloves. Working on carefully separating each part at the point of growth, Brother John wanted to avoid accidentally killing any part of the roses. He was always cautious when dealing with God's creations.

He noticed nearby another brother on his hands and knees, weeding around the rose bushes. He used a weeding knife that was particularly sharp, but the serrated edge on its side was extremely helpful with some of those naughty boxwoods.

This monk was fat and balding, even though he was only in his forties. Even in this cool weather, Brother John could see the beads of sweat trickling down the sides of his face as he was hunched over weeding. He had joined the monastery later in his life and was not yet a Professed Monk, although he certainly kept asking the abbot about it every chance he could. Maybe the higher-ups believed he was still hiding something or not letting go of everything in his past.

"Hello, Brother Paul Zizzo, how is God's work treating you today?" asked Brother John, a friendly smile adorning his face.

Brother Paul winced at the sound of another human voice before squinting and looking up into Brother John's blue eyes. "Eh, I suppose he is punishing me today for being overweight. I'm a sweaty mess."

Brother John was going to respond, but, as had happened many times before, he was cut off from saying anything at all, for Brother Paul was about to share every minute detail of his day.

"Yes, He 'who has called' us 'to his kingdom' wants me to enter with particular effort on my behalf. For some reason, I just cannot get in. I try every day to please the Lord, but no matter what I do, it seems wrong. Like, this morning, when we rose at three fifteen in the morning to go to choir and recite the Vigils, the abbot kept eyeballing me if I was not singing in the right pitch or if I was holding my Good Book the right way. He treats me like a bumbling fool. It was as if he was making sure that I did not have the Bible upside down! I mean, can you believe it? What have I done to deserve the extra scrutiny of the father and my fellow brothers?

"I am just a simple man. I was on the path to discovering that 'we are all one in Christ' when He called me to the monastery. I had a wife and children and a regular nine-to-five job. I had it all, but it did not satisfy me. Nothing satisfied me anymore. I became a numb man, a man of living death. I had no purpose, aim, or goal after I 'achieved' it all...or at least I thought so."

"Yes, yes, you have told me this story many times, brother," said Brother John.

"I know, I know, but with each iteration, perhaps I am getting closer to the Truth of why I am not a Professed Monk yet. After all, I have devoted myself now to this same work for *six* years. I have risen through the ranks and I am still not seen as worthy enough to commit myself forever to the Lord? Why? So, allow me to take your precious time while we toil out here and remind you about my coming here."

Brother Paul unbent himself a bit and threw his weeding knife back into the soil, wearing a stern face of mixed grief and anger. The anger must be what caused the abbot's hesitation, thought Brother John.

"Anyway, I had it all in the other world. I had the house and the cars and the family and the job, but my wife would make me lukewarm, terrible-tasting foods, which I could not ask her to improve upon without a scolding from her. My children were not grateful for their own existence, thanks to me and my wife. Instead, they spent their days putting their sticky fingers in drawers where they did not belong and drawing on walls they had no business drawing on. And if I tried to even pretend to scold them, the wife would beat me and the children would scream. Now, my things were nice, but the cars sucked me dry of money and my job sucked me dry of soul. I was no longer the cheery, upbeat man I had once been. I grew thin, yes, I did! I grew weak. I could barely make it out of my bed before my wife asked me what was wrong one day. You know what I told her?"

This was a rhetorical device that Brother Paul often employed and Brother John knew it, so he merely nodded his head in agreement and let him continue.

"I told her I was dying. I told her that 'narrow is the road that leads to life' and the only cure was to find God. Of course, she called me selfish and vile and a monster, but I realized nothing could hurt me when 'those who fear him lack nothing.' The very next day I left with just the clothes draped over my body and a heart open to Christ. I came here where they shaved my head, baptized me anew, and eventually gave me my own robe. I have worn this robe since that day of acceptance and never looked back. I am a man who looks ahead...but right now I cannot see beyond the abbot and his eyeballing..."

The sundial in the garden reached four thirty in the afternoon and now it was time for reading or private prayer before supper. So, Brother John and Brother Paul packed up the monastery's gardening tools and placed them back in the shed.

CHAPTER III

U pon closing the doors, it was as if Brother Paul had
never opened up a line of conversation with Brother
John. He walked quickly ahead of him, practically
running back to his room to pray.

Brother John walked slowly, contemplating the words that
Brother Paul had shared yet again about his life. For Brother
Paul had a life before, too, one that was much more complete
than he ever had. Brother John had only just started his life
with his love. They were newly married and were about to
have a family; his job was just barely bringing in enough; and
they only owned one beat-up car before he left it all behind.
It brought Brother John some comfort to know that had he
drawn it out longer, he still probably would not have been
happy in that life, and he would have had more to leave.

Upon entrance to his monastic cell, Brother John closed the
door and looked around. A moment of déjà vu enveloped his
psyche as he found everything in the exact same place it had
been for the past several months. There was a hard wooden
bed with its headboard shoved up against the wall underneath
a cross with a small wooden chair beside it. On the other side
of the room, there stood a small wooden desk with the Bible
laying on top of it and a chair tucked underneath. The room

had a window which was the only source of light available, although the monastery permitted candles when necessary, like during the winter months when it was completely dark by five.

This cell allowed Brother John the space to sit and think, which is exactly what he decided to do today. He took a seat in front of his desk, opened a page of the Bible, tilted his head down at the proper angle to read, and thought about Mary.

He could see Mary, when she came of age, joining a nunnery. She was still humming to the tuneful songs of the old English and Irish folks that were at once long-forgotten; penning her own signature in the air with the flick of her voice. Mary's voice topples that of a songbird. Like waves on the ocean, she sways in such a calculated manner—the box step. Her song takes the lead as she follows in its inviting steps. "One, two, three, one, two, three."

Brother John smiled, imaging her in the nunnery washrooms where Mary would hum and sway to her own heartbeat, the past whispering in her head, its echoes just as formulaic as the movements of her body. "The machine," as Mary would so fondly refer to it, was letting her dance. However, it was truly her soul that let Mary enjoy her own body. The body that was recycled from the scraps of leftover matter on the earth. Her body was made of the finite pieces of Shakespeare, Milton, Plato, and Aristarchus. Adam may have made Eve out of his ribs, but all the greatest beings on earth contributed to the making of this young woman—*Mary*.

Mary was like a new lamb, needing guidance on its spindly legs. Brother John could be her rock to lean against during hard times. He wished to smell her hair and watch her dance alone, but he soon pushed the thoughts out, crowding his head with sweet temptation. His job here was to focus on his studies to discover the Truth about life—its meaning in all of its beautiful glory.

Women were merely distractions from the holy moral and intellectual life. They carried extra fat on parts of the body men did not. Aristotle even believed that they had no souls! So why, on this perfectly beautiful day, should I be sitting here thinking about Mary? wondered Brother John. Energy should not be spent on women in general, let alone a *particular* woman.

With newfound energy and a guilty heart, the monk flipped to another section of his Bible and read until his eyes began to droop. He looked outside and knew based on the season what time it was, regardless of the peal of the bell. The sun was still high but past its peak now. Supper was being served until Vespers started at five thirty.

This time was wasted on searching for the Truth, thought Brother John. Perhaps later this evening I will find more success. He pushed himself out of his chair from behind the desk and opened the door to his cell. He heard his other brothers opening theirs as well and all of them headed to the hall where supper was being served on the same plastic trays carrying their plain white ceramic plates and mugs. It was a bit of a balancing act to get from the food to the table, but accidents were fortunately rare. The loud noise of a falling tray could ruin the contemplative spirit for hours.

The monks all took their places on the same side of the plain wooden tables, facing out. There was no conversation unless it was absolutely necessary, but most of the time a dish went around twice or a look from one monk would signal their needs to another and all would be performed without speech.

Brother John felt grateful for living in a world where idle chatter was finally looked down upon. He remembered in the outside world how frustrated he got with having voices clutter up his mind with airy nothings. Women, especially, were prone to chatter like birds without a melody to their songs. Their words served no purpose other than to obscure one's ability to think.

Here, silence was held sacred and voices were used to communicate something important or used to sing praises to the Lord in harmony. But to sit in silence was nothing out of the ordinary for these monks, and Brother John was able to sink deeper into himself as the day wore on. And the deeper he went, the closer he believed he came to the Truth.

***

The hall echoed with the sounds of clinking knives and forks, the setting down of mugs, and the pouring of water. The various sounds in their own way created a tune that would die down soon since suppertime was less than an hour long. Some monks could even listen to tapes with headphones on of sermons and chants and prayers. Tonight, Brother John ate his meal in silence.

The evening prayer time of Vespers came around once again and the pew found Brother John more withdrawn than normal as he absentmindedly grasped their backs to find his seat.

He sang from a faraway place where his mind could still roam around and explore. The inside of his head could be a much more illuminating place than singing the same set of prayers repeatedly.

Mary came back to him mid-vowel in his singing and he choked on it.

"Brother, are you all right?" asked a monk standing next to

Brother John.

"Yes, thank you," he said curtly, quietly clearing his throat and preparing to delve back into the prayer.

Still, he saw a vision of Mary approaching the garden at night. Moving like a levitating phantom, she glided across the green grass. He could tell that she felt whole, good, and free there. For it feels like her own knowledge of repeated patterns, reason, and compassion takes on an authentic voice in the way she dances when no one else is there, he thought.

But then the scene shifted to a Mary who had not saved herself and allowed the outside world to destroy her spirit in her middle age. Screaming aloud, Mary stabbed a quill into her wrist until the burgundy droplets became ink. She wrote "Goodbye, sweet earth. I wish I could remember how kindly you treated me then. But this man tore me down and built me back up in his image. I am nothing anymore. How did I go from having a strong sense of self-esteem to this—this selfless piece of a soul, no longer whole but halved? I am not an individual anymore but a dependent. I need him to live. *Adieu.*"

Throwing the bloody quill on the floor, she allowed the blood to continue leaving her body, becoming ever so pale. Slowly, Mary's breathing became raspier and her heart became faster. Mary was not afraid of death at this point in life because she could longer grasp life's beauty without him by her side. It seems that only a virgin can remain hopeful, enshrouded in bliss and happiness. An innocent who does not know what it is to bump into another and have their soul split in two.

Mary was a composition of all human experience, all human passion, all human parts. Yet, she met another with the same composition, a man who believed it right to rule over her soul.

He took it quickly, swiftly, and with it, her body and even her mind...but not all of it was taken. In her subconscious lay the very same little girl who had no concept of love. She did not know what romantic surrender would mean...her life. Mary was given to this man, this perfect being, this hyperrational mind, this animalistic lover, this ideal man. Mary gave in to love. She lost her stubbornness. She lost herself when she found him. He was her love, her soul, her life, her composition. Yes, she made him into a God, one who could rob her with her eyes open, one who could kill her if he had so chosen to. She gave in because she was a lonely individual, one who chose dependency over all. She got what she so deserved.

Brother John shuddered. If her life played out that way, how could he ever forgive himself? There were many nights when he was allowed to see a newspaper once in a while and the world was always burning. He often prayed, among his other brothers, to save those who had a certain spirit to them. Those people did not deserve to become cynical and broken souls.

Mary was one of those people whose spirit was too good to be allowed to die. She would thrive if only she could spend her life thinking and working behind the safe enclosure of a nunnery. Inside the stone walls is really equivalent to the inside of a person's own mind, waiting to be explored and routinely used. Not to mention, thought Brother John, that women need extra protection, as they are more fragile by nature and easily lured by the flesh.

Vespers ended before Brother John even realized that the monks were trying to exit the pew he was blocking. Now, at six o'clock, it was time to go back to their cells to pray and read more scripture until Compline.

Brother John's cell remained cold and empty with the few

wooden pieces of furniture filling it that were not his own but the monastery's. He had nothing to his name. Ownership of property was abandoned at the gate to the monastery, and crossing through its doors to the nave of the building was a promise to never own anything again.

But Brother John accepted this without much suffering as he had with him what was always his—his mind. He had his mind with him and it was the only thing that he needed to find the Truth, although he thought that the pen and paper he could have was helpful as well.

With a long, drawn-out sigh, Brother John needed to pull himself out of his depression over the state of the outside world and come back to himself and his goal to find the Truth. He pulled out his Bible and sat down, flipping through the pages he had touched so many times. The oil from his fingers left many unsightly stains. He read a passage from Luke 6:31 to "never do to another what you do not want done to yourself" and left his desk for Compline.

***

Compline was the last prayer for the evening. It always started at seven thirty and ended at eight, and in winter that meant rising and falling in the darkness. Thankfully, it was still the late spring, and the sun shone through the windows looking out toward the green fields.

The chants of the psalms filled the entire monastery nave with glorious sound. Their voices were deep and melodic as the men's voices combined to praise all that was good in Man. Brother John stood there with his chest raised, looking slightly up, his blue eyes catching the last of the evening light. He sang along with his brothers and spent much of the time releasing all of his sins, and everything bad within himself, out into the great nave, like one long exhale.

He breathed in through his nose and sang out through his mouth, exhaling, and thereby making himself lighter with each passing phrase. The times for chanting were therapeutic for Brother John as he tried to release the images of Mary he had in his head to prepare himself for a more clear-headed next day of searching for the Truth.

A loud thump sound echoed throughout the nave, to which Brother John swiveled his head around to see swiftly what made all that commotion. Brother Immanuel, one of the older monks, had fainted and hit his head on the stone-cold floor.

There was a small amount of blood on the sacred ground, which many probably saw as a fair sacrifice for their sins that day as the nearest brother helped Brother Immanuel up off the ground.

"Please carry our brother to his cell for an early retirement from the day's work," said the abbot.

A couple of the younger monks, including Brother John, foisted Brother Immanuel up underneath his arms and shuffled forward together toward the monastic cells. By the time they returned for Compline, it would most likely already be over.

"Are you all right, Brother Immanuel?" one of the fellow monks asked.

He could only mumble.

"He must have knocked himself senseless, poor old man," said another monk.

They shuffled along for several minutes until they finally reached his door and set him down on the bed. One monk took a wet washcloth and cleaned off some of the dried blood from his head. He wrung out the bloodied rag into a wash bucket filled with rainwater.

Brother Immanuel's face was filled with pockmarks from a nasty case of chickenpox he had as a child. Much of the water from the washcloth pooled in the marks, causing Brother John a sense of disgust, which he masked by asking about how far along he guessed the other men were in Compline.

"I bet they are already singing the *Salve Regina* by now and our abbot is sprinkling the holy water on our brothers' heads before bedtime. I feel sorry for breaking from the routine."

"Well, that's very selfish of you," said the semi-conscious Brother Immanuel now.

Turning green, Brother John apologized profusely and stayed silent for the rest of his time caring for the old monk.

Another monk sat beside Brother Immanuel and changed his washcloth out while another made a fan out of a piece of paper that was lying around to cool the overheated monk.

***

Brother Immanuel Gosbank had joined the monastery in the 1970s after fleeing from the draft. He was considered another hippie who refused to fight in the Vietnam War and would do anything from swallowing cotton balls to maiming himself in order to get away from the violence. He had considered himself a pacifist his whole life and used his paintings to spread peace on earth.

He was never much of a religious man until the day that that draft letter was drawn and came in the mail telling him he was of the eligible age and gender to be required for the service of his country. At the tender age of twenty, he was also eligible to join the nearby monastery. He was even raised Catholic, though his parents were only semi-dedicated. A life of being fed and clothed and bathed and *safe* forever seemed preferable to being violently blown up at twenty and sent home in a box.

The next morning, Immanuel Gosbank told his parents of his plans, burned the conscription notice, sold all of his belongings, and threw himself at the doorstep of the monastery where he was embraced openly.

Even today, he still had the '70s sideburns, though now they were barely there and as white as the tunic he wore to bed. The monastery also made him shave his mustache and his long hair off from the beginning. And if he could wear his normal clothes from his old life, then he would still wear bell bottoms and tie-dye shirts. All the monks would laugh at the spectacle if he was allowed to walk around as he came.

Thankfully, today, Brother Immanuel was a toned-down old man who could promote what he had always believed in—pacifism. Plus, he also told his brothers that the greatest gift the monastic life had given him was a chance to continue painting.

But his paintings were no realist masterpieces. He was a man with a wide, cheap, bristle brush, normally used for painting houses that he dunked straight into buckets of paint and splashed onto wood or, if he was lucky, canvas.

His paintings, he claimed, directly resulted from his emotions and his dealings with God on a transient plane. No one could interpret his symbols but himself.

Brother John had witnessed his art in action. Brother Immanuel stood there in his smock, covered in paint from a previous work, doing yoga and meditation in the middle of his bare cell. Then, in a fit of rage, he would collapse and nearly knock the paint buckets over in the process as he dove his hand toward one and whipped it out full force to land on the surface.

The typically wooden surface soaked up much of the first layer, so he would add more and more until circles and spirals dripped orange and yellow sap. The floors of his cell were always covered with the few newspapers that the monastery received, and he used those as inspiration for channeling his emotions.

There were exactly five times throughout the day when the monks had scripture reading or private prayer time alone in their cells. Brother Immanuel, although not supposed to, used that time to paint. He called it "prainting." Painting became his way of praying for all of those lost souls out in the world that needed his help. He prayed for peace with every movement he made, spreading the paint across the surface of his chosen material.

Brother John watched him through a peephole he found in his cell when he heard any kind of loud knocks or crashes against the floor. Normally, Brother Immanuel had landed hard on his knees enough to cause pain as he wept over the newspaper articles from the previous week. There was a recent school shooting and a handful of robberies in the area, and the country, in general, was always on edge with another country. There was always something on fire in the news, whether it was men themselves or their creations. The outside world, from the perspective of those papers, was a lot closer to hell than it was to Heaven.

Brother John often heard Brother Immanuel in his cell crying: "'The fool cannot be corrected with words'" for you must "'strike your son with a rod and you will free his soul from death.'" Brother John had seen through the tiny hole the self-flagellation that his brother had put himself through with a whip.

There were even horrific moments where he used his blood as a paintbrush, dipping the seven knotted cords of rope back into his open wounds to give penance for his sins.

The piece of wood would look very much like the thorns around Christ's head and it was rather a unique piece of art then. But Brother John viewed self-flagellation as no way to live peacefully with oneself on earth. Was harming oneself going to lead a man closer to the Truth? wondered Brother John.

***

Standing there now in Brother Immanuel's room, with the sun sinking, an eerie glow was cast on one of his latest pieces. There were seven separate dots over the top of a black background. The dots were hardly visible over the darker color, especially the longer it was exposed to the air. The other monks probably did not know what had truly created those little red dots. It was all just random paint smears on wood to them, but Brother John knew Brother Immanuel's secret.

Brother Immanuel was able to keep his eyes open now and thank everyone for their assistance.

"I thank you all. I think I had worked a bit too hard out in the fields today, planting all of those turnips. Did you know we are planting eighty feet of turnips this year?" His eyes looked like cloudy bits of jelly that it was astonishing he could see anything out of them at all, thought Brother John.

"Yes, I had heard the planting of the organic garden had started," said one of the monks.

"You should drink more water, brother," said another monk, "for 'the Lord knows the thoughts of men' and you cannot hide your need for God's precious gift to us from anyone. You must drink and water will heal you."

Brother Immanuel looked in the monk's direction and all the monks could visibly see his flash of anger that a younger man was telling him about God's words. The patronizing tone of a mother he had shaken off in a previous life made Brother Immanuel red in the face. But he knew where he was and that God was watching, so he took a deep breath and ceased acknowledging the monk who mentioned water to him for the rest of the evening.

Once the monks felt the chill in the air enter his room, they thought it better to leave him to his prayers and scripture, where he may repent for all the sinful thoughts he was bound to be having right then.

None of them spoke, only bowed and exited the cell. Brother John was last and closed the door to Brother Immanuel's room, thereby leaving him there laying on his hard wooden bed. He had not moved since everyone observed his red face and his jug of water remained untouched.

Brother John had heard the bell a few minutes before the monks left the room and he knew it was past eight, which meant now was the time to withdraw and get some sleep before the early morning.

It always amazed him that his body was so used to his routine now that he started yawning when the bell chimed. Brother John's eyes felt heavy with sleep and his body was limp with fatigue. The days were long and the nights were much too short for his liking, but since he followed the same routine every single day, his body adjusted accordingly.

Still, there was no time to waste when sleep time was so limited. He went straight to his room to prepare for bed and shut his eyes to the surrounding darkness.

For a few moments, Brother John laid there on his thin mattress with his single sheet up by his chin. His feet were unbearably cold, so he got up to grab himself a pair of socks. But he could not resist, as he went to get his socks, passing by the peephole and checking up on Brother Immanuel.

Looking through the hole, it was hard to make out anything in the dense darkness. But the moonlight coming through his window helped to distinguish a pair of feet sticking up right where they were left on the bed.

Did Brother Immanuel pass away or was he punishing himself for his sins by not covering himself in a blanket? It was surely too cold to go without one tonight, thought Brother John. Although, in the end, he decided that the most pragmatic option was to leave the problem until the morning, and he went back to his bed to shortly thereafter fall asleep.

CHAPTER IV

The next morning, Brother John awoke to the distant smell of bacon and eggs. Of course, the monks were vegetarians, but the guests of the monastery and anyone with the proper doctor's note were allowed to eat meat.

He remembered the smell from his childhood when every weekend his parents brought him to a diner that was fashioned out of an old dining car on a train. It was this long, dingy-looking tube that was low to the ground, even for a young boy. But going inside felt so cozy. There were booths attached to the side with little lamps over the tops of the tables and curtains covering the tiny windows. On the other side was the main show. The booth had swivel-top chairs down a long bar right in front of the grill and refrigerator. A little circular set of condiments sat right in between each seat.

The place was always packed, usually with older men who just wanted to find some morning camaraderie to take with their black coffee. When Brother John was a boy, his favorite part of those weekend mornings was watching the hostesses cook his bacon and pancakes right on the griddle-topped stove they had. He remembered the women, typical mothers, who could not help play-flirting with him. They always gave him extra bacon, fresh off the griddle. And they even used heavy iron weights to make sure it all cooked flat.

It was as if he had entered the World War II era, frozen in time. His heart always beat fondly at the smell of bacon, even though he had stopped eating meat since he made the commitment to become a monk as a teenager.

He wondered what had happened to those women. Did they ever have grandchildren to cook for? Did they still work there or were their ghosts there? Did those two women find happiness in their lives, or did the chaos rip everything they held dear to them away?

There were so many unanswered questions Brother John was left with when he stripped himself of his old life in order to find peace and stability. The routine of monastic life reminded him daily to be grateful for the fact that he even had lungs capable of filling with breath and a heart strong enough to pump his veins with lifeblood. He learned through doing the most minor things over and over again to experience those quietest, yet most necessary, aspects of human existence.

To be silent in this life meant to pick up on hearing the smallest of forces—to notice the things that really make the world move. From his heartbeat to the growing plants in the garden, there was life growing silently and thriving without the need to shout.

Brother John said a little prayer for those hostesses who served him his much-anticipated weekend breakfasts, where he could still remember swallowing all the saliva that his glands were producing upon smelling the bacon hit the sizzling griddle.

His mouth watered now as he pulled his plain robe over his shaved head and walked out of his cell to attend the first

Vigils. The monks would always have to begin with chanting prayers before earning any meal. This served to remind them, like Brother John in the diner, to wait and savor the moments before the release—before the ultimate satisfaction. In many ways, Brother John believed that this form of praise could be better than sex. Chanting and contemplating about all the things that were going right daily, all before the satisfaction of eating made for an even better experience. It lasted longer.

Brother John also remembered Brother Immanuel, laying there last night the way he was left. He decided that on his way to the great nave of the monastery, he would simply knock on his brother's door and see if he was also on his way.

Upon knocking on the door, Brother Immanuel remained unmoved. Brother John placed an ear on the wooden door to see if he could hear any movement at all on the inside. There was nothing.

Brother John went back to his room to glance through the peephole. Lo and behold, Brother Immanuel still lay there as before.

He must be dead, thought Brother John, clutching his hands and squeezing them together until they ached. He ran out of his cell again and called on a brother in the hall.

"Brother Daniel! Brother, please help me. I think we may need to get the abbot if Brother Immanuel is sick...or..." Brother John dropped off his sentence. What he really wanted was for someone else to be there to catch him in case he fainted. He was a rather squeamish fellow when it came to the sight of blood or the stench of death up close.

There were no locks on any of the doors in the monastery, as everything was communally shared, so Brother John simply had to push the door open to get to Brother Immanuel.

When opening the door, Brother Immanuel continued laying there, as still as ever, but, thankfully, there was no putrid odor in the room. The two monks approached cautiously until Brother John could see the tiny rise and fall of his brother's chest.

"Brother, are you ill?" asked Brother Daniel.

Brother Immanuel knew that Brother Daniel had not witnessed his wrongful behavior from yesterday and so he decided to speak to him. "Yes, brother, I am sick in the soul. I am punishing myself for the rest of the day—fasting and cold and lying as if I was in the grave."

"But would not it be better to come with us to sing the Vigils and then confess your sins to the abbot?" asked Brother Daniel.

"No, for I consider my sin a grave one that needs to be handled swiftly before it consumes me whole. I will ask for forgiveness tomorrow morning. Leave me now," commanded Brother Immanuel.

The two monks looked at one another before accepting his form of penance and turning around.

***

The monks met the others at Vigils and explained what Brother Immanuel was up to. The other monks agreed to accept his absence from the community for today, and the chanting commenced. A new day had begun.

Brother John thought about Brother Immanuel for the rest of Vigils. He could not help pitying such a man who wanted to punish himself so often for feeling his own emotions. There was no way to quell that which we could not control. A life of pain and misery is not what a man should look for; he should seek happiness.

An epiphany dawned on Brother John in that precious

moment. Life for Man was about finding happiness on earth. That is all that Brother John was seeking—a sense of peace and stability that brought him happiness and a sense of gratitude for all the things he had. But his journey required the space that monastic life gave him to feel it. Amidst the silence, there was the hum of gratitude for his ability to walk, breathe, dance, sing, think, talk, cook, read, and a countless number of other abilities he had. The very fact that Man's mind could create such a beautiful monastery reminded him of that feeling.

It was now time for prayer and breakfast. The monks walked out in a clean single-file line from the pews to the hall where the bacon smell loomed. No one had to say anything, yet they were all thinking about the last time they had bacon. Like a siren's sweet call, the bacon aroma gave each monk an extra pep in his step as they walked—not ran like they wanted to— toward food. Although it was only four in the morning, the monks' bodies knew that this would be the last meal until noon. They each had a properly proportioned amount of food, so the key was to pray over it and inhale as much of its scent in the meantime and eat as slowly as possible. The speed at which one ate allowed for a greater degree of satisfaction by the end of the meal.

"Let us pray before our meal," said Brother Paul. "Lord, I thank you for giving us this meal. We are merely vessels for your Word as You told us to 'renounce yourself in order to follow Christ.' You told us to 'discipline your body' and we have one monk today still upstairs in his room following your Word." As Brother Paul spoke, he was leaning closer and closer in to his food. Any monk who dared look up and open their eyes could see that his nostrils were flared, allowing the steam from the meal to tickle the inside of his flesh. The smell caused

Brother Paul to drool visibly onto his plate. He was not a thin man, so not eating for several hours on end was torture for his gluttonous design. "You, oh Lord, ask us to 'honor everyone' and so we do. We pray every day that others may enjoy the meals that You provide us and that no one will be turned away from us for a meal. For the meal is not ours, it is Yours. Amen."

The monks remained quiet for a moment, waiting for the abbot to make the first noise of his fork onto the plate before the others dared pick up theirs. The proper order of mealtime was God dines first, then the closest men to him, and finally all the piddly little monks. The rats followed not far behind the monks in the holy order.

But it was this very waiting that meant Brother John chewed much longer than necessary and ate in silence. He paid attention to the texture of his bread, where every hole was, and how the butter melted right into the little valleys in between. He felt his teeth squish through the scrambled eggs like they were savory air. And he satiated his thirst from the salt with fresh water from the well outside. His diet was very plain and simple, but it was just enough to sustain him and he loved every minute of acknowledging this food, giving him the energy to continue moving on.

Life *is* movement. Movement requires energy to burn and excrete, which Brother John took the time to remember at every meal. Each time he could eat, and with little exertion in today's modern world, his heart rang out with joy.

Perhaps it was this restraint and slow living that made outsiders compare the Benedictines to poets. Any man could become a poet if he lived in a world of silence and contemplation, where waiting for his next meal made all of his thoughts hone in on the details of each piece of food. Food became the poet's obsession—not women. A fresh piece of bread, sometimes still steaming, was more tantalizing than any female exposing herself, thought Brother John, quickly apologizing for having such thoughts.

But it was not only the room for contemplation that made us poets, thought Brother John. It was the scripture itself that gave meaning to every word and symbol for all of Man's everyday existence. It was hard not to come away feeling lighter than air after a day of reading such loaded text.

Not only did the physical reading of the text utilize our eyes and minds, but the singing used our diaphragm and lungs and throats and mouths on top of all of that. In this way, physically performing the same exercises every single day, whether or not we felt wholly there, provided us with a sense of belonging. We were locked into this story of being monks and monks chant and this is something that happens every day, like when the sun rises and sets. No sickness of the body or mind can keep a monk from chanting. Even Brother Immanuel, right now, lying in his bed, is performing the physical feats required for chanting. His blood is pumping harder and his lungs are filling with more air as he lays there still. That is his true punishment—to feel the life inside himself trying to move and being stunted all the while.

The Benedictine Trappist monks are a band of men who live to follow a routine and not the other way around. They use their rituals, their habits, and their routines to praise His name.

In Lauds, the monks chanted for the sun to rise again to grace our earth with heat and life. Brother John sang loudly, hoping that it was enough for Brother Immanuel to hear, though he already knew the chant by heart. Still, Brother John felt like sharing with the whole monastery how good it was to be alive and warm.

When Lauds and Mass were over, the monks received the "Bread of Heaven" in Holy Communion. This was made to sustain the monks in their praise of the Lord for the rest of the day, even if there was still dinner and supper prepared. The bit of bread was meant to remind them that His blood and body were enough.

Finally, the eight o'clock bell rang throughout the nave—its crisp, mulling sound shaking up the belly of the beast. The bell called all the monks back to their cells for scripture reading and prayer in isolation until Terce.

Brother John entered his bare room, approaching his desk when he heard the familiar noise of rhythmically ruffling cloth. Brother John moved to the other side of his room where Brother Paul resided. He was always one of the first ones to get to his room during the daily prayer times, like when he left Brother John in the garden a couple of days ago.

It always struck him as odd that a monk ever feel the need to hurry through his routine. Each segment came with its own time and there was no need to rush, even in the face of death anymore. The monastic life was based on its slow movement.

There was no peephole on this opposite wall of Brother John's room, but he heard enough—the rubbing cloth, the flesh knocking against the flesh, the muffled sighs exhaled. Brother Paul was "relieving himself" in his room.

This came as a shock to Brother John, for he had not committed such a sin since he was just beginning his monastic journey and he was certainly too intimidated to do such a thing within the monastery's walls. The walls could hear such things…at least, your neighbors could.

How would Brother John be able to look his neighbor in the face now? His eyes could never lie. Why did he now have to carry this burden of knowledge on his conscience? Curse Brother Paul! thought Brother John, while trying to expunge his mind of what he had just heard. So the man has a sex addiction, don't we all have our secret sins?

The point being, did this fact bring Brother John any closer to the Truth or to happiness itself? The flesh can be a wonderful temptress, but she is too fickle. Her pleasure lasts only a moment, in all-consuming ecstasy, but then it fades away just as quickly and all you are left with is a lonely, tired feeling.

Self-pleasure was a drug meant to mask and waste the feeling of accomplishment given by working. Brother John's past love came to mind as she would waste away her time on shallow things, like shopping and eating decadent desserts in restaurants. Her mind filled up with things that made her feel good instantly, little pick-me-ups serving her throughout the day to hide her sense of low self-esteem. She was ultimately worthless. She did not produce or create anything, she just lived off the fat of the land. Her life today must be the same and Brother John knew he could not breed such lifelessness.

Instead, he found life in the very place where people believe death lurks—the monastery. Here was a place where the monks worked and never consumed more than they needed to survive. Their bodies were not bloated with the sins of gluttony or laziness. Although, clearly, the monks still dealt with sins. But one could sympathize much more readily with the sins of monks than the sins of the layman, thought Brother John, who was now laying on his bed with his hands behind his head lost in thought.

Mary bubbled up in his mind again as he listened to the last few sighs coming from Brother Paul's cell. Although still very much a stranger, Mary must be a girl who fantasizes about her wedding someday and believes that her knight is out there somewhere waiting for her. Brother John could see her waiting for marriage before experiencing bodily pleasure and he could see her throw herself into art whenever a sexual urge struck as she aged.

Mary was her own kind of angel. One that in the modern age stuck out very much, but here she would be welcome and fit it. As a nun, Mary could freely do her art and she would be supported in it too. Her time tending the garden in the spring and summer would serve as her creative fuel.

Oh, Mary, thought Brother John. Mary, if only you could become a nun! If only I could know that you were safe, then perhaps I could sleep better at night. Knowing that you were in the nearby nunnery, stowed away but thriving, would keep my soul at peace. But, alas, here I am voluntarily and you can only join us in the same vein.

Brother John spent the rest of his prayer time trying to forget all that he had heard and forcing out imaginary telepathic messages that he hoped would influence Mary's soul wherever she was that day.

She was probably in school right now, learning the basics of biology or English grammar or ratios in math class, attuning her mind to the frequency of all the most intelligent minds of human history. School could be very similar to a nunnery, Mary, thought Brother John. We remain students of the Lord and learn about His teachings all day long. Our routine is just as strict and we are all a tight-knit community.

***

53

Terce flew by as Brother John was still lost in thoughts about Mary. The morning's work began, and he was outside, working in the garden once again. More vegetables needed planting and watering.

Brother Paul was nearby Brother John, and he knew that in order to live among his brothers, he had to maintain at least a cordial relationship with everyone.

"Good morning, brother," said Brother John, giving him the side of his face to avoid looking directly at him.

Brother Paul looked up like nothing was amiss. "Good morning to you. How have your thoughts about the Lord been this early?"

"Oh, pleasant…devoted," said Brother John, with a little smile included, to avoid admitting that it focused his mind on other things this morning. "And yours?"

"Wonderful, wonderful. You know 'by God's grace I am what I am' and no other. I am learning to accept myself and the others around me, for we are all sinners. I cannot help but sin every day, though I try to avoid doing such. But the Lord knows we are weak creatures. After all, He says that we must 'run while you have the light of life, that the darkness' of death 'may not overtake you.' I read that in John 12:35 this morning. I took this to mean that I must 'keep your tongue free from vicious talk and your lips from all deceit; turn away from evil and do good; let peace be your quest and aim.' As long as I keep Christ's name on my lips, then I may find peace. Do you believe the same, brother?"

Brother John nodded in assent and he pulled some little weeds growing around the foot of the rose bush near him. He plucked the roots out of the ground with ease, like a tick from his last meal.

For a while, there was a silence between them where a conversation was conveyed but unspoken. By giving human air to the sins, it would render them real.

Brother Paul's addiction to pleasure was left untouched, but the name of Christ was still on his lips from when he last opened them. Did that render all of his sins purified once more? Could the holy veil of a word endowed with such powers keep him from readily touching himself again this afternoon? Impossible, thought Brother John. He is lying to himself if he thinks such magical wishes.

It seems that Brother Immanuel's abusive nature serves much more to change his actions than some throwaway phrases from the Bible. I saw his own flesh break and blood pour forth from his open wounds, thought Brother John, beginning to feel lightheaded at the very thought.

"Well, brother, I believe that peace also comes from our routine and the stability from within."

"You sound like our Buddhist brothers."

"Remember that we do have a teahouse in our garden which comes from the Eastern tea traditions. I think we could perhaps learn much from them."

"Eh, they believe in nothingness. How could you feel anything?"

Brother John continued weeding with a furrowed brow, his thick brows shielding his eyes from the sun. He found it curious that all Eastern thought was about the space in between, the nothingness, being nothing. It placed emphasis on being the opposite or opposing force as much as the alternative—the complex yin and yang—to bring peace and harmony into life.

But that was like saying that the Good of Christ was needed

in a person just as much as the evil of the devil. But in Catholicism, and generally, in Western thought, those were diametrical opposites, never to touch if possible. Or if Man did give in to one, at least in the stories, it was always wholly. There was no in-between. You were either good or bad, whole or nothing.

Brother John found more footing in the Western ideas than the Eastern ones. Yet, he always revered how they paid attention to their every move, like everything in life was a ritual. There was a grace and acknowledgment of the materials we possessed, or at least manipulated. The plates and mugs and food at mealtime became almost anthropomorphized as we thanked it and God for giving it to us. The work in the garden gave a voice to our tired hands and the happiness of the freshly watered plants. The chants grew more harmonized as all of our breaths synchronized as one, while the power of attuning ourselves to details was something that both cultures could bring out in Man.

Brother Paul, with his balding head, put on his sun hat and kept working along the edge of the beds, plucking out any weeds peeking out onto the stone walkway. He worked rather quickly for being so out of shape.

Meanwhile, Brother John moved further down the bed, away from Brother Paul's general direction. Enough of an olive branch was tossed out, in Brother John's mind, to keep the peace between the two neighbors.

Regardless of if Brother John heard a repeat of yesterday's actions, he was better prepared today to focus on himself and his own growth down the path of Truth.

Maybe, thought Brother John, the Truth was Mary coming back to the garden to visit me. His heart beat a little faster.

Or maybe it is going through the motions daily, filling up my mind with memories of each beautiful moment I collected along the way. I think most of all I want to learn more, sift through all the information in my mind, and then pop out a beautiful gem of creative effort, thought Brother John.

He did not know exactly what the product would be, but he knew he wanted to create something. For all the things he knew, other people should see the world as he saw it too. Time and space were crucial for any creative throughout history to create a masterpiece.

CHAPTER V

That is what Brother John desired—to create a masterpiece. Someday, he would be old and full of knowledge that would just end up seeping out of him. He would have to share his struggles with himself and his own humanity with the world, eventually. There was no other option. Mary could not be his Truth or his peace. She only served as a distraction. Brother John plucked another weed from the dirt without hesitation, its tiny roots dangling in their nakedness and vulnerability.

"What are you up to over there, Brother John?" called out Brother Daniel.

Startled out of his absorption with the dangling roots in front of his nose, Brother John watched Brother Daniel approaching. He set down the weeds, eyeing the young man who had such dark hair that he would have a constant shadow of a beard on his face, even if he shaved it daily. He used to don the sharpest-looking beard in town before he became a monk. Brother Daniel was a teacher for only a few years after graduating from college. His popularity there was enormous because he taught a course on the American government and all the ways that it did not work. The high schoolers thought that he was going to be like the hip college professor that they would meet once they graduated…and they were not far off.

He was a teacher who never followed the textbooks and attended every teacher's union strike that happened and even organized some of them himself. Brother Daniel tanned easily in the sun and he used his darker tone to manipulate people into believing that everything he said was gold. He remained fit even when he decided to put down his classroom chalk and pick up his monastic cloth. Nothing about him had really changed since entering the monastery as an Observer, like Brother John. He remained self-righteous about how we are all meant to help one another in a community. Everyone in the monastery knew that this was an act of activism for Brother Daniel, a ruse for his students to see that life in a village was better than being alone.

And yet, thought Brother John, we were all alone here all the time. Even when we sang and ate together, we were still caught inside our own minds. There was no way out of our bodies either, as evidenced by Brother Paul's decisions.

Brother John kept weeding along the outer edges of the rose bush beds, saying, "Oh, I'm just weeding over here. The roses look like they could use some more room and the stone path is getting devoured by the weeds."

"Yes, I can see that. Are you contemplating your monastic vows of chastity and poverty and obedience?" shouted Brother Daniel, much too loud for the distance that was left between them.

Brother Daniel wanted to play the alpha male in all situations. Even underneath his robes, a man could see his puffed-up chest, his muscular arms, and heard his booming voice. Brother John wondered whether he would actually be called upon to even serve as a Postulant when the time came. His personality did not mix with the land of contemplation—he had no desire for silence.

"Always. Did I not shed my possessions and my lover and give myself wholly to this monastery?"

"Indeed, we all did, brother," said Brother Daniel, "but that does not mean that we are actively anti-sinners. Those people who are not chaste, are rich, and are hedonists who obey no one must be punished for their sins. Don't you think so?"

"You should talk to Brother Immanuel when he is finished repenting in his cell. For he would tell you we monks are pacifists. We do not engage in fighting, only praying for those who differ from us and, otherwise, leaving them be."

Brother Daniel sighed, rolling his eyes, attempting to make Brother John feel small. "You know, there was a time when Catholics would murder a man for betraying God."

"Yes, that was a darker period in human history where we had erred. But things like the Inquisition have not been around since the twelfth century. Man learns by not repeating history. We used and abused God's words," said Brother John.

"You think the Inquisition was over at that time? No, brother. The last execution of the Inquisition was in 1826, and in Italy, there is *still* a congregation that defends the Catholic doctrine from heresy. The Inquisition is very much alive even today, brother, just hidden and dried over time, but true activists of the faith can bring back the river."

The wind made the tree branches clap with applause for Brother Daniel as the birds sang for his march against the sinners of this world. He was a man filled with rage and a ravenous hunger for power, which made Brother John more uneasy than knowing that Brother Paul was a self-pleaser.

"I did not know that. I suppose my readings have been rather narrow of late. I do not read the latest news if I can avoid it. The world outside no longer interests me. I am only concerned with myself and how my life is unfolding."

"How very selfish of you, brother. Your life is but one drop in the vast ocean of human history, but the Inquisition has consumed many of you to last as long as it has. Besides, we cannot read everything in here. Have you noticed there are no medical books? What do you gain from your readings outside of the Bible?"

"I read the Bible as a poet would and try to live more slowly from it as a result. I also read some of the great poets, like Keats and Byron. I read Homer's epics, and I read Saint Benedict's rules daily. My mind has enough to focus on and I believe that the monastery only allows for that which is beautiful. I have the books I require."

Brother Daniel scrunched up his face, making his forehead wrinkles pop out especially far in his disbelief. "Since I have gotten here, brother, I have missed my daily dose of news and I have missed teaching my students about the horrors of the world. I want my mission here to be seen and heard by everyone on this planet."

"Perhaps your ambitions are too large for this monastery then," said Brother John.

And with that, Brother Daniel decided that there would be no hope of convincing this brother to join him in his fight and he turned around to find another.

***

Brother Daniel would not make it here long, thought Brother John. At the very least, the psychologist would see through his facade. The facade that he put on when in front of the abbot or any visitors of the humble, quiet monk. His voice would automatically drop to a softer, weaker tone and he would change his body language to avoid suspicion.

But his actual behavior was often brought out to each monk when they were alone, usually working on some task at hand. He probably did much the same thing at his school when he wanted teachers to join him on strike.

To minimize the uncomfortable moment, Brother John shook himself, jostling his robes against his skin, causing them to form goosebumps which were not helping him avoid the feeling of discomfort. In fact, there were days when he wished to throw off the uncomfortable robe, especially on hot summer days when the sweat became absorbed and held the horrible odor of his own stench. There was no need for chloroform in a monastery since a monk could simply pass out from his own smell.

Brother John hid his smiling face inside his cowl, which he quickly flung over his head for this purpose. Hiding expressions were something that every monk had done during his time here. That is why most people in the outside world believed that monks are always so solemn because that is usually the only side of them they get to see. The inner emotions that float up and rearrange their features get hidden away from view in the black cave of the cowl. This hood, like a woman's bridal veil, keeps the men sheltered from the outside even within the walls of the monastery. Their robes themselves, their habits, allowed the monks to sink deeper into themselves regularly, for the baggy form obscures the proper outlines of their bodies, leaving everything to a person's fancy.

With three strokes of the nave's bell, it was time for Sext. The second "little hour" of the day was passed by with haste, as most of the monks' stomachs were beginning to gurgle during the gorgeous harmonies. The chants were accompanied by the sound of seething, spitting guts. Man was an animal after all.

Falling from their heavenly prayers, the monks all went to feed on soup, more bread, some vegetables, and fruit. Brother John, in particular, loved fruit. It was God's dessert. He provided some of the most colorful and sweetly complex objects for Man to enjoy.

Biting into an apple was the first sweet thing he had tasted all day. It has such a crisp, refreshing taste that made his glands swell up in eagerness and satisfaction. The apple was sweet with just a hint of tartness coming in near the end. The tart bit came from the skin, while the inner white flesh was so sweet, Brother John thought it to be almost too much. How could something in nature be so good? wondered Brother John.

He always saved his fruit for last, no matter what it was: an apple, a banana, an orange. Any kind of fruit was saved as a treat. Brother John also left pause in between the salty food he ate and the sweet, usually drinking water or tea in between to cleanse his palate for the difference in taste.

The bread served with every meal never truly got old because as a staple food of the Lord's body, the human body always seemed to forget how delicious it was after each meal. Bread served the monks well as their staple food, and they ate it with as much pleasure as if it was a sirloin steak.

Salt also called forth the salivary glands in Brother John's mouth but not as fully as fruit did. Fruit acted as the drug needed for him to carry on happily and full for the rest of the day, or at least until the evening supper.

Focused on his apple and the peace it brought him, Brother John lost track of the time. When the great bell rang again to signal the end of the meal, Brother John only heard it in the far distances in his mind, like an echo.

"Come now, Brother John, we must help to wash up these dishes before resting on our laurels," said one of the monks sitting near him.

"Yes, yes, I think I went into a bit of a food coma there," said Brother John.

"Well, that is not a good sign, brother. You always drop everything at the sound of the bell. You cannot be gluttonous, even on the Lord's body."

"I will pray for my sins, brother," said Brother John, walking away with his face hidden in his cowl.

The little kitchen looked just as it did in the mid-nineteenth century when it was originally built. There was an unadorned cast-iron cookstove where a monk lit the fire inside and the stove on top grew hot enough to cook on. There was either a pile of coal or wood nearby to fuel it when cooking meals or drinks.

The sink was connected to the well outside and the cast-iron pipes led to the faucet, which gave the monks a bit of water to work with at a time. Usually, it was easier to go directly outside to the well and pump water into a bucket, fill the basin of the sink with water, and wash their dishes in that.

They all used aprons while washing the dishes to avoid dirtying their habits and as a matter of form. The monks all formed a working line, handing down one plate or mug at a time to the designated washer and then dryer and then replacer. The dishes were usually complete within half an hour.

Now, the time to return to their cells for prayer or rest or other activities to feed the mind was upon the monks until work time at two o'clock that afternoon. Brother John walked, in no hurry, back to his cell, still savoring the taste of the apple in his mouth.

Today, Brother John lay on his bed in solidarity with Brother Immanuel, who just had to last the rest of the day before his self-penance was complete. Lying there on the thin mattress, a chill took hold of his nonmoving body, even though it was still full of food. He pulled the blanket up over himself as he stared up at the ceiling.

Jolting upright, he scratched his neck where he felt something crawling. He nearly cried out in the middle of his empty room, like waking up from a nightmare. Indeed, a creepy, crawly spider, spooked at the fact that the object he was on moved, was crawling on down Brother John's sleeve and onto his bed.

He, himself, scurried up much like the frightened spider and ran to the other side of the room. A normal man would kill it immediately with his hands, which was his first conclusion, but a monk would save the creature and take it back outside into nature. Taking a deep breath, he looked around his room for anything that could hold an arachnid, but it was so barren in there that nothing but a sheet of paper would suffice.

Bending down at the hips, with quaking hands, Brother John tried sliding the paper underneath the spider's legs—trying not to injure any of them at the same time. But the little creature just kept running away from the large white specter, which Brother John could not help but understand. He imagined if he too were approached by a wave of blank nothingness, hitting him in the shins and trying to lift him onto its flat surface. The desire to kill the stranger dimmed as he watched how the spider reacted to stimuli.

He kept bent over, trying to scoop him up from another angle. The poor spider must have been so confused that in every direction, this white background to his world was coming after him. I would be petrified, if anything, thought Brother John, as he kept at his task. Finally, with a bit of speed and a little less concern about the spider's legs, which were surprisingly durable, Brother John scooped up the little spider who was now running faster than before, round and round on the page.

If he were to squish him in between the white edges of the paper, there would be a deep red and black splotch and no one in the monastery would know that Brother John took life, besides God. His brothers would not know that he had committed the sin. The killing of an arachnid was certainly a much quieter sin than what Brother Paul did to himself. There was no cry to be heard or screams or the crushing of bones, just a blip in the universe. And yet…it had a design. This little creature was fully formed and functioned enough to move and sustain itself. There was life even smaller than him who were considered living organisms that had instincts and would move away from pain and toward pleasure. The drive to eat was common among all of us. And there were creatures in this world much larger than Man who desired similar things for survival. What right did I have, thought Brother John, to take another life? In Romans 13:9, it states clearly "you are not to kill." I shall therefore take this spider outside back into God's creation, for the monastery is Man's.

Holding his attention to the spider, attempting desperately to find his way off the paper, Brother John quietly opened his door and slid down the hallway toward the exit. But his efforts at being quiet did not stop other monks from poking their heads outside of their rooms to see what was going on since no monk is to leave his room at this time unless due to an emergency, though his room served as his infirmary, anyway.

"Hey, brother, what are you doing?" asked the nosy Brother Paul.

"I am taking out a spider from my room back into nature," hissed Brother John.

"You should have let him live in peace with you," laughed Brother Paul.

"Not if I ever wanted to sleep peacefully again." Brother John opened the door to the world, allowing the light and wind to come in and further disturbing the resting monks from their routine. So, it turned out that good deeds can actually be louder than the sins we commit, he thought, placing one of his sandaled feet outside and leaning forward to drop the scared one off the paper.

Surely, the familiarity of the green grass and the feeling of the wind and the sun must make the spider calm down. He must know in some way that he is saved, right? wondered Brother John. Either way, recognition for doing good was not the aim. The aim was for life to be treated with respect. Life in any form should not be hindered from thriving until its flame naturally burns out. I, for one, vowed Brother John to himself, will *never* be responsible for another living creature's death if I can help it.

Upon closing the door and turning around, Brother John watched the whole hallways of doors swing shut as the monks all pulled their shiny, bald heads back into their cells. They knew that the disturbance to their reveries was over. Brother John walked back to his room alone, with his own thoughts following him and his heart feeling a little fuller than before.

A spider's life was saved today by a monk who thought about merely erasing him from existence a moment before. He shuddered to imagine what the outside world's people did. They gave no second thought, no time to interact with the living organism, no chance to feel good about saving the Good. For life must *be* the Good, thought Brother John. Life, at least, maintained the possibility and hope of something better, while death maintained nothing.

The idea of death was one that Brother John never liked to dwell on, even though it was all around him in the monastery— from the horrified-looking statues in stone to the bleeding Christ. Death and dying were built into the very fabric of the religious experience. The monastery even worked on caskets for the poor in certain seasons.

But he always believed that if he thought about dying too much that it might make him insane. Perhaps it was some kind of wives' tale to believe in such a fear since one was not supposed to fear death and going to Heaven. Still, Brother John struggled, and he feared.

There were even times when he felt jealous that he would someday die and be forgotten, while others kept living and having a world to hold and other living creatures to save. He would no longer be among the living species that he had called home for so long.

The thought of dying always brought him back to the most recent death that occurred within the monastery. One of the eldest monks, a man who had reached eighty-five, was ill in his cell for a week—he screamed in his sleep, awoke out of fever dreams so terrifying that he urinated himself frequently, and was generally lost in a foggy haze so deep that several monks had to come in to feed him and eventually an IV was used. His arms withered and shrunk so much that there was no way to give him food and liquids anymore. The poor monk was bathed and moved and fed—we all became his mother as he lay there dying.

The old monk once shouted out that he could feel the flames of hell on his feet, which were now full of pustules and boiling hot to the touch. He went from withered to puffy and bloated in a matter of days. If he knew that his body was cannibalizing itself, then perhaps he would have chosen not to be buried whole in one of our caskets. Though the monks still preferred to keep to the age-old tradition of burial over cremation, it was permissible nowadays. But this poor old monk had no clue what his body looked like now or how it smelled. He probably still imagined himself as an eighteen-year-old lad just entering the monastery for the first time in his life, only now, hell itself was opening up and trying to swallow him through the floor. Yet, he remained whole and not withered or bloated or anything other than the form he took when he was not ill.

We become strangers to ourselves whenever our bodies change, thought Brother John. Poor brother, at least he never had time to see the stranger that he had become. It was almost as if he prepared all of his brothers to disassociate his last days from the man they knew before his illness. By the end of that week, when he had drawn his final breaths, we really no longer saw him as Brother Simon.

Instead, if I remember correctly, we all saw him as a putrid body—something no longer to be touched or associated with. Our desire to put him into the ground as quickly as possible burned within us, though no one dared say such things. We pretended to treat him as Brother Simon, but it was so hard to see past the mortified flesh and the sinking eyes. This could not possibly be the same old man who, when animated, would draw sketches of bunnies and farmland or snored loudly in his cell or grinned with what few teeth he had left when he heard a funny joke.

This lump of bones, covered in decaying flesh, was not Brother Simon. Brother Simon's spirit must have fled as soon as his skin began bloating, just as the rest of us desired to abandon him immediately.

Brother John knew that for many days, all the abbot was hearing at confession was their guilt for feeling the strong desire to flee Brother Simon in his most vulnerable moments. That last week was so hard for all the monks. No one was saved from sharing the guilt that came with seeing a member picked off by death.

Of course, all the monks had their minds filled with illu-minated manuscripts adorned with the cloaked phantom of death with his scythe, the grim reaper, coming to collect souls. All the men envisioned the robe that often reminded them of their own robes and the violent weapon held in the dominant hand. They also had seen the manuscript of royalty being accompanied by the dancing skeleton of death to their own graves or a dance with the devil, sealing their miserable fate.

But how could death move? wondered Brother John. Movement was a thing only life could do. Perhaps that is what scared monks the most, that of holding onto the idea that the devil or a servant of the devil could cross between the living and the dead, like a missing link existing between the two words, as on All Hallows' Eve when the veil grew thin.

Or perhaps the skeletons were to show Man in all his naked glory—he was simply a creature designed out of hard connective tissue. Perhaps, the Bible wanted us to see that we were framed by natural material that the Lord himself animated, tired of, and discarded when He was ready. Brother John shuddered to think of himself as merely a pawn without free will. He felt so in control of himself and his activities and his joys.

Death, in whatever form, took Brother Simon mercilessly by the end of that horrific week. But Brother John, along with all the other monks, sighed with relief that it was not them. And they figured God would be more kind to them when their time came. Surely, they all thought that they would disappear quietly like other, anonymous monks before them in their sleep—never even noticing their absence the next day. Death for those lucky ones would be swift and sweet.

CHAPTER VI

Brother John's morbid time spent in his cell ceased when the bell rang loudly for work. Work was the most effective way for Brother John to stave off any thoughts about death. All of his worries and subsequent fears floated away, far in the depth of his mind, locked in a place where they would never escape until the next time an isolated, quiet time arose.

For now, Brother John left his cell as if he was running from a dancing skeleton, luring him to the dark pit six feet under, his long robe trailing behind him. Today, he decided to work on dusting the books in the library. The garden vegetables could wait for him for one day.

He headed down the hall, still as if running from something haunting him. Brother John passed the bare wooden tables used for meals and into a gorgeous room that appeared just as high as the great nave. There were tall wooden shelves, built all the way up to the ceiling, filled with books. The books were categorized neatly and stacked together by series, their spines were bound in leather with embossed gold text and beautiful scrolls. Many of the texts were still in Latin. There were saints' busts on top of cabinets filled with old newspapers and obituaries from the past. Everything was a sacred relic once a monk passed through the threshold of the rectangular mouth of the door to the library.

There were several wooden chairs and a few secretary desks scattered throughout the space for a monk to sit and study. He could pull stacks from the shelves and pore over them to write religious theses of his own ideas. The library was a place for the ultimate contemplation in Brother John's mind.

The study of the sacred sciences involved "divine reading" also known as *Lectio Divina* and all the greatest thinkers of the Western world emerged out of practices like these in the scriptorium and library.

There were still quills and ink for those monks desiring to hearken back to a more ancient time or pens for those who wanted to delve fully into the words without distraction.

Brother John had always had a weakness for this room. Heaven must look like this library, where each book is filled with a person's soul. He felt so strongly just then about the books and the amount of respect they deserved that he chose to wash the windows of the library first—to get his hands warmed up before dusting his beloved books.

Brother John carried a simple bucket filled with water and dipped a rag in it, making sure to twist tightly and squeeze out any excess water.

The windows were made in the mid-nineteenth century, so hot glass was normally cast on a round plate to cool before it was then polished and the frames were made of wood. The rolled steel frames were not invented yet. So, everything was slightly worn down and drafty. Brother John delicately wiped the dirt and grime off the large-paned windows. Some panels shuttered as he rubbed the rag against them.

Still, Brother John felt satisfaction in seeing the garden more clearly from the library. He smiled, watching bald Brother Paul trip over some vines as he worked in the tomato patches.

Although it was wrong of Brother John to laugh at his brother's inelegant behavior, he knew that the mockery was shallow and did not reflect on his moral character.

There were also limestone columns in between the windows, which made it difficult for Brother John to clean. He would have to step down from the window ledge of stone, carry his bucket and rag by the column in the way, and then step up to the next window for cleaning.

Brother John chalked all of his efforts up to a good cardio exercise, which was required for any monk who sat for too long in contemplation day after day.

The light shone more brightly through the cleaned windows that Brother John cleared. He took a moment to turn around on the stones and look out over the library and the scriptorium further in. He thought nothing was more beautiful than the sunlight hitting the spines of golden text, causing them to glisten.

Brother John's favorite place since he was born was the library. The sights, sounds, and smells were all familiar to him. It felt like the arts were the most selfish of professions. He loved looking down the aisles of books in a library. There were books with multi-colored spines, each sticking out at a variety of lengths on the bookshelves. In fact, Brother John could envision each story, each brain in a jar of formaldehyde, lying still for a long while until someone wanted to inspect it.

He noticed that any library he had ever visited before entering the monastery had similar sights, sounds, and smells, all of which made him feel safe. So safe that when he got to one, he suddenly felt a need to explore. Brother John was his own detective. He would crawl on hands and knees through corridors of books towering above him when he was younger. If one book were to fall from such a height, he would have died right on the spot. How many library-related deaths have occurred? He could have been famous had he succumbed to such a fate.

No, Brother John now envisioned himself becoming a great thinker among the monks. But for now, he was perfectly content living among the musky scent of yellowed pages that were flipped through quickly against his nose, or the soothing-colored rugs that would always burn his knees, or the various corners where privacy and quiet serenity laid a welcoming sigh of relief on the reader. Even the lighting was soothing. It was a semi-lit library and scriptorium with thousands upon thousands of books he may never even set his eyes on. To pick one book was to pick one human. For Brother John knew the stakes and believed that he had to filter through all the books in the world and choose the best ones to fill his mind with...just like with people.

There are nearly eight billion people on this planet. Most of whom he knew he would never meet. The key to his happiness was to select simply the people and books he could respect and grow from.

Although Brother John's robes were growing old and hole-ridden, his mind was expanding anew and brighter than before amidst these texts. In his own excited radiance, Brother John quickened his cleaning of the windows to tend to the books. The sunlight disappeared within the hour to be consumed by rain clouds.

Raining outside the library's windowpane, the thudding of each droplet as earth's breath smashed the tiny orbs against the pane, Brother John relished the moment. He remembered as a child the taste of pure butter shortbread enrapturing his tongue, while sweet, exotic spices from his cup of tea washed down the remains. The comforting light of the library of his childhood, the stacked books, reflected in the window. Tired lids opened and closed shut like heavy wooden doors when he read for too long. The lull soothed his heart into a rhythmical samba and danced with his dear friend, blood. The circulating droplets kept his body warm as he would keep adding caffeine into the mixture, faster and faster it goes, until the once muddled text now became clear again and the book soon had legs! *Freedom*! it shouted. Until its stubby, weak form fell back down and he must have drifted off to dreamland while reading again. All night, Brother John would sit when young, alone with his books, in silence, under the sky's fallen tears.

Brother John looked at a library like another person may look at nature…with pure joy—a kind of triumphant ecstasy of the soul. His love for libraries stemmed from his admiration for people's "blood, sweat, and tears." Their dreams and hopes and efforts were all neatly bound and tucked away on orderly shelves. Lives were preserved, and a rich chorus of voices was held together by the backbone of some fabric and glue. The ink imprints the thought onto a page, multiple pages of well-thought-out sentences and ideas. The power of words struck him to his core and bought total rapture to the harmony those pages created.

It is funny, thought Brother John, but when I feel over-whelmed and "trapped in myself" the only way to relieve it is to write. He took down a piece of paper from a desk in the scriptorium to jot down some notes. He thought that it almost felt like someone was releasing the air pressure. The individual is turning the wheel clockwise, slowly letting me deflate my head. My thoughts flow out onto the page, even if they're completely unusable. It still allows me some peace and quiet. On some days, I feel like it is a chore, but if I do not do it, I feel worse. This feeling is comparable to when people get "hooked" on exercise. They feel "so much better" when they work out that on a day when they are squeezed for time they feel awful all day. Somehow, my mind seems to be programmed similarly—only just exercise doesn't cut it. With writing, I seem to begin in a tired state and then I become more energized through the use of words. Just allowing every fleeting thought to slip from my conscious mind to the page gives me serenity. I remember the first time when I asked my mother if "serenity" was a word, and she pleasantly surprised me when she said yes.

Brother John tried not to cry over his family too much. He would never see them again since he threw off the yolk of his past life. Yet, they stuck along in his memories daily. Often his thoughts would disengage themselves from his paper, allowing his fingers to keep going through their tap dance routine when he wrote letters to no one. His mind wandered often to thoughts of Mary and her pale, little arms grasping up toward the sky and her vibrant green eyes. She was an earthy girl with dirt-colored hair and pink lips. Brother John often wrote letters to her like a romantic who, akin to a chess piece, moves each thought of his into carefully calculated action. If one incorrect move occurred, he may lose her. Humbled by his circumstances, he tried not to reveal too much, as if the world would laugh at his leaky heart. An organ that palpitates at a different tempo from the way his body moved when he was around her. But he was caught: two twins of the same celestial body wanted him. Mary was their inspiration. They are one and the same—soul and body—independent forces with a ruling presence. They cried out for Mary, shouting, "We do not *need* anyone. And yet, we *must* have someone!"

Writing in the scriptorium gave Brother John a chance to express himself. He relied on his readings from Aristotle and Plato to guide his thoughts when he was aching for something other than Saint Benedict. Aristotle brought the physical into view to analyze and touch, while Plato dissected the ethereal realm that seemed so far away. Hovering back and forth like a hummingbird, Brother John would dart from the poetic to the practical while contemplating and reading and writing. His "chewing of the cud" gave him the time to entertain different theories and ways to make himself happier.

His neck hurt every time he got lost in his writing because, inevitably, after a few hours, he found himself sitting with his nose to the page, hunched over like an eighty-year-old man. Upon righting himself, Brother John carefully folded the pages he had written and stuck them in his robe, pushing in the wooden chair, and picking up a feather duster for the books.

The poor books were so dusty, no matter how frequently a brother came in to clean them. It was as if, after a certain number of years, the books were required to wear the dust like an extra book jacket. All the particles floated around in the sunspots that came out after the rain clouds moved on across the land. Brother John watched them float down gracefully and settle on the floor beneath his feet.

Dusting the books occupied the rest of the workday for Brother John until the bell rang three times for scripture and supper. Tonight, the abbot was starting the reading in his usual monotone voice, while the rest of the monks picked up their trays of bread, fruit, and tea. Supper was always one of the lightest meals of the day. It may have been considered a snack, and the monks really intermittently fasted from noon on.

However, Brother John took his small meal with grace. He took the time to dip his nose deep into his green tea to take in all the steamy warmth filling his nasal cavity, he moistened the bread with his saliva, and he let the fresh piece of apple sit on his tongue for a good minute before chewing it fully and swallowing.

In the ecstasy of his endeavors, Brother John heard Brother Daniel Edgeworth rise from his seat with furious relish. He was inspired to lead the prayer for a while as the other monks ate their supper.

Brother Daniel stood up tall, puffing out his thick chest to poke out from his robe before opening: "My brothers, I call you all to the Lord's table to eat with him and be still through the night. This is our evening supper, which is made to hold us over until the morning. Take care to eat slowly and well, for the fight for salvation is about to begin anew."

The monks began eyeing each other back and forth as Brother Daniel continued: "My brothers, 'it is high time for us to arise from sleep' for we must no longer close our ears to the outside world. There are people out there in need. People out there who are heretics denigrating God's good word. They must be stopped!"

The abbot was turning red in the face. His head looked like a balloon ready to burst from the neck opening in his habit. "Brother Daniel, the point of being a monk is to pray for the world from the outside. We are not vigilantes."

Brother Daniel could see that he had persuaded no one to hear him out, so he took a step back in his tactics, relying more stringently on the Bible and its words. Clearing his throat: "Of course, 'I do not wish the death of the sinner, but that he turn back to me and live.' I do not wish physical violence upon those who have betrayed Christ. I only wish for us to take a larger role in making them see their sins and repent for them.

"You see, in Matthew, it even says 'love your enemies' and so we will use our words and the authority of the church to right the wrongs committed by the sinners over the oppressed men, women, and children who exist in this world. Aren't you all tired of waiting on the edge of the world? Don't you want to teach others how to live the sinless way of our Lord? I, for one, am ready to take our message to the people. I want to be a monk who serves the world. Isn't that what we should strive for? Brothers?"

Brother Daniel skimmed his eyes over the group of monks, now with all of their heads lowered as if asleep. The food was still slowly making it to their mouths, but they felt much more at ease hiding their expressions inside their cowls.

The abbot finally spoke when Brother Daniel paused for long enough to get a word in. "Dear brother, we feel your passion and believe that righteousness is a good trait to have as the Lord's servant. But you may not desire the monk's life after all. You are describing men who are still of the world. Monks are not. You are trying to alter the very definition of what a monk is and does. He is a man who has committed himself to a life of penance, free from life's distractions, to praise the Lord and save souls. The way to save souls is through contemplative prayer—not physical or verbal violence. We would only sin further if we did such things that were against the Lord's will."

Brother Daniel was scowling now, daring to stick his face further out of his cowl rather than in like the others. "Well, perhaps monks need to change from their medieval ways in order to accomplish anything. Who says that we cannot shape modern monk life?" He stood up on one of the wooden tables, which creaked underneath his weight.

"So, what brothers are with me, committed to changing how monks exist?" He lifted his mug of hot tea, looking for a face, even one face, to connect with in the line of monks. There were none. "Fine, well, maybe I will not make it to the Postulant stage after all. I cannot see myself being here for too long if I cannot feel my change prayers working on those soulless sinners out there who are belching and laughing at the face of God every day.

"Yes, can you imagine it? Men who rape women—"

"That's enough, Brother Daniel," cut in the abbot, his cheeks ruddy with anger.

"But I am just getting started, father! What happened to 'do not gratify the promptings of the flesh'"?

Brother John watched Brother Paul wince as he heard that last question.

"Do not you feel we should be outraged for the Lord who speaks through us?" asked Brother Daniel.

The abbot, who had never done such a thing before, slammed his fist against the meal table. The plates jumped up together before clattering down and all the monks hid deep inside themselves then. Not a sound could be heard in all the echoey halls of the monastery.

The abbot rose, walked over to Brother Daniel, and motioned with his hand to get down off the table. The somewhat startled Brother Daniel followed, and the abbot walked him back to his cell in peace. He was not seen outside of his cell for the rest of the evening.

***

The monks spent the final moments of their meal sitting in silence. This was not unusual except that tonight there was an electricity of thinking minds who tried so very hard to ask telepathically each other questions about Brother Daniel's punishment and how a man could veer so much from the monastic path. The men there became monks precisely for the peace and stability the lifestyle brought them and not to engage in this kind of violent rhetoric—Brother Daniel's days here were likely limited after this latest stunt.

The monks, in a single file, left the meal area to enter the nave for Vespers. Once the final line vanished into the air of the great hall, the men returned to their rooms for prayer at six. Brother John entered his room and headed straight for his bed. After serving as a witness to the drama at supper, he felt drained of energy and required a nap to keep him awake until his actual bedtime.

Closing his eyes, he fought a nasty headache that was coming from all the tension at hearing Brother Daniel lash out. He was filled with such anger, the likes of which were alien to Brother John. He stroked his temples in slow-moving circles, manipulating his skin until the circular strokes slowed and his hand fell by his side.

He dreamed about Mary on a plane, restlessly waiting to escape the environment that she had become accustomed to in school. She was older now and headed to the nunnery of her dreams. She wanted to detox from the way people behaved on a daily basis. She needed oxygen.

He imagined the plane beginning to move, and Mary shut

her eyes, trying not to look out the window as it started accelerating up to speed for liftoff. She squished between two people who were looking around the plane, ignoring her childish existence. Mary's eyelids cracked open a bit and she could breathe again. They were in the air. Tension built up inside of her as she continued the flight. Inside her head, the constant fiery image crept up of the plane burning—of the crowd descending, free-falling, and dying. But Mary attempted to sleep the trip off until landing. Somehow it worked.

Mary walked over to a taxi in which a large man took her to the hotel. He sat there, taking peeks at her from the front mirror. The wrinkles on his forehead made deep creases as he fumbled over some concerning question in his mind.

"How old are you, miss?"

"Nineteen."

"Oh, you look like a high school student."

"Nope." Turning red, Mary shuffled around in her purse for something nonexistent to take the blow that was just given to her a little easier.

Brother John imaged the cab slowing to a stop and Mary dragging her suitcases to the hotel. Grasping the door handle with one hand and her suitcase with the other, she yanked the door open and propped her suitcase in between. Bending down, she grabbed the second case and entered the hotel, which smelled like pine needles. Dragging her aching body toward the front desk, she asked to check into the hotel. This middle-aged blonde woman looked up from behind her computer screen, the droll expression making Mary uncomfortable. The woman opened her incompetent mouth, the thin lips contorting into a vowel-friendly shape. She answered: "Your name isn't on the list. You're gonna have to call the name it's under to add you."

Mary's eyes blinked rapidly as she contemplated strangling this woman to death or asking her to do it for herself. Somehow, Mary's hand subconsciously typed the number into her phone and called. Anastasia did not pick up but Crystal did. The crisis was averted.

Pulling the suitcases up to the second floor, she slipped the card key into the door and dumped her bags on the floor. Mary started feeling the tremendous exhaustion that she ruled out as hunger due to lack of airplane food. How dare they charge for food on a six-hour flight, she thought. Mary curled up on the newly made couch with the room service book. What could she possibly care to eat now? She made it alive across the country, to escape like a political refugee to a haven. And yet, Mary felt lonely and afraid. She had crossed the line practically unscathed into another world.

Brother John made it some place exotic and free like she was: Southern California. The place of glitz and glamor, sunshine, and wealth, but what she found was just a bunch of clouds, wind, desertion, and flatland. So far, California was turning out to be less than she expected.

She ordered food—a sandwich would take forty-five minutes to deliver from the hotel kitchen. Mary yawned and decided to take a brief nap until her sustenance came in the form of lettuce, turkey, and mayo on a bun. Drifting quickly into her own dream state, Mary had one of the most vivid dreams she encountered since her last night terror a few months back.

She imagined Brother John was lying on a beach, one presumably in California, with long hair dripping wet from one of his encounters with the salty waves—the mounds of pressure pushing him around in the ocean. Climbing back onshore, he lay there collecting sand all over his body. Each particle absorbs the water it stuck to, giving him a crispy coating. The sun's heat beating down on his fair-skinned arms, while his hands clenched mounds of nearby sand, and his body seemed to absorb greedily all the light that dared to touch him...

Snoring himself awake, Brother John realized he wanted Mary as much as he believed she wanted him. She was this young, independent woman who he just knew felt the need to want someone. She must have the same ideas about the universe and its organisms as he did. They had briefly discussed what was essentially physics and philosophy and art in the garden together that one glorious day. He could imagine the days meshing into weeks and soon into months when they would become inseparable if they could only be left alone together. It would feel almost like suffocating slowly or boiling at such a slow rate that it was unnoticeable to Brother John.

II

PART TWO

CHAPTER I

The sixth month of being an Observer finally ended for Brother John, who asked at the earliest chance he got to become a Postulant.

In a room where the abbot spent some time doing the bookkeeping and other paperwork for the monastery, he welcomed Brother John in. He was sitting at a rather antique-looking computer. It had the typical box shape and beige color. Brother John listened thoughtfully to the typing of the keys before he was addressed by the abbot.

"Brother John, I see that your time has come to ask to be a Postulant. Are you ready to bear such responsibilities in order to worship our Lord?"

"Yes, father," Brother John nodded.

"Come, walk with me to the garden and have some tea."

The two men rose, Brother John following behind the abbot's footsteps. They walked outside the front doors of the monastery—their hands gripping the iron and ornate knockers.

Strolling along the side of the monastery, the two men walked in silence, taking deep breaths as they headed toward the stone steps leading to the little tearoom built to commemorate a long-deceased monk.

The abbot was among the older group of men in the monastery and he gave off a cheery glow that only having wrinkles around the ears and mouth could enhance, like Father Christmas. But as a monk, he had to shave his white hairs before they resembled anything like the mighty beard that children were accustomed to.

The stepping stones surrounded by moss brought a lush forest smell to the nose. Brother John envisioned Mary undressing behind one of the trees under the moonlight as he watched every inch of her move.

Clearing his throat, hoping to hide the sinful image away from prying eyes, Brother John said: "I've always loved this tearoom."

The abbot glanced over at Brother John, carrying on his way toward the tearoom. "Yes, so do I. But have you ever followed the proper procedures for a true ceremony?"

Brother John watched the abbot's face light up like a young man's as he reached for a little bowl of rainwater that had been collected from the previous night. He briefly washed his hands in it and rinsed out his mouth.

"Come, cleanse your body and mind. This bowl represents a Japanese *tsukubai* and the act is purifying. Now, we may enter the tearoom."

The two men entered the minimalist room, which was covered with tatami mats and the chest with the tea items sat on the floor. There was one quote of scripture on the wall and nothing else.

"Brother John, these are tatami mats which are made from tightly woven rush grass, and inside each is a rice straw core. They retain heat and the smell of them calms the participant. You see, we are entering a space that is as sacred to the East as our churches are to the West. Both spaces are places of decor, ceremony, and tradition used to bring us onto a higher spiritual plane. Now, we must follow 'The Way of Tea' and learn from our Eastern brothers.

"For they also seek a life of peace and simplicity. The Zen Buddhists are wise and can teach us many things about the power of ritual. They even call this practice 'Teaism' like it in and of itself could be a religion. Of course, it is a sin to pray to something other than God, but I believe that the discipline that comes from preparing, serving, and consuming tea is one way to bring us closer to our Lord and perhaps get you closer to what becoming a true Postulant means. So, let us proceed."

The abbot bowed on his knees toward Brother John and said: "Thank you for coming today."

Brother John bowed in kind: "Thank you for inviting me."

The abbot then lifted a cloth that was covering the tea implements. He carefully folded the cloth and set it to the side. Then he scooted to the corner of his mat, bowed to the items, and took the folded fabric to wipe down each of the things from within the chest.

Every movement was numbered and calculated to such an extent that Brother John had never even seen done before. He was fascinated. There were such an array of utensils to be cleaned. He counted at least nine unique items, not including the chest it all fit back into.

He placed everything in a certain spot and then took the long brush-looking object and cleaned it in a bowl that he filled with water. The dirty water was then poured out into a separate bowl.

A different cup, cleaned earlier, contained the powdered tea. Brother John recalled its name a few moments after having drawn a blank—matcha. The bright green ceremonial grade tea was expensive. The monks only allowed themselves expensive communal items when they believed it brought them closer to God.

The abbot used a long, skinny scooper to measure the perfect amount of powder out, before adding more hot water to the freshly rinsed bowl. Then, the only sound filling the room was the sound of whisking. They were light scrapes that filled up the entire tearoom with sound—a productive sound.

Finally, the tea was complete, and it was passed from the abbot's hands to Brother John's. Brother John took his cue from the abbot to bow to the bowl of tea and then turn it clockwise in his hands before trying it.

Each of the monks took a sip of the earthy and vegetal-tasting drink. It was soothing traveling down Brother John's stomach, and he closed his eyes as he breathed deeply in the green essence. There was no grittiness to be found. It was all so smooth and at the perfect temperature for consumption. The bowl felt warm and uniform in his hands. A sense of wonderful calm, beyond anything that he had felt in days, overcame him and he began to cry.

The abbot finished the tea and rinsed all the items again before placing them back in the chest for another ceremonial day.

He rubbed Brother John's crumbling back, asking: "What burdens your mind, brother?"

"Why cannot all men reach this level of calm that I have just achieved?"

"Because not all men are sensitive enough to allow its appearance in their lives." The abbot gently raised Brother John's face with his hand. "You are of pure soul, just as this room is clean. You are ready to become a Postulant. Welcome, brother." The abbot hugged Brother John once more, bringing a new flood of tears. The room filled with sunshine, which seemed to be caught and absorbed by the entire area. All he felt for several minutes was warmth and light. It was glorious.

The two monks rose from their knees and walked outside of the tearoom—the most magical place apart from the dark crevices of the monastery. It was amazing to enter the heavy oak doors and feel nothing but cold and darkness filling the great nave. Some light did come in through the filter of the stained glass windows, but the feeling inside was completely different and it all felt so much further away from the tearoom in the center of nature.

To Brother John, he longed for many days afterward for that natural setting and the sensations that the tearoom gave him. Like an addict, he went during his work times to weed right next to the tearoom, occasionally cracking open the door to stick his head in and see the view. The room was also so pristine due to the amount of empty space and warm colors. The eye gravitated more toward it because a person could freely see to the other side of the room without any obstructions. Whereas, in the monastery, it was filled with statues and tapestries and pews and tables. Although, in the outside world, people may still call the monastery sterile. But the inside of the tearoom was on a new level for Brother John.

He longed to spend his prayer time walking through the gardens and ending up there every day, if he could, inside the tearoom. The clarity he imagined open to his thoughts may just bring him the peace and stability he continually searched for daily.

One day, Brother John was in the garden pruning the roses,

when he looked back and forth to make sure that no one was nearby as he shuffled off toward the tearoom. He squeezed through the door and saw the most beautiful strip of sunlight hitting the center of the floor. Brother John felt that spot call to him like a cat taking a sun nap. He sat down with his legs crossed and his hands resting on his knees.

The only noises he picked up were the birds chirping outside and the inhalation and exhalation of his breath. The strip of sunlight warmed the center of his face and the middle of his robe, shielding his vulnerable body. The Eastern practice of meditation was similar to a monk's chant in letting go of thoughts and focusing on the voice or the breath. Now, Brother John used this time to focus on his breath and let go of any and all thoughts that bothered him. Then, he shifted to relaxing his toes, his feet, his ankles, his lower legs, his upper legs, all the way up to the top of his head. With each inhale, he shifted up a body part. With each exhale, he let go of any tension. There he was in the center of a cloud, floating upon nothing. There was no pain, no stress, no tightening—only air. Hovering, Brother John stayed up there until he heard the sudden shuffling of feet near the tearoom.

Brother Immanuel, recovered from his repentance time and thriving at his art, managed to see the top of his head through the windows. "Hey there, brother, you know it is a sin to veer from the schedule of the Lord, especially from work."

In that miraculous moment, Brother John landed back to the ground with a thud—his muscles ached in certain spots, he felt tense in other areas, and his thoughts whirred nonstop now in his head. That moment was lost, and he felt sorry for it.

"Thank you, Brother Immanuel, for reminding me. I was just

so tempted by God's patch of sunlight in here that I thought I might praise him for it with prayer right there. I must have overstayed my time." And with that, Brother John rather ungracefully stood up and exited paradise.

Brother Immanuel was planting some of the broccoli seeds. The monastery planned on planting about twenty of those this season. He crouched down, making the holes in the dirt, eyeing Brother John. He seemed envious of the sense of peace he carried with him after that moment in the sun.

His wizened face looked more hollowed outside as he dragged his grubby fingers into the dirt, disturbing the worms and other creatures living there.

"You know, God has funny ways of showing us his love. Sometimes it is in the fingertips of an artist's hands as he works on a painting or in the death of a loved one who dies in peace. But sometimes, those messages are from the devil. Beware of temptations that lead you astray from the word of God, like that sunspot of yours may very well be a bad omen."

Brother John hid his smile in his cowl as he continued pruning. "I will take your warning into serious consideration, brother."

The two monks continued to work beside each other, but each worked in such distinctive ways.

Brother John worked slowly and calmly. He gently brought forth the stems that needed clipping and only cut in the best spot for regrowth to occur. Meanwhile, Brother Immanuel worked quickly, shoving his hands deep into the earth without taking the time to feel much of anything at all. His pleasure came in the form of paints and not dirt, almost as if he was too good for such lowly work. So, who, wondered Brother John, was the real sinner?

***

The work of the day slid into the prayer of the evening. Eventually, sleep called the monks to their cells to rest for the night.

As Brother John lay in his bed, he reviewed the things he learned in the tearoom with the abbot on the day he became a Postulant. The abbot taught him that there had been masses actually conducted in tearooms before, so the West was no stranger to Eastern spirituality. The Japanese tea ceremony is called *chanoyu*, literally meaning "hot water for tea." And an idea that comes from the ceremony is that of *wabi-sabi*, which means "solitary mellow." The ceremony teaches people how to accept the quiet simplicity and mellow taste of the tea and the process that comes with "The Way of Tea."

Brother John thought about how old and banged up the chest from the monastery looked. But he did not even notice it was hindering anything in the process of the ceremony. In fact, its authenticity elevated the feeling of connectedness that he felt in the process. The same went for the tea bowl, which he brought to his lips. It was clean but aged. This piece had been touched by many people before him, but recognizing that fact made the taste even more holy.

The entire tea ceremony reminded Brother John about the values of contentment, elegance, dignity, and respect. He felt a complete connection with the abbot for the first time, from the moment that he bowed to thank him for coming to where the bowl of tea was handed to him to drink.

There was this almost indescribable warmth radiating from the both of them, thanking each other with every ounce of being inside of themselves. During that ceremony, nothing else mattered beyond the four walls of the tearoom. And, in a way, nothing mattered apart from the host and the guest and their interaction—the tea utensils were merely there to get these two men onto the same spiritual plane.

The tools facilitated the emotional feelings of respect, reciprocating constantly between one man and the other, bouncing off each of their chests, building up more energy each time it took off and landed on the next man so that by the end there was only light.

Nothing in Brother John's life included that much light, as if the sun's rays could take up space in his soul. He reached that day a new level of being. It had improved his life so dramatically that Brother John was committed to involving the tea ceremony for himself in any way that he could in his daily schedule.

He began by taking his tea the next morning at breakfast with more intention. Though his outward actions may not have differed much, his internal sphere had significantly altered.

There was the teapot sitting in front with the hot water. So, he poured some of it out into his mug with his right hand. He swirled the water around, sanitizing and cleansing it a total of three times around, before pouring out the water into an empty bowl he had added to his tray. Then he placed the only tea they received. Instead of expensive loose leaf tea, he placed the bagged tea into his mug. Although he realized this did not look like much or did not seem special, he especially took this moment to bow to his mug and tea bag to thank it for providing him as good a cup as any when it was made and consumed with intention behind it.

The next step was to take the teapot and pour out enough water to leave an inch gap from the top. Now, to wait. Green tea is usually brewed or steeped for three minutes. On some days, Brother John counted out in seconds the entire three minutes and on others, he meditated and focused on releasing tension from his feet to his head for about three minutes. The tea was many times thought about in his mind as he waited. The one rule he made for himself was to not allow any negative thoughts to be held onto or stuck in his mind. He knew he could not control the thoughts as they came in, but he could decide whether to focus on any in particular or not, as they appeared.

By the end of the three minutes, Brother John was back on that weightless cloud, feeling no pain or sorrow. That glorious three minutes could last him all day.

The next step was to gently, without squeezing in any way, lift the tea bag out of the mug and throw it away. He also managed to get rid of the extra water bowl by this time too.

By the time he got back to his seat at the table and ate his food, the tea was cool enough to drink. He drank about a third of the tea with his breakfast food. But the rest of it was enjoyed afterward when his mouth was freed from the egg pieces and toast crumbs.

The most blissful part of his days now was slowly sipping on his green tea, which he was allowed to have at breakfast, dinner, and supper, though he sometimes chose only water when he was ill and could not enjoy the subtle taste of the tea.

The first thing he would do was hold the mug, after his meal, in his hands, letting the warmth penetrate the ceramic and enter his usually cold extremities. Then, he stuck his nose up close to the surface of the tea and inhaled deeply, its earthy notes traveling down his nasal cavity and carrying a sense of utter release. Once he took in its warmth through his fingers, its earthy smell, he then looked at the tea color in the white mug—the light yellowy-orange color made the water look so much more rich and luxurious. Finally, he brought the mug to his lips to taste the earthy flavors of the tea and hear his own satisfying sips. The whole practice hinged on the ultimate experience of tasting the item being worshiped.

To worship tea was easy for Brother John, since he was adept now at integrating new habits. Once the process became a routine that he completed three times a day, it remained part of his religious experience in the monastery. In an almost industrious process, Brother John used the mannerisms learned for the tea ceremony for other things in daily life.

For instance, he found himself meditating more and relaxing his body during chants. Together, the harmony of voice rose and soon Brother John, who had memorized every phrase of every psalm, was focused on relaxing his toes, his legs, his arms, his chest, and his head. There were other moments when he sat down more gracefully and upheld his posture to make sure that there was no discomfort while he sat. Or there were other moments that he found himself holding the Bible in his left hand only and flipping with his right, setting the book down when he was finished parallel to the edge of the desk in his cell. Each component of his life was done with purpose. The tea ceremony had slowed down time.

In its magical power, the process made life itself one long tea ceremony, where nothing was done without intention. Perhaps some may view his behavior as becoming obsessive, but he found it relieving. Suddenly, there was no more fear of the unknown in his life when each moment was manipulated by him. The tools he picked up to utilize to benefit himself during his day were treated with respect, for they each served him well.

Brother John spent more time dusting his room, even using a brush and dustpan, while on hands and knees to clean the stone floors. One of the most significant aspects of showing respect for the things around him was found in the act of cleaning.

He approached the floor of his cell with knees bent and slowly angling himself toward the floor. With as much self-control as he could muster, his knees gracefully landed without a sound. The only sound came from the brush sweeping away the hair and dust covering the floor. Over the next several weeks, he found a routine of starting in the far left corner of the room, opposite the door, and brushing with swift flicks from left to right in a zigzag motion back and forth until he reach the door and used the dustpan to take the dirt outside.

He did this at least during one scripture time alone in his cell, while Brother Immanuel secretly painted with his own blood and Brother Paul played with himself. So, they all held close to their bosoms their own secrets—what moved them to continue living behind closed doors. To each man, he alone knew whether his desires ultimately helped or harmed his own life.

This time, as Brother John brushed away the dust, he felt an odd numbness inside. The last weeks had been so clear and freeing for Brother John, but now the images of Mary came flooding back. He wished to sweep quickly away all incoming thoughts of her since he believed he had vanquished her with his new habits.

But there she was. Still nagging deep inside somewhere, only what used to feel like pain or sorrow or lust now came in the form of a numbing phantom. He could see her at a bit of a distance since some time had passed since he last saw her. Her influence was numbing but at least it was not painful. Instead, it served as an uneasy, numb hole where Mary had been so often after he first met her.

But before it was like experiencing a death when she left the garden that day, and in many, deeply suppressed ways, he had waited on her like the Second Coming. Such a notion was foolish since he wanted to remain celibate for the rest of his life, so this longing was unfounded. But could he bear to see her come and go away again?

The summer days were already waning. Where was the family who promised to help in the garden? Before the monks knew it, they would harvest all of their vegetables and collect wood for the winter.

Brother John no longer wanted to dwell on her. She was much too young for his lustful thoughts, anyway. He hit himself in the head with the butt of the brush, leaving himself a nice little goose egg. Thankfully, it was in a place covered by his unshorn hair so that the other monks would not notice.

He found himself poking the bump throughout the day whenever thoughts of her arose. Perhaps he could psychologically associate her with bad things, like the pain from physical injury, so that he could stop thinking about her and about saving her soul.

But she was such a perfect beauty—the epitome of childish innocence and a body on the verge of physically blossoming. She was as close to a perfect adult as she would ever be now, unless she chose to enter a nunnery and isolate herself from the ugly outside. A world where people lied, cheated, and stole from their victims; a world where her achievements learned in the home were considered "soft skills" that no one cared about; a world where a man who was lesser morally than her could take her purity away. There were so many things that would begin to strip her of her innocence and, therefore, her beauty.

Brother John witnessed it before happening to other girls, although they seemed more susceptible to giving in to the chaotic world and all the temptations it offered than Mary did. And that is precisely what made her special. She had a soul that appeared resilient to the moral decay of the world and that is why Brother John so badly wanted to not only save it but to coddle and encourage her soul's growth.

CHAPTER II

Brother John fell asleep with numbness inside of him, yet awoke the next day again without such a feeling haunting him. It was strange how the emotions affected the body. One moment a man feels an illness of the body, or perhaps of the soul, and the next moment it vanishes entirely. As many monks before him have said, the devil can play many tricks on man, and maybe they are right, maybe the devil has gotten into my head, thought Brother John.

Carefully, raising himself out of bed, the bells ringing, Brother John threw his robe over his head and exited his cell, sleepwalking toward the great nave of the monastery for Vigils. He squeezed his way in between one of the old, bent monks whose teeth always clicked together when he shakily lifted a cup of water to his mouth during mealtimes and another monk who was already going completely bald in his thirties. Seeing the frail older monk, Brother John observed his mannerisms. It seemed that as a man aged, he grew quieter, softer, gentler, more subdued. There was no need to scream anymore for what he desired, unlike the outcry Brother Daniel had made in the middle of their meal.

In fact, the older that Brother John got—the nearer he came to his feeble elders—the nicer he treated them for fear of his own old age. Every now and then, a sense of relief washed over Brother John that he would be taken care of once his body began to fail. The monks would always help him up and down the stairs or spoon-feed him or bathe him or generally care for him when he was sick until death. His cell would be where his world would come to a close and the handmade coffin made for him would finally receive its owner. The hills of the cemetery would hold his body close and dear, perhaps even under the shade of a tree forevermore. He knew that if he committed himself to this monastic life in this monastery, then he had a place to die and be buried.

There would be no violent car crash in another city or a camping accident in another state or a kidnapping in another country, landing him on the ground of an unknown place. His death was almost predictable now, staying enclosed in the walls of the monastery. Brother John knew his beginning and his ending because he had witnessed now many brothers die here.

He thought a lot about death while singing in the choir today, stuck between a world of dreams and reality in the early hours of the morn. In a world of unlimited data, especially in the outside world, Brother John realized he struggled to delimit his possessions. In his previous life, he had the Internet and grocery store aisles full of thirty different kinds of cheeses to choose from. There was a constant influx of commercials and a competitive atmosphere of who was living the best life. It wore Brother John out so much that one day he threw all of his things into the middle of the floor and started sifting through them. He eliminated all duplicates and items that no longer fit or things that lost their pair or items that were cracked but still being used—bags upon bags were taken to either the dump or the donation place in town.

In the library, Brother John encountered a featured section for that month on minimalism. It was a rather Eastern idea of eliminating everything in life that was not absolutely necessary. The idea became quality over quantity and Brother John became hooked on the idea of having nothing.

He remembered this as the start of his monastic journey—the need to declutter everything to make space for the thoughts in his own mind. From reading, he learned that the idea of minimalism can be to the advantage of a rational man. A man required tools to survive in life. But if there were too many things, like more than three choices at any one time, he would become overwhelmed. Brother John understood that our consciousness can only hold a certain small number of things in the forefront of our minds at once.

The Eastern notion that material objects are worthless in the grand scheme of things revealed that the spiritual realm is where we all should strive to be. The spiritual is where our souls rest in peace from our corrupted flesh is what both the Western and Eastern religions state. So, the idea of minimalism, or even essentialism, is the ability to pare objects down to their essentials—getting rid of distraction—in order to make way for the more important values in life.

Brother John delved deeper into how to stay organized: He got rid of extra paper, from bills to old college essays; unused kitchen items, like an extra electric tea kettle; old clothes, and so on. He found it therapeutic in a way because he discovered that with each decluttering session, he was better able to keep in his mind exactly what he had. And knowing this had allowed him to find things faster, actually use his things, and eventually move on to more improved things. He always knew that his highest values included learning and writing. Brother John wanted nothing distracting to come in the way of those flowing thoughts and those hours of study. So, he became as efficient as he could be by organizing and getting rid of valueless items.

Then, after about a year of decluttering all of his items, he relinquished everything and joined the monastery. He could finally breathe. Brother John could spend more time reading and listening to lectures. He could easily find what he needed because he knew where his things were. He could even visualize now where each item was in his cell. For example, his Bible was in the uppermost right-hand drawer of his writing desk. If he needed it, like during scripture reading periods, then he need not expend any extra mental energy. Brother John found he had more control over his environment now, allowing him to feel less stressed in both his body and mind.

Having a clearer body and mind meant more time to see the world around him. He had shed his old identity and was born again anew. The abbot told him once that as a man of God, like the nuns, he must also be married to Him. For monks, they must also maintain the virginity of their spirit in order to give fully of themselves to the Lord.

"Brother, you must forget your self in order to praise the Lord, for you cannot be saved without Christ leading you to God, the Father. Without Jesus, we are cut off from God."

Brother John bowed his head down, partially hidden in his cowl. "I understand, father. I remain pure in soul and stay silent to listen for and hear God in the growing buds and the flying birds in nature. For by becoming like children once again, heightening our sensitivity to the world, we can know Him. I am filled every day with more wonder and the more

I learn, the more I want to kneel down and thank the Good Lord. Every day here is like a miracle to me."

The abbot smiled and rested his palms on top of Brother John's head before walking past him down the aisle of the monastery.

The rest of the day passed by as usual, only given new life by the varied thoughts carrying on inside of Brother John's head. Yet, the evening brought with it a certain unease and restlessness for him. He turned from one side to the other, trying to get to sleep, when the noise of feet shuffling across the floor fully woke him up.

He quietly walked in the direction of the shuffling noise and placed his ear up against the right wall where Brother Paul rested. His cell door opened and Brother John heard him walk down the hall and open the exit door from there.

Carefully, opening his own door, he snuck out about a minute after Brother Paul left. He held his breath, for he knew that being caught would mean severe penance owed to the monks for his sins. Still, he had to know what Brother Paul, the one who could not stop pleasuring himself, was up to. Had he done this before while he was asleep?

Brother John opened the door to the outside and carefully peeked around it to find Brother Paul headed toward the garden. In the darkness of the night, Brother John kept low to the ground. In fact, he was so low that he was crawling around on his belly like a snake. He crawled several feet behind him until he reached the stairs and watched Brother Paul quickly enter the tearoom.

From the top of the stairs, Brother John could see inside the small right-side window in the front of the tearoom. A simple lantern was the only thing used in the space. Yet, its singular glow was enough to reveal that Brother Paul was not alone.

The soft yellow glow shone on a bare leg. It was meaty and long. All Brother John could think at the moment was that it was much too cool a night to be revealing the legs so much. He made his way down the steps after a good five minutes and crept as close as he felt comfortable to the tearoom.

The walls were made of thin pieces of wood, so any noise carried through easily. Holding his ear to the side of the tearoom, Brother John heard everything being said.

"Oh, my Madonna, please help me. I have sinned again and again and again. I can't help it!" There was a blubbering now coming from Brother Paul which made it very hard for him to understand what else he was trying to say.

"Shhh, honey, that's all right. That's why I'm here. Who's my baby?" asked a woman's voice, who Brother John did not know. She must have snuck into the tearoom at an appointed time to meet Brother Paul.

"I am," he sobbed.

Brother John had to see more of what was going on, so he decided to take the risk and peer into the nearest window, and what he saw horrified him. In the middle of the tearoom, to the left of the lamp, sat a voluptuous, half-clothed woman holding Brother Paul in her arms like the *Pietà*. He lay there crying as she touched him up and down. His robe was still on, but it rode up his legs revealing his fat, hairy ankles.

Their shoes were both discarded in the corner of the tearoom as the woman bent her neck low and kissed his mouth. They stayed like that for what seemed like minutes. A tear was still rolling down Brother Paul's large, ruddy cheek as he gave in to the sensations of his body.

"I am not supposed to find comfort in the body of a sinful

woman," he moaned, "and yet...I am not supposed to do anything for myself but for the benefit of others. How does this benefit my fellow monks?" But then he grew quiet as she drew her hand up to his thigh.

"You are the devil," he whispered. But he let her find his jewels, and she took possession of them as if it was second nature.

He sobbed, "I am not allowing Christ to form inside of me. I am not carrying out his actions. This is not holy; this is dirty and shallow. *I* am dirty and shallow."

A strong slap to his face cut off his wallowing as the creature grew hungrier.

"Who's my little animal?" She licked his cheeks, avoiding his needy lips.

"I am," he said, trying to hold on to her breasts.

"And what are your duties to me?"

"To love, obey, and serve you."

"That's right. Good boy. Now you know what would please me right now?" She pushed his head forward and down, down, and down again. He gave in as if his mind had been attached to her like glue, like the only thoughts he had when he was alone in his cell were of her. He did not please himself alone. She was there as a phantom in the room beside him, in front of him, on top of him.

These special nights were reserved for some time that Brother John had not previously known about. But Brother Paul could not always receive her services and so he had to dream many of them up. But he was addicted to her body and her smell and it seemed like any time he wasted away from her was like sucking the soul out of him.

It seemed that God did not give him life—this woman did.

Until this evening, Brother John had never realized what passionate creatures people could be.

***

When the woman had gotten her fill of pleasure, she reciprocated. Brother Paul was still crying, albeit at a more slowed, preoccupied rate, while she lorded over top of him and placed herself in just the right position. She rode him like a vile, thick-legged demon. Yet, in the stillness of the night, only Brother Paul's moans could be heard. The demon made no sound as if she was not even there or received nothing more from this exchange than stolen money.

Amidst the ecstasy of the act, Brother Paul whined that life was cruel to those who were weak. "You see, darling, other people have crushed me. The outside world saw nothing in me and so I ended up here paying for it. But I don't belong here. Look at me! Paying for sex and crying because of it! I'm despicable. I should be sleeping right now among my fellow brothers and praising Him in the morning, as we all seek salvation for ourselves and mankind as a whole. But look at me! I am not cut out to even save myself!"

"Then why did you come?" asked the temptress.

"...because I love the way you smell. You're intoxicating, my dear." Brother Paul tugged her hair to bring it closer to his short pig snout. He deeply inhaled and you could vividly see his flesh shiver with pleasure. "A monk is supposed to ask himself daily what brought us here, and in our search for God, we are supposed to reject our will. But I'm afraid that the more I do so, the stronger it fights back. I'll tell you a secret. Yesterday, when it was my turn to cook the eggs for breakfast, I tried to leave my finger on the gas coming from the stove, but I could not. My body, it seems, would not allow me to fight against it—to empty it of the will to live, which is the most powerful aspect of our will. Does that mean that I have failed to serve the Lord? Or am I a sinner for trying to destroy the very life He created in the first place? I simply don't know what He wants!" The tears rolled on again as he blubbered, "Christ is supposed to animate us! He is supposed to guide my thoughts and actions with his Holy Spirit. His love is meant to pour forth from my soul and show me the way! Yet, here I am in your arms, and I have never felt more love in my life! Am I animated by the devil then? Hold me!"

The devil woman held Brother Paul close to her sizable chest, smothering his face. She held him like he was a baby. Her body was warm and soft, and Brother Paul seemed to calm down whenever he was held close and as affectionately as this woman was holding him. But even he knew he could not hide behind a dream forever and that his time with her was limited. The sun was on its trajectory to rise again in the morning, and Vigils began even before that time.

But lying in her arms made Brother Paul feel safer than ever before. He could hear her heart beating, her smile taking shape, her warm brown eyes glimmering, her powerful arms holding him. Surrounding his body with love, she was an enigma of its presence.

Meanwhile, Brother John, watching all of this unfold, wondered if his brother could breathe on his own without her. She seemed so essential to his life at that moment, like her leaving would cut off his supply of oxygen.

The woman reached her suntanned hand out for Brother Paul's and he gave it to her effortlessly. The spots of moonlight slipped through the leaves of the trees and through to the tatami mats beneath their feet, while the crunchy noise the sticks made under animals' feet outside as they ran around made for a musical interlude of sorts. A drizzling rain hit Brother John's body as if begging to be noticed and he felt the soothing warm drops sink into his skin and fill his own insides with warmth and comfort.

Brother John continued to peek in through the window and saw Brother Paul gazing up into the face of his mistress. She looked purposeful and strong. He must have known that nothing could hurt him when he was with her. She said, "Fetch me that bowl of water from outside."

Quickly, Brother John squeezed himself up closer to the front of the tearoom so that nothing would stick out to the view of the person from around the corner where the bowl was for rinsing the hands and mouth before a tea ceremony. The bowl was still filled with rainwater.

Brother Paul complied, handing the bowl to the thick-legged woman. "Thank you," she said, "now on your knees."

He got back down on his knees as she smiled and dipped her finger into the icy water. Lifting her dripping finger up to his forehead, she made the sign of the cross. Both monks shivered. A woman of sin could not possibly purify a monk's soul. She could not hear his confession and speak to anything higher than her primal soul. Had she, in fact, damned him for all eternity in that one gesture?

Brother Paul kept his eyes closed, trying to make sense of this move. Was he being baptized into a new sort of religion and, if so, what? Was this just make-believe or did he just commit himself to something entirely new? It was impossible to tell at the moment. All Brother Paul seemed to know was that this woman cared for his ugly soul.

"There, now you are mine *and* God's. Allow me to show

what animates our Lord," she said, snaking her way over his body like a predator to its fresh prey. In a sudden convulsion, Brother Paul moved his body against hers while his head avoided her kisses as if his mind was in revolt, but his body was begging for more. It appeared as if he wanted her to force herself on him so that he had no control—no say in the matter. His life was in her hands, and he trusted her as he had never trusted anyone else or anything else with it. God never moved him spiritually the way this woman did.

He clearly desired to have her forever. Brother Paul has her consent by the way his body responded under the weight of hers. He tried giving himself over to the Lord's will and what that looked like was having this woman slap him on the backside until the area turned bright red. Then she pinned his wrists down, threw his own robe above his head, and unabashedly used him to pleasure herself. Leaning forward on top of him, she whispered all the evil things she would do to him. He tried to struggle under her weight, to no avail. Finally, Brother Paul gave in and she took him, used him, and made him into her pleasure. And he loved it.

***

Brother John could not stop watching. The entire scene was unbelievable, like it had been a nightmare. But there came a point when he could no longer sit by silently while his heart pounded like madly wild bells within his body. He had to escape this sinful bastion of pleasure and return to his own room unnoticed.

So he slowly backed up the way he came, slithered on his belly back to the exit, and squeezed into the tiniest amount of space possible between the wall and the door to let himself back inside. There appeared to be no one in the halls and the ease of sneaking back into his cell was almost suspect, but he took the opportunity, regardless.

Laying there in his bed, Brother John attempted to ignore the images coming up repeatedly in his mind, like the roiling water inside a tea kettle. Still, the images persisted and the more he tried to push them out, the more of them came and stuck there. He saw her thighs and his disheveled robe; he watched her lean in to kiss his weak little lips; he heard the guttural moans coming from his mouth. Brother Paul's tears shed, and the confessions made throughout the evening were meant to serve as a justification for continuing his behavior. It was bizarre and disgusting. He sniveled there in the arms of a prostitute for what felt like hours.

The early hours of the morning were approaching—Brother John could feel it in his bones. He knew the monastic routine now as if it were instinct. After shutting his eyes and allowing his body to unwind, Brother John fell asleep until the three-fifteen bell rang that morning. Peeling back his eyelids, Brother John could already tell that they were going to be red as sin. How did Brother Paul get away with his night frolics without being caught just by his fatigued look? wondered Brother John, who tore off his sheet and forced himself up by sheer willpower.

Nothing in the world felt more holy than sleep right now. But Brother John knew that suspicion must not fall on his head, so he headed to the great nave. Sliding in the pews, he stood by another monk who felt mighty high on the edicts of Christ that morning and felt the need to lecture someone about it—Brother John was the selected target.

"You know, young man, when I was in my youth, I knew God called me to this vocation to serve as a peacemaker. I did not enter to gain anything. There was no ambition of mine to achieve in coming here. I just wanted to give myself over to the Lord to animate with his loving spirit. And boy, today, I woke up without a single pain in my old body. God is good! He wants me to continue serving him through a mass, like this one, for which I can sacrifice my own ego to God and meet him up there in the ethos where our voices go to renew my utter surrender to him. He wants me to work on His land to show my obedience. He wants me to pray for the Good of mankind and to serve as an olive branch between our world and Heaven." The older monk smiled his semi-toothy grin, much like a fool. He was so ecstatic about his lack of pain that it made Brother John more fearful of old age and the horrors of what was to come. He smiled and shrank back simultaneously, hiding the side of his face visible to the man in his cowl.

Vigils began and Brother John was able to call for help, for release from the images of what he witnessed last night, so he put extra breath from his diaphragm into each and every phrase, in turn, making him one of the loudest monks there that morning. He got lost in the chants of the early morning, allowing the constancy of the routine to bring him the freedom to let his thoughts wander. Unfortunately, they wandered back to the tearoom and what it meant to him before last night and what it meant after.

Before last night, the tea ceremony with the abbot marked a notable peace and stability in his life. The air and sun coming through were pure. But then, covered by darkness and unveiled in the moonlight, a sinful deviance of lust and instability caused the room to appear small and putrid. There was no room to breathe within its four walls, no matter how thin they were. Brother John would suffocate the next time he approached the tearoom.

The distractions of last night drowned out all holy thoughts. Brother John could not even fathom being the one who was actually involved in the sinful act. He peeked from around his cowl about the nave, looking for a single sight of Brother Paul. Craning his neck around to the left, he did not find him, but searching to the right there he was—the sinner himself looking as innocent as ever, chanting along with the rest of the monks in perfect unison.

Brother Paul's eyes did not appear red, though Brother John was quite far away. Still, the question bore a hole through his skull: How many nights had he spent with this Madonna? It was astounding to see nothing amiss. How many other men were committing sins each and every night? Was this how they maintained their constant search for God in the monastery? By sinning regularly in it? Was Brother John missing something?

Without looking suspicious, Brother John covered his mouth to yawn and take peeks at Brother Paul throughout the mass. Brother Paul carried on in such a natural fashion that Brother John began believing that perhaps he had dreamed up the whole thing! There was nothing natural about his obsession with sex, yet the power of Christ did not smite him immediately within the confines of the monastery. *Nothing* was stopping this man, and Brother Paul knew it.

CHAPTER III

Feeling sick to his stomach, Brother John made it to breakfast but could not eat anything, nor could he enjoy his green tea. Something very wrong was happening here, and he needed to figure out what it was. In the hollow pit of his stomach, he searched for signs of Brother Paul leaving on previous nights: Had he heard any footsteps outside his door? Did Brother Paul ever look tired or disheveled? Were there moments when his head drooped with sleep? No, there was no recollection there...besides his desire to get back to his cell quickly at every solitary prayer time. But surely no one else was in the room, which is why Brother Paul often amused himself.

In a moment of sheer frustration, Brother John determined to go back out there tonight to the tearoom and see if he was there again. He would nap during prayer times for the next two days, it seemed. But if that is what it took to understand what was occurring in this monastery, then so be it.

The *Rule of Saint Benedict* discussed the idea of true and false monks. The latter was a monk who came to the monastery to achieve a personal goal and not truly to serve God, while the former came to seek God in all of his divine light. When a new follower comes to the monastery, they make a vow to

Conversatio Morum or "fidelity to monastic life." He agrees to follow all the rules that Saint Benedict lays out and takes each day one at a time, and only time reveals whether a new member is a true or false monk. It seemed that Brother Paul was a false one. He did not pray to a point where he lost sight of his own existence; he did not sing to relinquish hold over his own will; he did not work to obey the orders commanded to him by his own Lord.

***

The night approached within what seemed like the time it took to hear the first ring of the bells. Brother John exited the monastery a little after midnight the same way he did the previous evening. On nearing the tearoom, there was a lamp brightening up the single room with the tatami mats. The moonlight helped shine up the darker corners of the room. Inside, there was a visible hump wearing what looked like a monk's habit with a black scapular.

To Brother John, the hump appeared to look like a black bear. He cautiously squatted down underneath the window he used the previous night. Peering in, Brother John sucked in his breath, nearly choking himself violently in the process and thereby exposing his presence to Brother Immanuel.

Yes, Brother Immanuel was pouring over the newspapers of the day just like in his room, only this time, it was even gorier in its execution. In here, the tearoom mats were covered with layers upon layers of newspapers to ensure the complete absorption of his blood that was currently running down his back like rain down a windowpane and covering his long fingers.

Leaning forward, Brother Immanuel, with his pockmark scars shaded in more deeply by the lamplight, hovered over the newspaper articles, circling with his bloody fingers over important sentences. There was a hunger in his eyes and a snarl on his mouth that was obscured by the crook of his esteemed nose. It was as if his soul was a book and his life a vast piece of art spread out on canvas.

His black eyes kept scanning and scanning over the pages on the ground, his back curved into a C-shape with the bones peeking out of the top of his habit. Brother John could not understand his brother's desire to do his ritual out here in the middle of the night. Why would he need the darkness to cover up his sins, unless he was some kind of warlock? wondered Brother John.

Brother Immanuel rocked back and forth, the gashes in his back opening and closing like haggard mouths. They all tried silently screaming out the pain that he must have felt to have the cool night breeze whip against his open flesh. Every time the breeze entered though, he closed his eyes and smiled as goosebumps caressed his body.

After several minutes passed, Brother Immanuel unfurled himself and lay there on his stomach over top of the articles, like he was trying to absorb their messages through his skin. His habit was clearly hiked up in the front above his chest as he lay there. It looked rather uncomfortable. But there he lay in a kind of stupor until he shot up and threw his entire fist into the can of paint he had lugged here.

His whole fist dripped with more red. Convulsing into the canvas, he threw his fist at it and left marks there. No one would know how much of the blobs were a mixture of his own blood and the red of the paint itself. Brother John wondered what was driving these spasms. They came in waves, one after another, after another.

Brother John noticed the bloody cords of his whip resting on the edge of his stack of newspapers, allowing for the most absorption. Occasionally, Brother Immanuel looked over at it and spit. But then he would cry out, sobbing, and viciously whip himself until his knees buckled. And as his brush gets picked up again, it whirs across the canvas as he muttered something about "men who look like soft petals smell like butterscotch" and about how he "demands arms and thighs remain open!"

The man was lost in a passionate fantasy. His frenzied mind was on display and Brother John had never before witnessed such a loss of self before. He looked like a man without reason—an animal filled with instinctual rage. Was this the Holy Spirit? No, surely this was the devil's spirit animating Brother Immanuel tonight—another false monk was in our midst, concluded Brother John, plucking nervously at the bits of grass and moss beneath his feet.

Round and round went his bloody, red-painted fingers—the hands that mimicked God's creation. A beautiful set of hands that were meant to be a baby's entire world crumbled into a nightmarish phantasm of ghoulish tricks played on those innocent few men and women who still peopled this hellish earth.

The only thing keeping Brother John silent witnessing this atrocity was the doubt building up in him. He was unsure of whether the spirit inhabiting him was of God or Satan.

For God could very well be present in the uncertainty of this moment and the absurdity of Brother Immanuel's choices. And being a monk was all about experiencing His presence after all. Brother John could not figure out the meaning of tonight's punishment, so he ceased the rapid flood of thoughts and looked back in through the small window.

Brother Immanuel was hunched over again like a bear, panting and trying to catch his breath. He rarely spoke to people since he believed that his love of language required silence to uphold its integrity. Language, however, was created by Man and Man was deeply flawed—certainly not good enough to worship, in his opinion.

So, he moaned at times and remained silent at others in the tearoom. His wounds were clotting as he hugged his knees up to his chest. The skin weakly stretched to cover up as much of his backside as was left.

Tears moved his back like ripples and he dipped his dirty red brush into the salty glimmers falling from his eyes down toward his cheeks. The tears further watered down the red, which he used as he crawled on his knees toward the canvas. With quaking hands, he dabbed at the canvas—a thin streak of pink appeared but was barely visible once it dried.

His tears made no sound on canvas, and it was in that artistic silence that Brother Immanuel screamed.

He screamed in the most bone-chilling way. It was as if the tribesman of a past age had just pulled the heart out of his sacrifice—a most primal scream.

Brother John ducked behind the corner opposite the monastery for fear that someone had heard the scream and would come running out toward the garden, but no one came. Minutes passed with the ringing scream bouncing off the inner skull of Brother John on an infinite loop.

On and on and on it stayed lodged in his mind as he attempted to comprehend why a monk would defy St. Benedict's rule of silence. God would certainly be displeased at hearing one of his own suffer so this night.

When Brother John gained enough courage, he propped himself back up underneath the windowsill. Now Brother Immanuel was lying with his habit up on his backside up to his neck. He lay there, exposed. The news articles stuck to his body as he shook all over.

His body was in the complete physical expression of one suffering in mind, body, and soul. There was no Brother Immanuel left. He had exited his body a long time ago this evening. Now, he was meeting with the infinite.

Brother Immanuel sat up, layers of newspaper sticking to his back while his robe fell down, crumpling the papers. Some of them peeled off, cascading lightly down with their heavy, doomsday words printed on both sides.

Reaching around to pull off the rest of the papers, Brother Immanuel winced, slicing open his finger in the process. Blood poured forth anew and as he sat there watching it bubble, he watched intensely. The red blood formed a convex lens on his index finger until the form could no longer retain its shape and it seemed to explode and pour off of his finger and land on his bare legs where his habit was hiked up.

An eerie smile matched the shape of the convex lens of blood as he stared at his leg for ages. In slow motion, he finally scooted his way toward the canvas and pressed his split finger onto it, wincing once more at the sting from the pressure placed on the split walls of flesh.

Brother John could imagine just how many germs were worming their way into his skin all over. His brother was a walking cesspool of bacteria now. Upon suddenly feeling sick, Brother John scurried up, light on his feet like a squirrel rummaging through leaves for a nut, and ran into the forested part of the land. There, behind a tree, he excommunicated the evil thoughts from his mind not once, but twice for good measure.

Brother Immanuel, it seems, heard nothing when Brother John returned. He was still sitting there in front of his canvas, dazed. The painting at this point was a series of blobs and lines in varying degrees of red. There were brown, aged blood spots all the way to light pink water spots. Every color in between those seemed represented in some area on the canvas.

Brother John recalled one time Brother Immanuel was talking about people in the future, finding his paintings and linking them back to him. He desperately wanted to leave a legacy and become famous, even if he never actually stated it aloud. In some way, the idea of never being forgotten brought him a strange sort of peace.

We had all heard here at the monastery about medieval whips found at monasteries in Europe. They were kept in glass cases in museums and whoever's blood stained that whip was now famous and preserved in the memory of human history.

Fame could keep a name alive in spirit, but what did we care? wondered Brother John. Most of us abandoned the world ages ago, and we even abandoned our christened names for other religious ones, which were more preferable. My brothers should not seek fame.

But Brother Immanuel remained determined. He sat there taking in the canvas as a whole, unafraid of the time and the impending sunlight.

***

Time passed. Brother Immanuel sat there like a gargoyle defending the monastery from ghosts. There was a certain amount of discipline he was exerting in remaining so still and silent, especially after his earlier outburst. Now, he let the grand silence of the night keep him. His eyes hardly blinked.

After some internally set amount of time passed, Brother Immanuel opened his mouth, but nothing came out. His white hairs on his head quivered with each attempt at talking.

"Huuuhhhh…heeeeehhh…helloo? God, are you there?" his raspy voice cracked. "I am here to confess three faults to you on this early Friday morning. I do not want the abbot to hear my sins. I want my God to hear me directly."

He sat there on his knees with his head down and his hands in the sign of prayer.

"Here I am, Father, outside in the wee hours of the morning, donning my habit, which I put on to travel outside to the tearoom. I abandoned my simple linen tunic to talk with you. I conform in many ways to the monastery's rules, but tonight I could not resist. The temptation to paint was too strong. My greatest sin is to be remembered for my art.

"Oh Lord, I came here to escape the war and spare my own hide. Yes, I was always a pacifist, but I was also too afraid of death which, as you have told your children, is nothing to fear as long as we follow you. Well, on that day that I came to the monastery, the place I now call home, I saved myself. And ever since saving my own skin, I have wanted more. Now, I suffer from wanting to be…famous. There, I said it. I want other people to recognize my name.

"My art is made by your spirit, though. When I call forth your presence, it moves me in mysterious ways. Tonight, you have been hard on me, Father. I am torn up, bleeding profusely. I suppose that is what I get for being selfish and desiring to stay alive while others died in Vietnam. I am a coward and no soldier in your army of love. I am unworthy. I see that now.

"I also know that you knew me before the war. You knew

when my hedonistic passions brought me to women. I painted them and I slept with them and then I deserted them to start the cycle all over again. Sometimes I still have dreams about all the lovers that lined up to follow me and my art. I told them how to position themselves with their legs wide open. And I even began taking on pretty men. I touched them all as I painted. Before, my art had distinctive shapes that represented people, but I vowed once I reached the monastery to never paint reality again.

"Dear God, I only paint for you now. Can't you see? I only paint for the One who moves me. I see things in my paintings now that astound me, dazzle my mind's eye, and allure my soul in ways I had never known before! Something overtakes my body and moves my arm to follow your commands. This is true postmodern art. An art that is both new and old and visionary in its process! Lead me, oh Lord!

"Your hand moves mine, and it is showing me that life on earth is cruel. Following your passions, as I did for so long, is not the way. Drugs, sex, and explicit art are only ways of marring our path toward You, God. I see that now and I am deeply, truly sorry. I carry my sins with me always and I have sacrificed myself for Your will. My passions are to follow You, to feel You working inside of me, to express Your will on canvas. Speak to me!

"My Savior! Butcher me! Cut me into a thousand pieces for your glory, only let me not be forgotten! Please! Please! Pllleeeaaassseee! Amen."

Brother Immanuel sobbed violently into his open palms. It was clear that he cried tears of sorrow for himself. He came to this monastery seeking life and fame for himself and not to discover a God he thought he had already found.

This man could not even consider his art being the product of the opposite force from that which was the Good. Moved by the very devil himself, Brother Immanuel painted evil's image in his own blood.

Brother John looked back at the painting and the thin pink line that was barely visible could almost resemble the devil's tail. There was nothing logical about this act. There was nothing there to say that the Lord's spirit was really moving him. There was nothing *good* in his art. Yet, he roamed around the tearoom, convinced that his art was holy.

Brother Immanuel and his reformed, holy art struck Brother John as immensely funny. This horror show became so absurd in a matter of minutes that a Postulant could only come to laugh at the poor man. Somehow, he had come to a false conclusion that this art meant anything when it really meant nothing. The blobs and lines were simply the ravings of a lunatic who thinks he has found God.

All this time in the monastery and he is still on his search for God, thought Brother John, feeling overwhelmed with exhausted pity. There was nothing anyone could say to Brother Immanuel that would reveal who he really was. After thirty, it was very hard to change a man's mind. So often, he was set in his ways and living his life according to those principles. The man was old now and nowhere nearer to the Truth than he was on the day he entered the monastery.

All of that scripture and all of those chants seemed to have shed little light on his attitude toward God and how he could embody Him. The man was still a child. Brother John's heart bled for him.

***

The piece of art was complete. Brother Immanuel nodded

in the face of it, never noticing the possible devil's tail in his image. Rather, he collected his whip, soaking its seven knotted cords in water and rinsing his blood-soaked brush. He covered his red can of paint back up with the lid, took his canvas off the easel, and folded the easel up. He shoved everything, including all the bloody newspapers into a bag, probably taken from the kitchen for foodstuffs, and walked out the tearoom door after blowing out the lamplight.

Brother John stayed by the side of the tearoom, away from the windows and doors, hidden by the night. He sat for what felt like half an hour on the cold, dewy ground, thinking. He thought and thought some more about how funny Man is in believing that he can commune with Christ through his art. And yet…many people believed that, so why should Brother Immanuel be different? Was he not allowed such a privilege? wondered Brother John. No, he was not allowed because St. Benedict did not believe in lashing ourselves to death. The Benedictine life was filled with discipline and happiness in our toils on this earth. We were martyrs of the spirit, but not of the flesh that God gave us.

Once the idea of Brother Immanuel's sin was solidified in his mind, Brother John shuffled off into the darkness. His stiff, cold bones squeezed once more through the doorway and into the monastery, where he crossed to enter his room.

Inside, he took off his shoes and lay down on top of his bed with the sheets still underneath him. There was no use now to try to sleep deeply. He would only have enough time to pass out and wake up to the bell's ring in two hours.

The hours passed by much too quickly and Brother John felt like he had been hit by a speeding vehicle. His body was seething with fatigue and hunger pains from two nights now of disrupted sleep.

Sleep was a thing of faint memories to his body that longed for such a gift. However, discovering the secrets of this monastery's people was Brother John's principal objective. He was still young enough to bounce back from such endeavors, and so this early morning, he told himself to stay silent and hide all pain as an exercise of faith.

There were no mirrors around in his cell, so he simply combed his fingers through his hair, swatted at his habit a few times to expel the wrinkles, and blinked his eyes a bit. The great bell was nearly through with its ringing and Brother John heeded the call.

Vigils began shortly after Brother John snuck into one of the pews in the front. It was three thirty on the dot and the sun had yet to rise. As with yesterday, Brother John looked over his shoulder to see Brother Paul still appearing as innocent as ever.

But now he turned his head, hiding his glance behind his cowl, to spy Brother Immanuel across the room. Brother Immanuel was hunched over it looked like in pain. His back was probably on fire. But there was no blood soaking through his habit like one would expect. Perhaps he had collected some bandages from the cabinets upstairs and covered up his wounds. Although how he could cover his whole back with gauze and bandages escaped Brother John.

Still, Brother Immanuel otherwise looked just as innocent as Brother Paul, only with a slight bend. They both raised their voices in harmonious prayer, like the rest of the brothers.

It was utterly unbelievable to Brother John. How on earth did these men get away with their crimes when they had confession at least every week? he wondered. Unless they talked directly to God and avoided telling the abbot their true sins…that must be the answer.

Brother Immanuel would not have lasted this long in the monastery if anyone knew why he really joined and how little he had learned since the '70s.

Time ticked on while the monks sang in unison. Brother John kept peeking over his shoulders back at the two criminals. From their throats emerged the same notes that intertwined so well with his. Their voices met and danced together off the limestone walls of the great nave as they had every day for over a year now.

How could our voices meet without repercussion? Why was the voice of the devil allowed to sound so sweet and pure? wondered Brother John, as he tried carrying his voice louder than the others in protest. His attempt at being heard, calling out the impure among the group, was drowned out by the other voices coming up to meet his.

This morning, among all the other ones, all men were equal. And Brother John had to learn to accept it. If he was to survive here, he must learn to put blinders on like a horse and focus on his own journey—forget everyone else and leave their problems to their own minds.

Determined to forget what he had seen the previous two nights, he caught himself looking at Brother Daniel, who was acting rather strangely. He seemed too giddy for this early morning chant.

The morning was usually a time for contemplation that was trapped between dreamland and earth. It was not for those who were up and enthused to take on the day. Something about his raised chest and smiling demeanor made him stand out amongst the rest.

Well, another sleepless night will not kill me, I suppose, thought Brother John. He kept his eye on Brother Daniel, who was only looking ahead as if at a golden prize. Nothing he sang was registering in his face, yet all of his mysterious thoughts were hidden behind his thick skull.

There must be something happening tonight in the tearoom. A monk cannot look as determined as he looks today without reason, but today was just a normal Friday. There was nothing to celebrate.

CHAPTER IV

The night approached rapidly and Brother John slept for several hours before midnight rolled in again. Midnight was the time when the devil came out to claim its newest collection of impure souls. It was in the darkness that things abhorrent to the daylight could emerge.

Brother John headed out the same exit door and down the garden steps to the tearoom. Tonight, there was a light drizzle that marred Brother John's steps. He pulled his cowl tight over his head as he walked cautiously toward the tearoom. The same lamp was lit again and gave off a lusciously warm glow that made Brother John envious. He wished to be inside the room, wrapped in warmth and peace, but alas, here he was, stuck outside on this chilly night in the rain.

Brother Daniel, with his stunningly pitch-black hair and youthful face for his age, appeared quite handsome. He was holding in his hands a book and talking to a group of people sitting cross-legged on the floor mats.

They looked young compared to most of the monks. There was not a single gray hair on their heads that Brother John could glean. Brother Daniel had mentioned to his high school students that he used to teach before he joined the monastery.

One blond boy raised his hand lazily and gave a slow reply to whatever Brother Daniel was talking about. The entire scene was certainly more tame than what Brother John had stood witness to on the previous nights…that was, at least, until he listened to what he was saying.

"My students, my peers, my fellow soldiers, we are here to fight against the materialism found in this world. You have come here to listen to the words of Marx. Now, Karl Marx was famously an atheist, but his words were truly the closest to God's as I have ever heard before. He is just more blunt about it.

"Unfortunately, due to his lack of beliefs, he has been banned by the monastery. His books are hidden away in a part of the monastery's library that I have found. But, my friends, he should be taught to all of those men and women who want to make a difference out there in the world today. I am trapped for now here, away from the world. But you, and you, and you are *free*. Free to go out there and change our evil capitalistic culture.

"For God wants us to give up all worldly possessions. We are a sinful lot who should spend the rest of our lives praising Him and living in a world of peace and stability. There should be no more poor people and those that are in need should be helped by others. We are merely shells for the Lord's presence to fill.

"Communism is the way. It is the modern term for Catholicism. I have spoken to my brothers of the monastery. I have taught them about the last bastion of the Inquisition in Italy. There are still proper defenders out there of the Catholic faith from selfish heretics.

"If you spend enough time learning Marx the right way with me, then we can surely change the world. This group can and will use force, though Christ did not want violence nor did the monks because only that can bring true peace.

"True peace is something right now that can only be found in isolated places like this monastery. But I want to see peace all over the earth. I want you all to remember we are fighting for equality, brotherhood and sisterhood, and justice. All women and men are to be treated fairly. But capitalism ruins it with competition and the idea that money means success and happiness for some but not for others.

"Let me tell you, my friends, it's a rigged system. Money is just paper."

And here Brother Daniel whipped out a dollar bill and rubbed his backside with it, while the students laughed and clapped.

"It is worthless. What matters, my students? Well, God gave me a voice to share with you all today that people matter— *other* people. We are one big, happy tribe that could live in peace and harmony if only material wealth was gotten rid of. America tries to place the fittest people on top and the rest on the bottom. We, the majority, are not one of the 1 percent—we are the 99 percent—the majority. Do we not matter?

"Capitalism creates a dichotomy between the few and the many. Why do you think the French Revolution occurred? The poor just kept getting poorer while the rich got richer. And I, for one, am *sick* of being victimized for my class status.

"I say that we form a *violent* protest outside of the local bank. I say violent because, again, that is the *only* way that people will listen nowadays. We must shed blood to get noticed. The cameras will not come unless someone or something gets destroyed. This will be your final senior project by the end of your time in school, my friends. I will see to it that it gets done. Now, who has questions?"

A girl with a lip piercing sucked in her saliva before asking: "Why was Marx so against God then?"

"Good question," said Brother Daniel, "he was *not* against God. He simply did not believe in Him and he thought religion was merely a way of people protecting themselves from being hurt. No one wants to believe they can die or bad people can get away without some form of justice. It is just human nature. This does not mean though communism and Christianity cannot live together as one."

Brother John continued listening through the side of the thin wall. He did not want to risk being caught when Brother Daniel was standing right there and looking out at the heads of his students by the window. He crouched down in disbelief, another sinner who told none of his sins to the abbot. And he could be the most dangerous out of all of them simply because he meant to harm other people and not just himself.

***

Goosebumps knocked down drops of rain that had conglomerated on top of Brother John's skin as he sat there, uncovered. His habit felt wet on the outside, though luckily water had not yet penetrated all the way through to his skin. An icy breeze brought the hairs on his arms up to attention as he kept his ear close to the wall.

A man's voice asked: "Cool, so what kind of weapons should we bring to make those dirty capitalist businessmen listen?"

"Pepper spray, flares, glass bottles, flammable items to make Molotov cocktails with. I think anything that goes up in smoke will send quite the message, at least enough to bring the news cameras around our block," said Brother Daniel.

A young woman asked: "Does the monastery know about

this plan?"

"Of course not. I have told my brothers about the Inquisition and fighting for our future, but none of them seem to be taking me seriously. However, no, the abbot knows nothing."

Brother John shook his head. The abbot knew after that brief outburst of his that he would not make it very far in the monastery. He was approaching the time to become a Postulant himself, but Brother John knew that the abbot would not allow Brother Daniel to climb the ranks. With this knowledge, Brother John felt the need to stop the impending protest, but how could he when he was not allowed outside of the monastery? he wondered.

The answer was swimming around somewhere in his gray matter. It was just time that he needed. Though all Brother John truly wanted was peace and stability! There would be no peace, though, with the impending threat of violence in the near future. Brother John sighed as he resolved to get Brother Daniel found out before he put these past three nightmarish nights behind him for good.

Squatting up on his toes, Brother John took one quick peek in the window at the group, who was now continuing their discussion of the principle of Marxism and justifying why they must cause a scene.

"Once you graduate from high school and possibly college, do you or you or you want to work your life away in a factory—isolated from people and the final product of your efforts? How can a man live that way? Capitalism is something we must simply grow out of, like feudalism, and grow into communism where you are no longer taken advantage of but treated as equal human beings! That is the dream for Marx. He wants us to *all* get our fair share and live the life that is best for a person.

"No more the slaves of the factories, no more are we the products of class conflict, no, no we will be the classless men and women of the future! A future that looks a lot more like what these monks in this monastery experience today, but that none of you may enjoy.

"You cannot join the monastery if you are a woman or a child; you cannot join the monastery if you are under twenty-one or over forty-five; you cannot join a monastery if you are in debt; you cannot join a monastery unless you are a member of the church. I am sure that nearly all students today, due to their student loans and young age, are prohibited from joining the place of peace and equality. But at your age, you can do *so* much! You are free to try new careers and fall in love with different people or even more than one! Life is so *easy* when you are young and it is unfair that you should be left out in this unfriendly world where its economic system sucks the lifeblood out of you. You can only find a sense of peace when you are not perpetually worried about where your next paycheck is coming from to keep the necessities of life at hand."

Brother Daniel by now was sweating, with beads of it rolling down his forehead and into his eyes. The salt burned them, but he persisted in engaging his students and awing them about life at the monastery.

But what Brother John seemed to recall when Brother Daniel entered was a significant decline in the quality of the peace inside the monastery. He was a loud, aggressive man who used his good looks to persuade. He was what some would call a born leader in the way he used his extroversion to convert followers to his Marxist ways of thought.

However, in the few months that Brother John joined before his arrival, peace and stability were found in the silence. There was no persuasion to do anything but what each monk decided to do for himself amidst the scheduled day.

A monk is most at home in a place where routine is king. Brother John was no exception as he went about living his life and enjoying the little, seemingly insignificant features of each day. He thought back to his moment in the tearoom with the abbot before becoming a Postulant. The ceremonial nature itself is what made the wait for the tea and its consumption that much sweeter. Or there were moments during chants where the harmonies were just spot-on that day. At times, even eating silently at breakfast next to a monk who you respected made the act even more heartwarming.

To be surrounded by people who valued similar things to you was what Brother John craved and not any forced sense of equality. The equality stemmed naturally from the behavior of all the selected monks in this monastery. Brother Daniel was not meant to dwell among them. He had not earned the privilege of peace, and it was clear now that he never felt it before. Brother Daniel, it seems, had only seen peace from an outsider looking in. He was still in the place where his students were psychologically. His envy and rationalization for why peace was unattainable to him were becoming ever clearer to Brother John.

***

Brother Daniel was pacing up and down without a moment to catch his breath, his sweat forming pools on the floor where just the night before newspapers would have laid there already soaked with blood and tears and paint. But now the tatami mats soaked up his sweat and were squashed underfoot as he walked, as if in a trance.

The students' heads followed back and forth, maintaining eye contact with whatever part of his body was visible to them. They were sold. They wanted to pay with their souls for what he was offering. There was no sum too large at this point to dissuade them from giving up their lives for this man and his future—the future of equality.

He was captivating to watch since he exuded nothing but passion as he spoke and paced. Brother Daniel was even more convincing in his convictions tonight than the abbot, thought Brother John. However, there was that visible sense of pain at not having known peace in his demeanor.

Brother Daniel turned to face his students once more, full of new words to throw out at them and to observe what stuck. "My friends, one of the key things that you must take away from tonight is that you control *nothing*. You may very well think you are in charge of your life because you thought about growing up, getting an education, learning to play the piano, going to college, etcetera, but those opportunities only came about because God wanted them for you. God is the determiner of all things. Your unique name and body are only to be known and remembered by God, your Creator."

Falling to his knees, Brother Daniel made himself small. He touched his head to the floor and squished his body into the mats as low as they could go. Much like Brother Immanuel had done the previous night of laying nude on his newspapers, Brother Daniel lay on the floor, praising the Lord.

"Follow me!" snapped Brother Daniel, as the students shuffled hastily onto their knees and bowed down.

The tearoom was silent. Brother John remembered the abbot telling him once that solitude made people appreciate the little things and open to experiencing more love. He longed for that solitude in his cell, especially at night during the most important time for silence. But instead, here he was, squatting in the rain underneath the window of a tearoom filled with a monk and his radicalized students. There was nothing stable or peaceful about this community that was more like a powder keg waiting to explode.

"There is a monk in all of you students. There is a godly spirit inside that is longing to get out and love this world, but that love is trapped inside by the confines of a materialist system where money keeps the doors to love closed. Money silences all hearts and trades them in for greed. Do you want to be greedy and fat pigs living off the land that you cannot even call your own?" Brother Daniel eyed his audience from the left to the right, looking over the very tops of everyone's heads as he turned. He was lost in his inner world now, where he saw the utter destruction of the earth by capitalism.

With a visible shudder, Brother Daniel escaped the poisonous images by replacing them with rhetoric about how glorious a communist system would be if executed properly. "I did not think any of you would desire to live in a world for the greedy. I bet you want to see a world like this monastery here where we humbly follow God in his footsteps, where we grow organic produce with our hands in the soil, where we sing the praises of One who is higher than ourselves, and where we love our fellow monks more than ourselves. There is an idea when you become a monk that you lose all of your property and worldly possessions upon entrance, only to gain a community that will never let you starve.

"Just last week there was a monk who was sick and stayed in his cell for days without leaving. He had his meals brought to him and fed to him from a spoon that a monk would serve to him every breakfast, lunch, and dinner. He was allowed an extra blanket to keep warm under as his fever wreaked havoc on his body. He also was brought an assortment of books from the library to read while he lay there in bed, resting. It was that kind of care that healed him much faster than any quack doctor could do or governmental health system. All the monks prayed for him all day. In my own mind, his name stayed there in my thoughts for as long as he was unwell. This kind of communal energy and care served to make this elderly monk well again in just days.

"Tell me that is not how you want every person on earth to be cared for. No man should die homeless on the streets, hungry, malnourished, in debt, and alone. Nothing makes me more upset than seeing the homeless in the park who are passed by blindly by people who *think* they are in control of their own destinies. 'No, no, no!' I want to shout at them. 'God is in charge! God has a plan for all of us and you are no better than this homeless man!'

"It is our job in the world currently to show those who are godless that He is up there and in control of all. And we, the worms of His earth, should bow our heads in shame—for if just one person commits the sin of pride, then so do we all. We are all sinners on this earth. It will be by the miracle of God's grace that we ever know peace. But, I love you all and I want to at least try, try to know what it is like! Are you with me?!"

Brother Daniel swung his head around the room, finally landing on each face. Some young women had tears in their eyes and some young men carried a fire in their breasts that burned brightly that night, nearly matching that of the lit lamp nearby.

"Yes!" they all shouted, throwing their closed fists up into the air.

The resounding yes caused Brother Daniel to bow once again, yelling, "Amen! Praise the Lord!"

The lecture seemed to have come to a conclusion after Brother Daniel's last words: "Meet me two weeks from today in this tearoom. We will ascend together, my friends, up to the heathens' den in protest. Bring your weapons."

A stirred-up mass of blackness exited the tearoom door without caring much about being caught on the grounds. They hollered and whooped, some holding hands, some jumping from stone to stone in all manner of disgrace. Once the students funneled out, only Brother Daniel remained, still pacing as before, boring his eyes through the matted floor. He kept at this pacing without speaking. The silence surrounded him in contrast to the loud exit of the students just a moment before.

Finally, he sighed heavily and blew out the lamplight. Brother Daniel returned the place to normalcy as if nothing had gone on in the tearoom that night, before exiting himself and heading back toward his cell in the confines of the monastery above. Meanwhile, Brother John had seated himself as on the previous nights behind the corner, opposite the monastery and away from the front door and windows. His bones were cold and stiff as he brushed off the tiny droplets still landing on him from the sky.

Dawn was approaching and with it a newly felt anticipation for the day ahead. Even though Brother John and all the other monks knew what their day looked like according to their strict schedule, they could never know what each of them would do. Men revealed subtle changes daily and great changes over time. Discovering their true selves in the darkest hours was part of the learning process for Brother John. If he was to sleep next to these people night after night, he needed to know who they were and what they cared about.

Sneaking back through the outer doorway and into his assigned cell, Brother John lay in his bed, determined to fall finally asleep, at peace with the knowledge that he possessed from some of his closest neighbors. They were not the monks that he saw during the day.

***

Peeling open his eyes at the sound of the first bells of the morning, Brother John walked down the hallway to the nave for Vigils, one of the major choral offices of the day. It lasted just under an hour as opposed to the "little hours" of hymns, psalms, scriptures, and prayers, like Compline. But his head felt foggy and his steps slow. The lack of sleep at this point, after three days of waiting and watching, was taking its toll on him. He felt tranquilized. There was a veil laid over his face that night, which he did not notice until the morning. It comprised a thick fabric causing blurry vision and was weighed so heavily over his head that he could hardly produce one foot to place in front of the other.

In his thick fog, Brother John noticed other monks staring out of their peripherals at him. So, he slunk into the restroom and plunged his face in the cold water held within his palms— surely this would wake him up and pull him up out of the fog. But alas, the fog stayed, and he was now colder than ever. He was, in fact, so cold that his lips turned blue as he walked back toward the nave to join his brothers in song. The psalms rang up into the high ceilings and touched the hand of God. Brother John envisioned seeing God's index finger slowly twirling around the mix of harmonies to fit His perfect ears. We must surely sound terrible to Him this morning and He needs to adjust us accordingly, thought Brother John, who was at that moment attempting to corral a yawn through his fist.

Now looking through bleary and watery eyes, the nave looked horrifying to Brother John. The gargoyles looked twisted more than usual and Christ's wounds flapped open every time he blinked while Madonna rolled herself into an irregularly shaped blue ball. There was nothing beautiful about the vision in front of him, and the harmonized voices of prayer brought with it an ominous undertone of doom to his ears. His throat closed, cutting off any ability to make sounds for several seconds as he mouthed the words until his voice cracked back into submission. This morning, Brother John wielded absolutely no control over his own body.

A new fear gripped him as he stood there, unable to do anything—paralyzed by his lack of control.

"Brother," said Brother Daniel as he tugged at his sleeve, "are you all right?"

Blinking in quick succession cleared the tears and things went back to their more normal blurry state. With a sigh, Brother John said: "Yes. I'm fine, thank you." He stood there next to Brother Daniel in shock that he was right there and up close for him to analyze, unlike the last two brothers. The contradiction between his daytime politeness and his nighttime fire did not go unnoticed by Brother John.

He could practically touch the crow's feet marked around Brother Daniel's eyes that were glimmering in the candlelight surrounding them. He was that close. Brother Daniel had brown eyes that gleamed and meshed well with his black hair, causing him to always look devious. But now that Brother John had seen proof, he knew what to think of such a man. A man who was too young and headstrong to let go of the outside. He had to be stopped before those students did something rash, thought Brother John.

CHAPTER V

Brother John sat still in a nearly vegetative state in front of his green tea that morning. The hot steam wafted over his face, making him even drowsier. His eyes grew heavy and his head kept plopping forward, nearly falling flat on the wooden table. The other monks took note.

"Have you not been sleeping well, brother?" asked one of the monks.

"I am fine. Carry on with your breakfast, brother," Brother John mumbled. He would have to make it until eight that evening before he could get any proper rest. There was no excuse for missing the day's work when a monk was not gravely ill. Besides, sometimes a lack of sleep can do wonders for one's creativity, he thought, cheering himself up.

But no other thoughts came to his mind all day besides ones about sleeping. The temptation to shut his eyes in between the routines of the day took precedence over all else. The opportunities arose mainly when he used the restroom and was in his cell for prayer time.

With eyes closed, the world of Mary in the monastery's garden came alive. He envisioned her walking toward the tearoom and pulling him in after her. The monotony of the monastic life was suddenly shaken up by her quivering legs and sighing mouth. She was too young and pure to agitate, but that was exactly what made her so irresistible.

He recalled in his mind when the abbot warned: "You know nothing changes after the final vows are made. You will have to get to know your brothers in Christ. You will see them evolve and change over the years. You will watch your brothers above and then below the ground. And during all of that time in your life, you will see all the relational tensions, as I do, between the monks of this monastery. Everyone here enters wounded. They need help and a compassionate hand. Are you prepared to be one of those helping hands, Brother John?"

"Yes," he said. "I am prepared to heal those wounds with moral teaching and spiritual guidance as needed."

The abbot nodded. He seemed content until his wrinkles grew more defined as he scrunched up his face. "Brother John, please know that you also will need guidance...and sometimes the only answer is to just *be*. You will need to remain in the moment and let God guide you. This involves an enormous amount of faith in the Lord when a mortal man cannot help you out of the darkness.

"Many monks before us have said that if you can survive the first two weeks without losing your mind in the solitude, then you can last a year. You, my brother, have now surpassed those two weeks as a new Observer, and I am proud of you. You have seen yourself in a new way—alone. It can be very difficult to face yourself in a somber, silent way, but it also leads you to holiness. I have high hopes for you, brother. But remember that you give *and* receive help from our community."

In his fatigued state, Brother John was trapped under a cloud of darkness. Can I make it out alone? he wondered. Can I hold out knowing what I now know about these men? Who else knows?

Wiping his sweaty palms on his habit, Brother John was only half-conscious and deliberating sloppily about what he should do with this burden. The brothers must surely see that I am disturbed, thought Brother John. They know I am aware of sins committed within the grounds of the monastery. They can smell it out like a pack of bloodthirsty hounds.

Did Brother Paul, Immanuel, and Daniel know of each other's evenings? They must since they were each coordinated on a different day. Does the abbot know? What other monks hide their secret longings in the night? wondered Brother John.

The idea of confronting each monk somewhere alone bubbled up in his subconscious before emerging to the foreground, where thoughts explode on the scene of the conscious mind.

"I know!" He sat up, shocked by his own revelation. "I will confront each man in the garden when they are out of hearing from the other monks. We could even move into the privacy of the tearoom for more space."

The idea stuck with Brother John right through to the evening meal. One of the other monks was selected that night to read during the meal, giving Brother John the excuse to hyper-focus on every word and lose himself in their meanings.

Tonight, the selected monk read from Matthew 5:10 and the words "endure persecution for the sake of justice" rang out in the meal hall. Brother John knew it was addressed to him. He must address the sinners for the sake of his own sense of justice and peace. For peace came from knowing all of his brothers and living beside them without having any further questions. There was no fear of the unknown about them, as there was now in his heart.

These three monks must be known to me, he thought. They are enemies to my inner peace until I understand their behavior. What caused them to sin and hide it from the very person who was meant to absolve those sins—the abbot?

Soaking up the rest of his vegetable soup with bread, Brother John saved his green tea for the very end of the meal. First, he bowed his head down to meet the tea and take in its soothing, vegetal smell. Next, he took the mug up, cupping it in his hands and experiencing the warmth it provided. Finally, he sipped slowly, just a bit of the perfect liquid. He let it sit at the back of his throat for a few seconds before swallowing, feeling its warmth slither down into his bowels. All Brother John could envision were nutrients being soaked up by his intestines and his body regenerating to full health.

A man's health meant everything. It allowed him to do his daily routines and accomplish his values, and he could only maintain those values with his health. Eating well, exercising, and sleeping were all necessary and here Brother John knew where he was lacking.

So after Compline ended, he headed straight to bed and did not move until the bells rang out loud enough to wake the monks six feet under in the outer courtyard. He arose as refreshed as he could be in a monastery where its residents get up before the sun.

Yawning and stretching out toward the limestone ceiling, Brother John decided to corner the first night's sinner, Brother Paul, in the garden today. What he would ask and how he would approach him was strictly prohibited from crossing his mind, since so much was left to chance and he had never confronted another brother before.

But honesty was a key virtue to a monk, so Brother John

knew he must inquire into what he saw. It was the only way to bring peace to himself and the monastery as a whole.

So far, he believed he had faced his suffering with grace. The knowledge and visions of the woman with the thick legs promenaded across his memory since that first night.

But he had to choose which work time he would use to inquire into their evening endeavors. There was one work shift from nine thirty until Sext at eleven forty-five in the morning; and there was another one from two until private prayer at four thirty in the afternoon. But who could wait until the afternoon when there was tension in the air? thought Brother John. He was simply too preoccupied with this problem in his midst to focus on his own peace.

In a fit of frustration, Brother John kicked the trash can with his foot in the kitchen while getting his breakfast tray. A few of the brothers looked up, but they all thought he had simply run into it and Brother John made off as if he had. It was an accident, just like this one-off meeting that each of his nearest neighbors had over the week. They were not repeated each week nor, even worse, multiple times a week. Brother John could not fathom how sneaking about in the dark and risking being kicked out of the monastery made *any* of it worthwhile enough to do.

All things a man does should be able to be seen by the light of day. If it requires darkness, then perhaps it should not be done. In a simplistic way, Brother John moved within these confines as to what was moral and what was not since boyhood.

Work at nine thirty finally came around and Brother John stepped out into the luscious green grass. The spring was progressing, and the sun had done so much good already for these happy plants that had been covered in leaves and snow and feet for many days beforehand.

Keeping his eyes on the fields, Brother John saw Brother Paul far across the way. He was bending over and throwing seeds into the freshly dug-up mounds of dirt. Brother John approached, clutching his root shovel to his side in the hopes of it providing some stability that he had lost.

Gulping down whatever lump was forming there, Brother John opened his mouth to speak. "Brother, I see you are planting some of the heartier potatoes. They will be delicious in our fall stews."

Brother Paul only half glanced up at Brother John. He never could enjoy the moment. There was a storm brewing in his head of all the complaints he could make about kneeling on the dirt or his fingers freezing on the ground or his lower back aching when the day had just started.

Brother John could feel the complaints on his brother's tongue, ready to flow out, so he stopped him before things got too out of his control. He wanted to maintain hold of the situation.

"I just hope these potatoes know—" started Brother Paul.

"Yes, it is cold out here," cut in Brother John. "But then we must work faster to keep ourselves warm. Besides, we will all complain in the summer when we are watering out here how hot it is. Be thankful for what you have."

"What I have is fine enough," said Brother Paul, though he shifted his body when he said it.

"Is it really, brother?"

Looking baffled, Brother Paul sat up straighter and stared down at his newfound enemy. "What are you trying to imply, brother?"

"I saw you in the tearoom earlier this week with a wo—"

"Stop!" Brother Paul shot his hand up toward Brother John's open mouth. "For Heaven's sake, do not speak of that devious kind around me. Have you no fear of accusing an innocent man, Brother John? For I am innocent. I have made my confessions to the abbot and there is nothing more to it."

"But why? Why are you not at peace here, brother?"

"I have a weakness…as does everyone here! I bet you have one, brother. I just do not know it yet. But it is a sin to hold my weakness over my head like blackmail. You know, the abbot says that we all arrive here wounded, and you and I are no exception," Brother Paul hissed.

Brother John could only get his answer if he was completely honest with Brother Paul, so he said: "Brother, I am not here to threaten you. For my own peace of mind, I want to know why you chose to take such a risk. Why do this place and its rules not suffice?"

There was silence as Brother Paul threw a few more seeds into the dirt, patting over and around them aimlessly, lost in his own thoughts.

Finally, he said: "I am not confessing to you. You do not need to know. Go find your peace in the Lord."

"But you are *ruining* my peace. We are brothers here—a community. We will watch each other grow and change until we are underground! Shouldn't you be more open to your neighbors in Christ?"

"Perhaps one day you will see that each man owns his weakness, and it is only between himself and the Lord."

Brother John pursed his lips, but he could not come up with any other way to argue his case. Meanwhile, Brother Paul had already moved further away down the line of dirt, ready for new seeds, with his back turned to Brother John's face.

***

So, it was true that Brother Paul was in the tearoom earlier in the week with a woman, thought Brother John, as he lay in his bed the next morning. He did not imagine it, although now came the problem of not understanding *why* Brother Paul did it.

Perhaps there was a better way of extracting the information he desired. A new tactic would come to Brother John as he cornered Brother Immanuel today in the garden.

Upon the bells ringing at nine thirty, Brother John ambled outside toward the garden. There were more patches of broccoli being planted in the organic vegetable garden, which Brother Immanuel was in charge of.

"How many are we planting this year?" called Brother John as he got closer.

"Oh, I have on my list here seventeen plants," called Brother Immanuel.

"And how are things with you, brother? You seem to be bent over more than usual lately. More flagellation than before, huh?" said Brother John.

Confused, Brother Immanuel looked up at him and laughed. "Yes, I know it might be a bit medieval of me, but I still follow in that tradition."

"Do you also follow a tradition of going into the tearoom at midnight often?"

Brother Immanuel visibly flinched under Brother John's gaze. His wounds must have reopened from such a sudden movement. His blood, at least, would be honest, thought Brother John.

His back turned away from Brother John, Brother Immanuel continued to play ignorant. "I do not know what you mean, brother."

"I mean, I saw you earlier this week splattering blood everywhere in our sacred tearoom. Why? Why risk getting kicked out now? How long, Brother Immanuel, how long?"

This tactic was much more earnest, and Brother John hoped it would work in providing him with more answers than the previous day.

Brother Immanuel was an old man who was closer to the grave than most of the monks there. He was less afraid of losing his plot in the ground than others. Still, he hesitated before answering: "In more than fifteen hundred years of monastic life, do you not believe that a monk has sinned? We sin every day of our lives. We were born sinners. The Lord knows what I have done. I cannot help but love my art. I bleed for it in the hopes that it will help others. And that is what God calls 'perfect love.' Evil is 'self-love' and that is not the sin I have committed, brother.

"I am a compassionate man. I maintain my own daily sanity in the isolation by losing it one evening a week. My heart bleeds for the men and women out there in the world. I only see them through the veil of a newspaper, but I can feel their pain. It tortures me. We are supposed to pray to help these people. I must give myself wholly to God and He wants me to be selfless, even though it hurts." Brother Immanuel looked afraid, like a maimed deer looking at his hunter approaching.

"But the monastery teaches balance in all things, especially the *Rule of Saint Benedict.*"

"Yes, but that balance is not static, nor can it remain untouched by the lives of others. Have you learned nothing here yet, brother? We were awful, disgusting maggots who walked this earth before God sent his Son down to save us and even now we still sin terribly."

"How can you gain peace, brother? How can you avoid the bloody whip?"

"By not feeling the guilt…but the guilt eats at my soul every day and the solitude forces me to watch the worms eat their fill, while the newspapers solidify the problems that they gnaw away at daily. By taking on God, I am taking on the world and every problem is mine to help bear. You should start learning to do the same, brother. Learn to carry your own cross and then that of others."

Brother John was certainly getting further along in his questioning with Brother Immanuel than with Brother Paul, but it was still not clear what he could do to help his neighbors.

In a moment of renewed confidence, Brother John asked: "Your art is for you, though, right?"

No time elapsed when Brother John saw a light behind his brother's eyes before it went out, and he gave his verbal answer: "No, brother, the art is for those other people out there."

"But they surely will never see it."

Brother Immanuel began to sweat under his arms, even though a cool breeze had come in while they were talking.

"Oh, they won't? What about those archaeological digs that occur in ancient monasteries? They recently found whips and crosses from the fourteenth century. Someday, long after I am buried, if it must be so, my paintings will be found."

It was noticeable now that Brother Immanuel had not only said too much, but he wanted to say more. The words "I will be famous" formed only in the air between them and were carried away by the fresh breeze.

Brother John needed nothing more from Brother Immanuel now. He knew that there was a man underneath all the guilt who wanted to paint for himself.

He smiled a little toward Brother Immanuel, bowed without another word, and left him behind. Brother Immanuel carried on the conversation in his mind, debating with himself over how much or how little information he had revealed. His soul might have just glimmered through his long-built wall.

Brother John worked in his own patch of plants, weeding where the vines of invasive plants were suffocating the growing vegetables. He got lost in his work, thinking about Brother Paul and Brother Immanuel and their hidden desires. Both were out of balance here and so much so that they would do anything to regain it again.

One man lost himself in women, the other in art, but both used their madness to create some sort of artificial peace. While here, Brother John was finding peace in everything he touched. What was it he had that these men did not? he wondered.

The question plagued him until all the monks headed off for bed after Compline. He rolled around, sleeplessly, on his mattress. The wind had picked up outside and a terrible draft in one of his windows caused him to shiver through his single sheet throughout that night.

***

By morning, Brother John felt much like he had after his last adventure. The night that he stayed up to watch Brother Daniel sin.

Brother Daniel was in the garden working on planting the last line of large onions in the field before the final frost of spring. His vibrant and youthful black hair made him stand out among the sea of similarly dressed monks in the field that day.

Brother John identified him in his periphery before he had even turned to face his direction. The man must feed on the blood of the young to maintain his good looks, thought Brother John. His looks were certainly a key part of what made students desire to follow him anywhere, even to the most solitary of places—a monastery.

"Morning, brother. How are those large onions coming along?" inquired Brother John.

Brother Daniel blinked, shielding his dark eyes from the sun, as he tried to look up at Brother John. But his brother was much too bright to see, so he lowered back down his head and asked: "Brother John, is that you?"

"Yes, in all my glory," he laughed.

Brother Daniel smiled and got out of his squatting position above the ground with relative ease. He asked: "Aren't you supposed to be doing some of the corn farming this morning with the other monks?"

"I sure am, but I find that in order to maintain peace, there must be a balance between work and play. So, I decided to come on over to the onion patch to have a chat with you."

"About?" Brother Daniel immediately put himself on the defensive.

Clearing his throat, he chose the more direct approach with Brother Daniel. "Brother, I saw you earlier this week in the tearoom with a bunch of your students. You were discussing some kind of pro—"

Yet, again, the sinning monk jumped forth to cut him off from giving the idea any standing in reality.

"Quiet!" ordered Brother Daniel with burning eyes that could not be hidden inside any cowl. He was now much closer to Brother John's face—so much so that Brother John could feel his breath on his own cheek.

"Brother, you know that the Vocation Committee, the abbot, and the monastery's psychologist will determine your ability to serve as a Postulant soon. We are both going to have to be put to the test if we are ever to reach our final vows. Don't you want that?"

"And don't you remember my little 'scene' at our meal not too long ago? They were never going to let me become a Postulant after that and I never wanted to, anyway. I miss my students and they need me. I light a fire inside of their souls to change this crumbling world for the better. I am the leader they need."

"Sounds like you are playing God then," smirked Brother John.

"No, I am a man of this earth and with it, I shall fall...but not without fighting for it. I want to see a Heaven on earth. But after all of my experiences in this world, I have come to the conclusion that only violence creates the fastest and most radical change."

"The whole point of a monk's journey is to spread peace."

"Oh, shove it!" cried Brother Daniel. "The real Catholics fought in Inquisitions to remove the heretics from power. We must go back to forcing those who choose not to believe to believe again. Whatever medieval objects of torture we must bring back, we will. Those people who mock our God and spit in his face deserve every bit of pain that comes their way." Brother Daniel was seething now and spittle flew from his gaping jowls like a rabid dog. His handsome looks gave way to only a frightening appearance where redness and veins were all that a man could see. He was overflowing with hatred.

"Why are you so filled with hatred for those who live in other ways than you, brother? Those people can only be shown when the Good is modeled for them."

"Oh, yeah, and is that working? Those people need their faces shoved in their sins like a dog to his own excrement left in the middle of the living room carpet. Enough time has passed in this world that there is no longer any excuse to be ignorant of God's glory or Christ's sacrifice. Anyone who denies Him now is in cahoots with the devil."

"How did you even make it into the monastery in the first place?" asked Brother John.

"I know my views are radical. I am keeping my mouth shut... for the most part. Why do you think I try to meet with my students in secret?"

"You do not confess your sins to the abbot?"

"Of course not. I aimed to learn all that I can here about the current culture within God's favorite places on earth and no one has a backbone. So, I do not belong here any longer. Everyone, by now, knows that. You know, I have talked to every monk about joining in my cause."

"Have any of them joined?"

Brother Daniel already knew how much he was going to share by the way he said: "Yes, but I will not tell a traitor who joined."

"Are they going to this pro—"

"Stop. Don't say that word in the middle of the day when other monks may hear. Yes, they are going. I will say nothing more."

Feeling deflated, Brother John looked down at the patches of fresh dirt, wishing he could hide in one of them like a seed. He thought that life would, indeed, be much easier as a seed. He would take root, sip his water from the ground, and grow toward the sunlight. There was no need for morality as a plant.

The two men knew they would accomplish nothing more by talking, so they each turned their backs to each other and walked in opposing directions over the monastery fields. Brother John walked back toward the sunlight, while Brother Daniel returned to his more shady spot away from the sun. Their work carried on that day without another interaction.

CHAPTER VI

I n this world, there was still good and bad. People were morally good or bad with possible gray actions in between. There was still a battle raging between God and Satan—between the selfless and the selfish. Brother John knew arising that morning that his neighbors were on the wrong side and that today would prove it.

It began during Vespers when Brother John tucked himself into the pew beside Brother Paul with his balding head much lower and more visible to Brother John's eye.

"Excuse me, brother, may you hand me a Bible over from that pew?" asked Brother John.

Brother Paul handed it to him without a single glance, as if he no longer existed, as if his neighbor had disappeared forever. There was no more connection between the two of them, even in the confines of the monastery. A certain callousness froze Brother Paul's heart since the last time they had spoken about his sins.

"Thank you…brother," said Brother John, holding the Bible in his hands as carefully as a baby.

The chants commenced, but the voices all sounded distinct and separate to Brother John's ears. He could no longer hear any harmony between the raised voices as if God had rejected their efforts to please Him. He was not there to touch their reverberating echoes today. In fact, there was nothing up there, not even a lonesome bat that squeezed its way into the nave.

The gargoyles appeared more hostile, with one, in particular, looking like it was grimacing at their song. Their singing made the statue of Jesus wail in pain—his face more distorted than usual. Brother John was tired this morning, but he could have sworn that what he was seeing and hearing was true: the Madonna cried, the cherubs screamed, the wooden engravings of sheep bled. There was no peace today inside the nave. The gaping aisles along the sides, guiding followers of Christ to the altar, seemed filled with the dead spirits of those who could not rest in peace.

Brother John could see through his blurry eyes the hems of dresses gliding to and fro and the overcoats of men rippling behind them. Their bodies were moving with whatever caused their death still stuck in them or appearing on their faces— the horror of the realization of death's hand reaching out to them before their final breath. Eyes wide, Brother John kept blinking rapidly, closing his eyes, and then staring back at the aisles. They were crowded with the dead. Some ghosts even added their voices to the song. No wonder it sounds so strange and disoriented this morning, thought Brother John.

The dead sang the Vigils in the darkened hall of the nave in a monastery where other sinners lived until they would walk the aisles like the rest of them. There were some monks hidden in their cowls and habits that Brother John sighted in the aisles. He so badly wanted to speak to them and ask about their sins and whether their brothers committed any while in the monastery. Perhaps they could explain to Brother John what he should do to stop the impending protest.

Brother John had never before imagined ghosts walking the aisles beside him, so this must be a sign, he thought. Today must be the day, and I am being called to intervene. The monastery wanted me to keep my neighbors at peace so that they would not roam this nave looking for revenge that may never come.

Holding his Bible close to his heart, Brother John kept a close eye on his neighbors for the rest of the day, right until midnight struck. If the abbot did not have a clue what was going on, then Brother John must take control and restore order. For the routine was key to the peace and stability of the monastic life.

Living inside a cloister like this one, the monks had to abide by the rules. Saint Benedict would have called for his neighbors to care for one another in this community and help those along the path toward peace and happiness. Feeling much more resolved about his decision, Brother John cracked open his Bible to the next hymn and tried to harmonize with Brother Paul next to him. But anytime that his voice reached the same level as his brother's, Brother Paul would move higher or lower, softer or louder in his voice. He refused to have anything to do with him.

In his desperation to make everything harmonious again, Brother John asked: "Brother Paul, would you like to walk with me to breakfast?"

Brother Paul narrowed his eyes and pointed toward the wooden depiction of Jesus on the cross at the altar. "No, I am loyal to Christ alone and no one else. For He is my only judge."

Moving aside to get out of Brother Paul's way, Brother John left the pew and walked alone behind his brother. His head hung down as he searched his mind for any clue that would allow him to figure out when and where exactly this protest would take place. Thinking back, he remembered Brother Daniel telling his students that high-level bankers would be punished. But where was the nearest bank? wondered Brother John. The monastery was isolated on a hill, miles from town. They were utterly alone.

He would have to just follow his brothers and their form of escape, hoping that with the Good on his side, he could put a stop to it. But with the clock still progressing forward, Brother John was afraid of losing sight of one of the men. They could even watch out for him and the possibility of being followed today. How could the abbot not feel the difference in the air? wondered Brother John. The change was palpable.

Brother John entered the kitchen to grab his tray with breakfast, and he found a seat next to Brother Immanuel.

Brother Immanuel was staring down at his plate of bread. He usually refrained from eggs since they could have become chickens, so his plate looked rather sad. Sometimes he even left out the butter, since it came from the milk of a cow. So, it was dry bread and water on most mornings for Brother Immanuel. The man who loved animals more than people.

In a way, Brother John could empathize with his neighbor about the innocence of animals but could not when the line was drawn at people. People could err, that was true. But many did not mean to err. They could also do good and be aware of it, unlike animals who were without a conscience. Trying to understand Brother Immanuel by taking that proverbial "walk in his shoes," he attempted to warm up to him more slowly than last time.

A form of small talk seemed necessary. Brother John began:

"Good morning, brother. How are you?"

Brother Immanuel did not look up for he knew already who it was that had come to judge him and perhaps even change his big plans. He murmured: "Just fine. Peace be with you." But that was all that he said as he placed a bit of bread in his old mouth. He deliberately chewed as slowly as possible to avoid having to converse with Brother John, who was sitting next to him, waiting for the next chance to speak.

"Brother Immanuel, I do apologize for my behavior recently. I meant no harm to you or judging you for what you were doing in the tearoom that night, but I must know now if you are planning to join Brother Daniel…"

Brother Immanuel's shoulders abruptly rose like a cat's back as he heard the name of Brother Daniel. "I will tell you nothing!" he hissed.

"Oh, please, please, brother! I know he means to commit a violent act today. I must know when and where it is so that I can stop it! The monastery is not a place for violence!"

"It will not be here," said Brother Immanuel. "Of course not, the abbot knows nothing of it, and if you dare say a word…" He left the threat lingering in the air as he turned away to keep eating his dry bread. In an awkward position, Brother Immanuel stayed angled away from his brother, which brought more attention to them than before.

"People are staring, brother, go away," muttered Brother Immanuel.

But Brother John remained determined in his interrogation, since they both now understood the gravity of the present situation. There was to be violence, and it was planned for today, and at least three of his brothers were involved. Taking hold of Brother Immanuel's robe, he tugged on his sleeve.

"Listen! Brother Immanuel, you most of all advocate peace. You are a pacifist! You came here to escape Vietnam! Why are you turning away from us now?"

It was difficult to see Brother Immanuel's face from the angle he was at, but Brother John could feel his arm falling into the sleeve he still clutched in his hand. With a deep sigh, he said: "Before the war, I saw all people as good and merely misguided by the devil. But since being in the convent and reading the newspapers, it seems evil is very much a *choice* that people make. There are evil people out there, brother, and it pains my heart to know that fact. Before I expire here in the monastery, I want to try one time in my life to bring justice to those who chose to live the evil life."

"And who are these evil people you speak of?"

"The businessmen, of course. The people who sell magic tricks that in the best case do absolutely nothing and in the worst case cause moral sin or death or both! These 'innovators' play God and mess with nature. They harm animals who they think are less worthy of life than themselves. These are the people who have lost their faith and no longer fear God. We must remind them of that fear, as that is the only way to save their souls or, at least, to save the souls of the other victims they intend to feed on."

"But aren't you playing God then, brother?" asked Brother John.

"Preposterous! We are the servants of the Lord and His will runs through our veins. Each of the members of this community has been haunted in some way by God toward this singular goal: Right the wrongs committed by heretics."

"This is just Brother Daniel's way of speaking! He is making you take part in his crime. Don't fall for it, brother. He is not meant to be in this monastery—he even told me himself! Please abandon this goal and come back to our paradise here in the monastery."

"Brother, have you seen the ghosts walk up and down the aisles of the nave before?"

Goosebumps threw up every hair on Brother John's arms as he heard those words exit his brother's mouth. "Yes, yes, just this morning. I thought I was merely seeing things from being tired…but…"

"Oh no, brother, we have all seen them now. They are the victims of the businessmen walking those aisles aimlessly, just waiting to be released from their time in purgatory. We must help them!"

"Has the abbot seen any such phantasms?"

"We have not spoken to him of such things in confession for fear that, like you, he would try to stop us. We do not ultimately obey the abbot of the monastery, we serve God. This is His sign to us to do something when the problem arrives inside our own walls—not as mere newspapers, but as ghosts themselves! We have seen the Truth, His chosen few, and so we must answer the call."

"But how do we know for sure that what we saw was real?" asked Brother John.

"We must have faith in our Lord. Multiple reports have been made now and to investigate would only anger our Lord. We must have faith."

Brother Immanuel bowed his head and remained seated away from Brother John for the rest of his breakfast.

***

Brother John sat in deep contemplation, trying to make sense of what he had seen. Could it have been people in on the conspiracy and dressing up as ghosts with sheets over their heads? he wondered. Could they have been mists or drafts coming in through the old stone? What could cause such distinguished shapes of people if not for real ghosts? With his mind thoroughly boggled, Brother John's earnestness to discover the Truth became toothless. He stepped back from the pursuit for the next stretch of the day while still keeping his eyes on his neighbors.

During the first work shift at nine thirty, Brother John caught sight of Brother Daniel talking to one of the other monks in the garden. They were working on weeding around the newly planted potatoes. He overheard him saying, "The darkness is when the devil in all of us comes out." Brother Daniel lifted his head and noticed Brother John nearby, so he left the monk alone to continue weeding. Brother John took this as a sign that he would find out nothing from the leader of this impending protest. Still, he thought he must at least try.

Continuing his march toward where Brother Daniel worked, within hearing distance, he asked: "Brother Daniel, you know why I am here. I need you to help me. Help me find peace again within these limestone walls. Your fight against businessmen should not be through violence. I cannot sleep, I cannot eat, I cannot focus on my daily routines when I know that there is an uprising afoot and many of my neighbors are in on it!"

"If I were you," grimaced Brother Daniel, "I would stay out of this and find your peace back in your own mind. Stay out of our way. You can turn away and forget our existence and then you will find your supposed peace. But I, for one, could not eat, sleep, nor find peace knowing that the world turns without us. Our prayers have shown no effect for thousands of years now as monks. It is time that we teach the next generation to do better than us—to take down the heretics as in the Inquisition!"

Brother Daniel thrust his weeding knife into the soil and stood up. He came close to Brother John's nose, breathing on him erratically like a bull seeing red. There was no way to stop what had been building up in him for years, perhaps for his entire life, thought Brother John.

"All right. But I will follow you and I will do everything in my power to stop what is happening today."

"How do you know it is today?" asked Brother Daniel.

"I saw the ghosts in the aisles during Vigils," said Brother John.

A smile emerged on Brother Daniel's lips. "Ah, then you are one of us."

"Brother Immanuel just told me how the sign is about the ghosts and those are the victims of the businessmen."

"They are indeed."

"I don't believe that what I saw was real. Tell me how you made ghosts appear."

"If you don't have faith in ghosts, then maybe you came to the wrong place, brother—not me."

Brother John scowled in the face of Brother Daniel, who mockingly smiled back at him. The two faced off without a word for several seconds, thinking about how they would get the other out of their lives.

"Brother, I am sorry to tell you that if you have seen the ghosts, then you at least understand why we must do what we are doing. Yes, it is today. You have figured that out yourself, but unless you join in our fight, I cannot reveal any more."

Hearing this offer, Brother John contemplated a viable solution to his present problem, which is when he said: "Okay,

I will join. Tell me when and where and what to bring."

"I don't believe you for one second," said Brother Daniel. "Prove to me you understand our cause and that you will not go and tell the abbot of our plans."

In a sheer panic, Brother John scrambled around in his mind for ways to appease his brother. "What if I recruit other monks to attend? I mean, I have no clue who you have already convinced, but if you tell me, then I will find them and convince them to come...with whatever weapons you chose."

There was no way that Brother Daniel could believe in a sudden change of mission, but he did want as many monks there as possible. "Okay, bring me two more monks by tonight, if you can find any, and you can come. I will meet you at midnight in the tearoom, where all the rest of the protesters will be until we move out."

I knew it! thought Brother John. Darkness is what suited such sinful behavior and so it was in the tearoom for each of his neighbors out there in the middle of the night. He bowed to Brother Daniel and exited the garden entirely.

His legs took him straight to the library. The library would be of no use to him in terms of what weapons to bring to a protest, but the library was Brother John's immediate place of comfort. Like a familiar food favorite, Brother John entered the library and hid in between two of the stacks, furthest away from any sign of human life. He only wanted to be surrounded by the spines of books.

Sitting on the floor with his legs crossed, he closed his eyes. Behind his eyelids, diamond shapes were sitting there, performing wiggling dances whenever the sunlight became obscured by the clouds. In came his breath and out, in and out, in and out, then a deliberate focus of his mind's thoughts on his toes, up to his legs, up to his torso, up to his arms, and then up to the topmost hairs on his head that waved in the musty air. In a matter of minutes, Brother John had cleared his mind until the wave of nausea struck him about what was coming. His situation could only disappear for short moments, like the rays of sunlight that were caught behind clouds.

***

"Brother, are you all right? Did you fall? Or are you meditating?" asked a concerned monk, looking down at Brother John sitting in between the stacks.

"Oh, I thought no one would find me here. I am meditating, brother. Perfectly fine," said Brother John, embarrassed to see that his first victim had come to him only to see him so low.

"Would you like me to help you up?"

"No…what I would actually like you to do is join me with your cell neighbor to attend Brother Daniel's little 'event' tonight. Do you know what I speak of?"

The monk shook his head and rolled his eyes. "Boy, he's gotten to you too? Brother, don't go! We are not here for violence."

"Listen, I promised to bring him two protesters in exchange for learning when and where the event would be so that I can stop it!"

"I see. Well, during our private prayer time, I will ask the brother to my right if he will come. But we are there to stop it?"

"Yes. Just pretend that you are convinced to join in on the violence and then follow me to try to stop it. Are you in?"

"Does the abbot know?"

"Supposedly, he knows nothing."

"I'm in." The brothers shook on it and Brother John believed

170

it was much too easy to recruit two monks that it could not have been but some kind of sign.

***

It was midnight when Brother John and his two recruits were headed down to the garden and into the lamplit tearoom. Sure enough, there was a large group of students and monks crowded into the small room. All the tatami mats were being stomped on and dirtied by the dozens of feet passing through.

"Ladies and gentlemen, I believe our last recruits just arrived, and the van has now pulled in. Please remember to take all of your things with you as many will not be returning tonight to this same location," said Brother Daniel, who looked ridiculous wearing his habit of peace next to the students covered in black with ski masks over their faces. There was a great juxtaposition between the holy and the demonic standing together.

Another student dressed in black had a large van that he drove up as close to the garden as he could and into which everyone packed in. There were several backpacks that Brother John accidentally came into contact with—they were immensely hard, and the sound of glasses clanking together sounded on each bump along the way.

After about a twenty-minute drive, the van stopped at the local bank. The bank had gorgeous white pillars resembling the classical architecture of Greece. They made the building imposing and, to Brother John's mind, that must mean security within the bank must be extremely complex and of the highest priority to the owners. Still, Brother Daniel appeared unfazed as he stepped down from the van with a handful of items.

Standing in front of the bank, Brother Daniel raised his voice to a new level, short of shouting, to Brother John's ears.

171

His voice rang as one of his students supplied him with the addition of a megaphone: "Ladies and gentlemen, my students and my brothers, we are here tonight to show the world that in order to effect change, there must be *action* taken. For much too long, I have watched aspiring students, including myself, decide to take the road of peace and quietude to change the world—to model how another human being should behave amongst his fellow men—but nothing has come of it, friends. *Nothing*! We do this not for ourselves either. For as the Psalms say, 'Not to us, Lord, not to us give the glory, but to your name alone.' We desire a world where God reigns and the weak are helped by the more fortunate and all ills are made well again, swift justice is brought to those who err, and all is right in the world of sinners—only then may we rest in peace. For having done our work for the Lord, we may enter the gates of Heaven and live in true eternal peace there. But to achieve such a utopia on earth, I have learned that it takes the servants of the Lord to carry out his will and *smite* the heretics!"

There was clapping from his captive audience as Brother Daniel took a moment to soak in the glory.

"This is what brings us all here tonight. Though it is unlikely anyone will be here from the outside world as we commit this act of justice, the whole world will know by morning. There will be news cameras here and journalists and reporters from all over the area and showing the entire world what He wants. It is through our actions tonight that we remind the heretics that we are here to protect the Catholic religion and the monastic way of life, thereby bettering our world and making it cleaner for Christ's glory. So, helping me tonight is Brother Paul and Brother Immanuel. Would you two please hand me the prepared Molotovs?"

The two monks stepped forward from out of the group and handed him, from their own bags, the bombs. The lamplights glittered off of the glass. An unfamiliar sensation of panic grew in Brother John's gut. Now he knew the full plan: Brother Daniel was going to light the bank on fire by throwing his homemade bombs through its massive windows. His thoughts circled chaotically trying to figure out the proper way of stopping him and the crowd from attacking in such a horrific manner.

Meanwhile, Brother Daniel held the two glass bottles in each hand. He had one monk on either side make the sign of the cross over them and read a passage from the Bible. Surprisingly, the speech from the megaphone had stirred no soul in the entire town. The bank was in the downtown area where businesses resided but few people lived. Brother Daniel's plan would succeed if no one in the crowd stopped it.

III

PART THREE

CHAPTER I

Brother John looked over at his two recruits who kept looking back at him, waiting for some sort of plan. But there was no plan. Brother John simply had to throw himself now into the pit of the unknown and fight for the Good.

Squirming in between a few of the students, he made his way up to the front and ran right for Brother Daniel—he had two options: crash into him until they both fell on the lawn or try wrenching the bottles individually from his hands. Brother Daniel, however, was taller and weighed more than him, so knocking him down seemed unlikely. In a split second, Brother John nodded to his recruits, who followed behind him in the crowd, and they all charged toward Brother Daniel.

Brother John got a hold of the bottle in Brother Daniel's right hand while the other two monks went for the left. He seemed only mildly shocked Brother John was trying to fight him, and with the way his students reacted in response, it seemed they had been looking out for such a move too. Immediately, the students grabbed onto the cowls of the disobedient monks, choking them with their own collars, and pulling them off of Brother Daniel.

The other monks were startled but remained standing there

waiting for the deed to be done, while the students actively participated in making it happen. Out of their backpacks came bricks and more glasses filled with fuel and pepper sprays and paint sprays. There were even rocks that the students had collected on their way over from the monastery.

As soon as Brother Daniel got his right arm free from Brother John's grasp, he threw the Molotov cocktail through one of the eyes of the bank. The window shattered, and the lamplights attached to its face made the pieces glitter like falling snow. Brother John shouted, "Violence is not going to change the world! You must see that! Brothers and sisters, please!" But his pleas went unheard under the megaphone a student grabbed who was shouting, "Burn down capitalist pigs! Burn down capitalist pigs! *Burn down capitalist pigs!*"

As soon as the bomb broke the window, the students let rain their bricks and stones and glass bombs. Throwing everything they brought with them, it looked like a scene from when mankind first awoke on this earth as nothing but primal beasts. They were savages attacking the unknown. No thought or moment of consciousness appeared to furrow their brows, only sweat from the heat of the growing fire.

The flames licking the outside of the eye of the building blackened the classical pillars. The flames moved deeper and deeper into the bowels of the bank. The money might be safe, but the rest of the building was not sealed safely away. The men who built this structure must have shuddered in their graves as the building suffered so.

At this point, Brother John could only weep. There were no words to express his sense of overwhelm. How could the days have gone from inhaling fragrant teas, singing chants together with his brothers, and pruning the roses in the monastery garden come to this? Now, his world was filled with the smell of smoke, faces covered by masks, and the sounds of screaming savages.

Once all the students and even some monks threw everything they brought at the bank, some students went up to the front of the building face that was still untouched by the fire to spray paint vulgar words and pictures. They vandalized every part that was not already blackened by smoke.

"Well, it looks like we accomplished nothing in trying to stop this protest," said one of the recruited monks to Brother John. He could feel the blame placed on his shoulders for having exposed other peaceful monks to this violence. The weight was unbearable.

However, Brother John could not leave until the student who drove the van took the monks back to their home, for he did not know where they were, having never traveled outside the monastery before arriving there. So, he waited. The entire protest felt like it lasted ages when, in reality, it was only about ten minutes. They knew that the alarms inside were triggered and they would need to escape before the police arrived.

The students fled on foot back to their vehicles, which were within walking distance from the scene, while the student with the van drove the rest of the monks back. The tearoom filled up with the brothers as the student clapped Brother Daniel on the back before heading home.

Without saying a word to Brother Daniel, Brother John exited his beloved tearoom and ran across the garden. It was nearing one in the morning as the cool night air reddened Brother John's ears. But he was determined to wake the abbot.

Upon knocking loudly on his door, the abbot opened it with a look of worry in his eyes. "Is everyone all right, Brother

John? Is one of our brothers ill?"

Brother John shook his head from side to side before blurting out all that he could muster together in his addled mind: "Brother Daniel led a group of our own brothers and his students to vandalize and utterly destroy the local bank in the name of our Lord just now."

With a fury lighting up his eyes, the abbot moved Brother John aside with the back of his hand and sped toward the great bell. He rang the bell at this unusual time, waking all the sleeping monks, who must have been alarmed at such a deviation in their routine. Then, the abbot walked with each heavy step echoing in the cell hallway of the monastery, shouting, "Every brother to the great nave, *now!*"

The sleepwalking monks hurried down to the nave with their eyes half-closed, though they were alarmed by the bells at this hour. Meanwhile, the monks from the tearoom tried to ease their way back in and toward the nave without being recognized as coming from anywhere else but their cells.

The abbot and Brother John following closely behind were the first monks in the great nave. Taking a quick look in both aisles as they entered, Brother John sighed with relief that he saw no ghosts there this morning. He turned toward the abbot, who asked: "Brother John, give me names. Right now."

"The only monk who should be held responsible is Brother Daniel, father. He is the one who has been recruiting other monks and students to join him for months now. My other brothers are to blame too but only in their confession time with you. I do not believe they should be thrown from the monastery publicly like this."

The abbot lowered his head as if he was not surprised by Brother Daniel's further sins. "Yes, after that last fiasco, I should not have been surprised that he would continue to sin, but this is unheard of. Has he learned nothing from his time here? Some people choose evil and he is one of them."

Other monks began trickling into the nave as their footsteps could be heard approaching from several feet away. The moonlight was the only thing lighting up the interior until the abbot lit a single candle to help illuminate his face at the altar.

"My brothers, since it seems that you are all here in attendance, we have a very grave sin to speak of. Brother John here has just informed me that tonight, a group of sinners left the monastery and vandalized the local bank. The head of this operation was Brother Daniel." If the abbot could see the accused's face hiding in his cowl, he would have pointed him out for all to scowl at, but it was still much too dark, so he remained hidden in the crowd.

"Yes, I am afraid no one is surprised by this Observer's behavior. He has not been able to mesh in here well. I, perhaps foolishly, thought by giving him another chance that God would enter his soul, but it seems I am mistaken.

"It is my duty in this monastery to direct my flock of sheep to act in the way of the Lord. We are here to fill ourselves with His undying love and remain moved by His spirit alone. And I, your abbot, 'I have not hidden your justice in my heart; I have proclaimed your Truth and your salvation, but they spurned and rejected me.' Brother Daniel may be the instigator of this violent act, but all of you witnessed, at least once, his atrocious ideas. No one informed me of this in confession. So, 'how is it that you can see a splinter in your brother's eye, and never notice the plank in your own', my brothers? Brother Daniel was given permission by all of us to do what he did today and some of you, I am told, even threw the objects of violence yourselves! Lord have mercy on your souls!"

The abbot's forehead was the target for many of the monks' focus as a vein pulsated through the thin, pale skin that grew redder with time. The more furious the abbot became, the more the vein moved like a snake trapped within the skin of this monk, just waiting to break free. In horror, everyone stared, waiting for the vein to finally wiggle its way out of his face. Growing queasy from the sensation, Brother John looked down at the floor.

The abbot continued: "You are all taught the *Rule of Saint Benedict* and you all know the tiny book by heart. If read daily, the book would have told you that you must 'love the Lord God with your whole heart, your whole soul and all your strength, and love your neighbor as yourself.' Loving our neighbors is a key aspect of the Bible. Instead, neighbors were pitted against each other by those who embraced the rules and by those who refused to follow them. But brothers, 'do not repay one bad turn with another' for that is not the way of Christ. In fact, we are supposed to take the pain that comes our way as a sign to do better, as a form of payment for our original sin, and as a way to prove ourselves worthy of God in the face of suffering.

"Saint Benedict has never advocated for violence and any violence that occurs upon a brother. Well, he must accept it, as I said. He must never fight back. We are a community of peace and self-improvement. You can only work on yourself and hope that others will follow your example. We are a monastery filled with love. I have no tolerance for violence of any kind, which is why tonight we are excommunicating Brother Daniel and he is to leave the monastery by this afternoon. He is no longer welcome to this monastery."

There was an explosion of murmurs within the crowd before

the abbot. A bone-chilling fear swept over the monks who could not imagine such a sentence for themselves who had devoted their whole lives to the Catholic church. A lonely, empty circle formed around what was presumably Brother Daniel himself, standing there in one of the further back pews. He stepped forward and walked down the nave at this point right up to the abbot. Then, he spat at the abbot's feet before removing his cowl and turning around toward the cells, presumably to cool off and collect or give back anything that was temporarily known as his.

The abbot's face was shockingly red by now, with the vein appearing purple and bulging. He had never been treated with such disrespect before today. The only way to release the valve was to look up to the ceiling and pray to God, which he did for a newfound grace and peace in the face of such low behavior. His visible frustration slowly cooled as his face grew white once more.

"You are all dismissed; however, I expect everyone in confession to confess anything and everything they knew about this protest tonight, and they must submit to physical punishment as a consequence. No one shall sleep peacefully tonight for their sins," said the abbot as he descended the steps of the altar and walked past each monk without looking at any of them.

The abbot was disgusted by all of his sheep. He was not seen for the rest of the day. Brother John thought about his own involvement in the scheme. Was he merely a bystander? No, he thought, he must have been at least a step above such depravity. Still, along with all of his other brothers, there was a grand feeling of guilt.

Brother Daniel was the only man to break the profound

silence that day as he cursed terribly in his cell, throwing what little was in there against the wall before he handed a box filled with things back to one of the brothers who maintained an inventory of certain items for the new monks: Bibles, habits, cowls, sandals, weeding knives, sun hats, toothbrushes, toothpaste, bandages, things that every new monk would require.

Carrying nothing but the layman's clothes on his back that he was given in order to return his habit, the abbot escorted Brother Daniel out of the monastery. Several of the monks followed behind, watching something that many of them had never witnessed before—the excommunication of a brother and physical removal from the property. It was a story that they would surely all hold in their minds as the consequence of disobeying the abbot and, furthermore, the Lord.

***

That day happened about six months ago, thought Brother John, who was now a Novice within the monastery. He was only two years away from making his final vows and becoming a Professed Monk. The stretch before making his final vows was the longest one of a couple of years before even being allowed to ask the abbot. But once a man came this far in the process, it was highly unusual for him not to become a monk for life.

Taking comfort from this knowledge, Brother John felt a sense of ease and peace returning to his life from the day that Brother Daniel was a brother no more. His havoc on the monastic life ruined more than just Brother John's experience but many others' and they were happy to see him leave, though they hid their smiles in their cowls.

Brother John had never again witnessed the ghosts walking

down the aisles of the nave, so he hoped that Brother Daniel had somehow orchestrated such a show to scare more brothers into joining his protest. In fact, there were really no "signs" anywhere anymore. Life was lived by the book and routines had been regular since that day.

Everyone had given their confessions to the abbot the day after Brother Daniel left, they repented for their sins, and they all could start anew. The entire day felt like the birth of each man, and a sense of sheer happiness permeated throughout the halls of the monastery. Although Brother John noticed the large, gaping wounds bleeding through Brother Immanuel's habit the day of the confessions, and Brother Paul had blood staining his front half—it must have been the chaffing.

Since the day of the protest, Brother John decided to never set foot again in the tearoom at midnight, regardless of what monk decided to use it. Since coming so far, he no longer wanted to change the ways of his brothers. He knew that Brother Immanuel and Brother Paul were still probably up to their old ways and there were other monks who most likely replaced Brother Daniel's tearoom slot. But as long as he remained ignorant of what his neighbors were doing, then he found some sense of peace and stability.

There was no imminent threat of violence any longer and the other monks who were still on their journey to finding peace just needed more time to find it. They sinned because they were unhappy. Fortunately, Brother John was *not* unhappy. He *loved* the monastic life in every way, from the early morning chants to the reading time in the library, to the work hours outside amongst the plants, to the meals that filled his stomach as well as his soul. The monastic life was for him.

Each part of the day facilitated his personal growth and

mental well-being. The early mornings before the sun awoke allowed him to see sunrises in all their glory. Brother John could sing to his heart's content at such a sight and prolong his enjoyment at seeing the light. Then, he ate with his fellow men in respectful silence at breakfast, thoroughly enjoying the aroma of his cup of green tea. He ate slowly and with intention, remembering to chew every last piece and swallow every last drop.

Then, he went back and forth between work and private scriptural reading times. The combination alternated between using his mind and body to fulfill his very soul. Life was too good when both his mind and body hummed with enjoyment. The sun felt so good on his skin when his mind was fatigued and the quietude of the library felt so wonderful when his muscles were tired. Each task was further split up by times to refuel with mealtimes and other times to chant and release some of those emotions building up inside of him.

Brother John optimized his life within the confines of the rules. He could feel his best when he moved from task A to task B throughout each day on repeat until one day melded into the next. His life became one long day. Night served as merely a period to the end of one date and the beginning of another like a coda.

For Brother John, this was truly living. He woke up each morning ready to conquer the day as the best version of himself while maintaining enough energy to improve even more. Every day that he was still breathing, he partook in activities that he learned to appreciate and be grateful for— some which he had been doing daily and others that he picked up more recently as hobbies. The world would never cease to amaze Brother John.

***

Life continued without any bumps for Brother John until one morning when he was in his cell and awoke to hear moans. He launched himself out of bed and followed the sounds. He reached the side of the wall where Brother Immanuel was and the peephole. Glancing through it in the darkness, he figured it must have been the early hours of the morning. He could only see Brother Immanuel laying on his stomach with his feet pointed downward. Why he was not on his back like usual was the question in Brother John's mind.

The moans continued as Brother John wondered how long he had been sleeping through his brother's obvious pain.

Opening his cell door, Brother John went to his neighbor's door and, knowing that there were no locks on the doors, while trying to avoid waking up the entire hallway of sleeping monks, he pushed open Brother Immanuel's door and stepped in.

Brother Immanuel did not attempt to even raise his head, though Brother John made it apparent that he had entered his room with the shuffling of his feet across the stone floor.

"Brother, are you all right? Where does it hurt?" asked Brother John. But then an involuntary gasp escaped his throat as he saw Brother Immanuel's white tunic covered in blood all over his back.

"Oh Lord, are your wounds still bleeding? Have they not closed up? Are these new?" asked Brother John, pulling up Brother Immanuel's tunic and instinctively dropping the fabric back down with his hand over his mouth to halt a scream.

A wave of nausea and seeing stars caused Brother John to drop to his knees and bow forward on the cold, hard floor. He placed his head down to alleviate the heat that had rushed up into his ears, filling them with hot white noise.

What he saw was so wretched that the devil must have been inside of Brother Immanuel this whole time, for nothing more grotesque had ever been revealed to him.

Brother Immanuel's wounds had not been able to clot fully. He had a bacterial infection growing in several of the individual, puffy mounds on his back. The microbes entered his wound, which fed them, and they continued to spread to form what looked like a yellowy film. Meanwhile, the battle was raging right in front of Brother John's eyes as Brother Immanuel's immune system was bloated around the wounds, trying to kill the bacteria. He must be in the midst of a fever, thought Brother John. The wounds held puss and blood, which were seeping out like the tears falling from the face of a crucified Christ. His whole body looked ravaged and unclean. There were even black spots on his back, like something from the pages of the history of the plague. It was as if he was always just wearing a temporary skin meant to deceive others into caring for him, but underneath was a series of festering wounds that moved and grew and changed all the time.

Brother John felt guilty as he noticed his genuine disgust toward another human being. Decay exhibiting itself in real time on another person's body made him hate that person. Perhaps it was a form of self-preservation, but all Brother John knew was that he *hated* his brother.

"Brother, you need to go to the hospital *now*. Your wounds are infected. How long have they been like this?"

Brother Immanuel only moaned.

Brother John turned and exited the room, heading straight for the abbot's cell down the hall.

"Help! I need you to help get Brother Immanuel to the hospital. His wounds from flagellation are all horribly infected!"

The abbot, hardly hearing the words that awoke him from his slumber, took a moment to show the gravity of the situation on his features. However, once the meaning of Brother John's words made sense, he ran to the office where all the bookkeeping was done for the business side of the monastery and picked up the landline phone, dialing 911.

The hospital was so far from the monastery that it took nearly thirty minutes for anyone to arrive to pick up Brother Immanuel. Within that time, the abbot and Brother John ran back to Brother Immanuel's room to aid in any way they could.

"The Good Book says, 'Be brave of heart and rely on the Lord' now in all your humility, Brother Immanuel, and 'bless those who curse them.' For you are a good sheep of the Lord. Please say your prayers while the ambulance comes to help you. Stay with us, brother," pleaded the abbot.

But when the abbot lifted back up the tunic of Brother Immanuel, Brother John noticed just how red and swollen the entire area looked and it seemed to be spreading to the sides of his torso. Brother John bent down and quickly touched the skin, which was warm. The deep tissue seemed to be fighting...and losing.

That single poke caused Brother Immanuel to howl in pain.

"Sorry! I'm so sorry, brother. The ambulance will be here soon. I promise not to touch you again. You have an infection, brother...brother...brother, can you hear me?" Brother John noticed that after Brother Immanuel cried out, his head lifted and fell back down again with a thump. He stopped moving after that as if he had passed out. "Do you think he has fainted away...or...or moved on?" asked Brother John, who

189

was committed to keeping his promise of not touching his disgusting brother again.

The abbot reached down and felt for a pulse. There was none.

The ambulance came to pronounce Brother Immanuel dead at two fifteen in the early morning of February 9, which was a Sunday. The timing of his death did not go unnoticed by the rest of the monastic community—he died on a holy day in the dead of winter during the coldest of months.

The men from the ambulance said that it looked like necrotizing fasciitis had killed him, which meant that flesh-eating bacteria were killing Brother Immanuel's deep tissue and organs were starting to fail because of it. The dead of winter was embodied inside Brother Immanuel's body on this holy day.

CHAPTER II

A doctor arrived shortly after the ambulance medics declared Brother Immanuel dead. The doctor filled out the proper paperwork and worked with the abbot to make sure that his body was as prepared as it could be to immediately enter one of the burial spots in the monastery's cemetery.

He had no living relatives left to speak of, so things were fast and fairly easy as they lowered his body into the ground in a simple box made of pine. The rest of the day's prayers concerned their fellow brother, who had passed so suddenly of his own doing.

But in order to preserve his sanctity as a monk of the Catholic faith, his death was not even allowed to be *thought* of as a suicide. He accidentally fell prey to the outside forces of bacteria entering his open wounds that were merely created to give penance to the Lord.

However, the lesson was not lost on the monks that this is one of the reasons why the monastery did not support or permit flagellation. Saint Benedict did not advocate for such self-abuse, either. Death could always be a potential outcome for any brother who defied Saint Benedict's rules and created open wounds within the flesh.

***

The next morning everyone arose and attended Vigils to proclaim once more the verse, 'Lord, open my lips and my mouth shall proclaim your praise,' followed by the psalms. Each monk seemed to still be dreaming as they sang.

Brother John had awoken suddenly to the bells from out of his odd dream that morning. He had dreamed of Brother Immanuel still laying on his stomach with his feet facing downward. He replayed the moans repeatedly in his dream as he and the abbot tried to think of ways to heal miraculously Brother Immanuel. The abbot came up with a plan to mix together a medieval salve and rub it on his back to heal all the wounds within minutes. Bringing out a mortar and pestle, he ground down several herbs and honey and made a paste. The sticky goop was laid thickly on Brother Immanuel's back and he writhed at first before they both heard an audible sigh. At least the salve seemed to have soothed the wounds and numbed the pain. Taking advantage of this opportunity, Brother John proceeded to squeeze out the puss-filled mounds on Brother Immanuel's back. He wanted to expel the evil humours which he thought were trapped in his back. So, bending over the sick monk, Brother John took both thumbs and worked with opposing pressure to push out the evil and what came out appeared to be nothing more than cottage cheese—completely edible, if one were to get over the fact that it came from a sick man's back. Still with mild disgust, and some amount of curiosity, he continued onto the next pustule and the next and the next until his entire back had been released of its impurities. The bells woke Brother John up right when Brother Immanuel was wiped off and he rose from the bed well again.

Thoughts surrounding the mystery of death clouded Brother John's mind as he hid any yawns in his cowl. The voices of the monks regained their harmony ever since Brother Daniel left, though now, without Brother Immanuel, it all felt a bit hollow. Still, the act of waking up the diaphragm, the lungs, the voice box, and the mouth created a wonderful way to start each new day, believed Brother John, who was focused on forming each sound out properly with his mouth.

Stuck on an O-shape, Brother John's mind began shifting to thoughts of Mary. He had spent many months now without the thought of her entering his mind and haunting him. But today, perhaps weakened by thoughts of death, he wondered about her whereabouts. He wondered what she was doing in school, what kinds of friends she had, if she had a crush on any boys, and if she still kept that beautiful, sincere innocence about her. By now, she may very well be another year older and that much closer to becoming a teenager—the most dangerous time for those who are still innocent.

A sense of fear and dread shook Brother John's frame as he thought about losing the only pure vision of a real person he held for so many months now. She was like his Madonna in the flesh, which nothing could sully. Her body was a temple and her mind a sponge for knowledge. Brother John could see her sitting at her wooden desk and perfecting her notes in history class with specific colors and dots and lines to signify each point's level of importance. He could envision a smile appearing on her face as she answered a question correctly, building up her self-confidence with each right answer. The hunger to know more stayed with her even when the school doors closed. Someday, she will feel closer to the Truth than ever before and that will drive her onward to do great things with her life.

Finally releasing the O note of the verse, Brother John was able to move his mouth around. He inhaled deeply for the next chant and thought more about Mary until Vigils came to a close. Breakfast was spent in much the same way until the later morning private prayer time. The sun had finally arisen by eight o'clock and Brother John sat below the tiny windowsill of his cell.

Crossing his legs and lowering his wrists, with open palms toward the ceiling, he sat there taking deep breaths. He breathed in for four counts, held it for four counts, and exhaled for four counts with his eyes closed. Once a rhythm in Brother John's breathing was established, he focused all of his thoughts on his toes all the way up to his head, relaxing each part of his body as he moved up. By the time he had reached his head, all the world had slowed down and the problems that once seemed insurmountable became more manageable.

***

Meditation was a method of slowing time down for Brother John. It was a segment of time just for himself to think about where he had been and where he was going. The time for analysis gave him more of an ability to take stock of the moment. Looking from the outside in, Brother John could interpret his experiences from a more rational standpoint. For instance, when Brother John first noticed that Brother Paul always left his work in the garden promptly to attend private scriptural reading time in his cell, that should have encouraged some suspicion in him. But it did not until the day he heard those sounds he could never forget.

Brother Paul continued to follow his own routine. Perhaps he believed that his lifeblood was connected to his member and that it required all of his attention. His sex addiction must have been the subject of every one of his sessions in confession with the abbot.

But it was apparent to Brother John that happiness could not come from a place of addiction, of any sort. But Brother Paul followed the routines that all the other brothers did. Still, any moment that he found alone, Brother John began noticing that he was constantly pleasuring himself.

There were even days when he waddled around like he had chaffed himself so badly the day before. The monks would notice if he stole all the lotion from the community restrooms, so he must have gone without. Brother John could not imagine how raw the skin must have gotten with only saliva alone to help.

But it was an insatiable hunger for Brother Paul, who must have spent every waking hour thinking about his next little death—a thick-thighed woman with him or not.

Before coming to the monastery, Brother John knew a man who had a similar problem. He told him that sex addiction is just like drug addiction, in that you will go to any length to find a fix. The need came from a feeling about himself that he was not worthy of anything, including sex. He was lucky if he got any from his hard work at finding it.

For this man, the low self-confidence came from bullies at school, but for Brother Paul, it came from the Bible. Every day he was told that he was sinful and worthless, so rather than taking that to be humble and do better—Brother Paul used it to stay low. The only pleasure he found in his life was in the moments where he forgot himself entirely and that was through sleeping or sex.

It appeared that sex or any kind of self-pleasure soothed

Brother Paul's internal pain. His invisible wounds were poked and prodded every day, seven times a day, in the form of Vigils, Lauds, Mass, Terce, Sext, Vespers, and Compline. For the Prophet said: "Seven times a day have I praised you."

That did not even include the scriptural readings alone or during meals, when there was another chance to be reminded about his inadequacy. Perhaps Brother Paul thought that by taking himself out of the competitive environment of the outside world that in here he would not struggle as much with his self-esteem, but the sickness still seems to be holding on.

With her pretty little teeth in his succulent, fatty flesh, the mother of sexual pleasure is feeding off of Brother Paul just as much as he is on her. Like a compulsion, the bell rings to signify the beginning or abrupt ending of his self-pleasuring endeavors.

The entire monastic ritual for him must have been about his next fix. The time spent pursuing them was so much easier in a way when his days all looked the same. But after each "session," he must have felt even emptier than before—having relieved himself of all the tension building up in him for those few hours beforehand. To then feel empty must have put him in a terrible mood all over again until he thought about the next sinful act. For without such a lifesaving float of an idea being thrown out toward him, he would surely drown in his own depression.

Trying to find the Lord so far had proved hollow for Brother Paul if he was still behaving in such a way. There was no mighty hand slapping away his own from his member. No matter how many tears he shed over it or wallowing he did on the floor, no sign seemed to come to tell Brother Paul to repent.

So, alone in his cell, believing he was out of God's chosen few and possibly even out of sight, he could not resist. He thought about his woman in the tearoom that he could hold and feel sorry for himself in her arms. Brother Paul could cry at her without having to find answers or even pray for forgiveness. For she just *held* him. Brother John had seen her simple acceptance of this broken man.

The thick-legged woman just held a weeping man with no self to speak of and holding him carried him through to another day. But the cycle repeated itself with no movement forward. It seemed that Brother Paul would die a sex addict inside of these holy walls. He would die without having improved his sense of self-worth. He would die without having experienced sex stemming from pure love. He would die without knowing what true happiness felt like.

Brother Paul was not at peace in this monastery, thought Brother John as he meditated on the soul of this human being. Brother Paul lacked the stability of the soul that Brother John had achieved. There were demons there pushing and pulling him constantly that it must have been exhausting enough just to get out of bed in the morning.

It was just a matter of time before old age alone would end the endless cycle of hellish addiction that Brother Paul was caught up in. Feeling an enormous sense of pity for his neighbor, Brother John rose to his feet from the windowsill of his cell and pressed his hand to the side of the wall nearest Brother Paul—who was still quietly groaning on the other side.

***

Returning to his windowsill, Brother John focused on his

breathing and checking in with his body. Relaxing all of his tense muscles, his thoughts drifted to those about Brother Immanuel.

Before he began meditating as a regular practice, Brother John had never quite picked up on Brother Immanuel's strange desire to maintain a perfect posture at all times. Perhaps he even leaned a bit too far back at times. He also never noticed any stains on his habit, though the black scapular he wore over it hid most of the stains.

Now, thinking about his brother and his ultimate demise, it became clear that Brother Immanuel had been practicing self-flagellation for some time before Brother John had ever even thought about joining the monastery. He kept his posture upright to avoid having his habit stick to his wounds as much as possible, and he also did not want to lean forward in the event a wound should tear open afresh. He had done his penance for the day and needed to heal at least a little bit before the next session.

He often went to his cell during private prayer times at a slow and solemn pace. Poor Brother Immanuel enjoyed the suffering and dragged out the procession before the release of pain for ages. His entire days, to Brother John's mind, now seemed like one long procession before being slaughtered as a sacrificial lamb repeatedly.

Brother Immanuel's only guidance from the Bible must have been: "Serve the Lord with fear" and the oppressive feelings of guilt that he carried in his heart. There was one day when Brother John heard Brother Immanuel weeping more loudly than usual and the sound the whips made against the air caused shivers to ravage his flesh. It was only later in the day when Brother John heard the news that his sister had died from cancer that same day. He had not seen her since he escaped service for the monastery.

The only way to relieve the guilt he felt about not having been there for his sibling as she fought this invisible demon was to self-sabotage his own mortal flesh. Brother Immanuel knew he owned nothing of material worth, nor did he have social capital of any major sort in the outside world. The only thing he had to give and punish was himself.

His own mind must have constantly been whipping itself regardless, but he needed to show others what his insides already felt—pain.

Brother Immanuel was the definition of a masochist. As a monk, he was already isolating himself, picking himself out from the crop, and choosing to become a man of God. He was held to higher moral standards than most people, and Brother Immanuel must have felt the pressure.

The pressure of being perfect and failing over and over again killed him. He wanted to be the perfect savior, like Christ was. How hard could that be? he must have thought. But each time he believed he failed, the consequences were meted out just as severely. If he were to be better than others, then he must take punishment worse than others.

By this logic, Brother Immanuel beat himself senselessly with his nose on the page of a newspaper so that all the outsiders could see that he was different, maybe not perfect, but different. He carried his guilt alone and must have felt at least some sense of pride for having carried the weight by himself.

Brother John had never seen Brother Immanuel yell at someone or beat them. Although there was that one day when a rage burst forth behind the mask of his face. But he made himself pay dearly for that outburst. He kept his rage in check and the cloud of guilt that he considered his own was always over his head.

Feeling an immense empathy for Brother Immanuel, Brother John sighed out loud. His neighbor on the peephole side of his room would never rise again. He was buried with his guilt deep down in the dirt outside in the fields of the monastery. He never considered that the people in the newspaper could never feel his suffering or hear his cries of pain like Brother John could. He was alone until the end.

There was no happiness allowed in Brother Immanuel's world while other people suffered. He had created this unrealistic fantasy for himself, where he could only experience peace when everyone else did. For he followed what God taught him, he had original sin that must be repented for and so did everyone else, and unless those sins were fixed, then suffering would continue ad nauseam.

Unfortunately, as hard as Brother Immanuel tried to right his own wrongs along with everyone else's, he failed and suffered immensely from it. Still, during his struggle, he must have found some licks of pride or bites of pleasure in his wounds. Otherwise, he would have quit the entire struggle much earlier on.

Brother John thought about where such a person could find relief from such agony. Perhaps he found it at the moment before losing consciousness, which had happened a time or two in his cell before. Or maybe he found a certain pleasure in the ritual itself, much like Brother John did. Or there could be a kind of masochistic sensuality in using one's own blood to create art. He may have thought that he paid the price to at least leave his art behind as some piece of greatness that came from suffering. For the very idea of the starving and suffering artist was just as well-known here as being an isolated monk. It was established in a society already that only through great pain could great things be achieved, so if the monastic life had failed him, then perhaps the artistic one would not.

Brother Immanuel's art still just looked like messy pools on canvas, but if people on the outside knew what this man had done to his hide, then it would immediately be endowed with more meaning—the wondrous ravings of a madman or the holy subconscious images of a saint. The messages surrounding each piece would surely make them sell now, especially that he was dead, for plenty of money. Brother John wondered if the monastery would end up selling all that was left of Brother Immanuel.

***

Unwinding himself from his seated position at the windowsill, Brother John peered through the peephole to see Brother Immanuel's paintings still leaning up against the opposite side of the wall.

They were still there, a tribute to a suffering soul, and Brother John could only sadly shake his head. He went back to his crossed-legged position for one more ten-minute session of meditation before the bells would ring for Terce.

Finally, what monk could avoid contemplating the last days that Brother Daniel was still a part of the monastery? He had caused so much destruction to the monastic way of life that no man within the walls had yet gone a day without him on their minds. Since he still walked this earth, the common thought was about where he was and what he was doing. Most of the monks seemed to believe that he went back to his students and was training them to become little warriors for his cause.

But what really was his cause? Why did he need all of this power? It seemed that Brother Daniel, when cut off from the outside world, lost his identity, which was wrapped up in his status in the eyes of other people.

The isolation grew even worse after his mealtime fiasco where the abbot gave him his first reprimand in private and then everyone else had to follow a strict protocol for the repenting brother. Brother John remembered that for an entire month Brother Daniel had to recite his prayers alone, eat his meals after all the other monks, not have himself nor his meals blessed by his brothers, and no one was allowed to speak to him—he was shunned by the only community he had left. What that must have done to a man who loved power must have been devastating.

The only thing he probably could think to do was to dream about a way to escape the hell he had put himself into. He must have brought his students around during the same month that he was being shunned.

In fact, Brother John did seem to recall a sense of control and confidence that Brother Daniel exuded in the way he walked about halfway through his month of punishment. Either his plan was hatching to bring his students over or they had already started to meet.

When Brother Daniel tried to recruit Brother John, he had such an intensity on his face that it frightened him. It was as if the only thing driving him to carry on was the ability to gather followers. He lusted for the power to control minds. It seemed like he was constantly seeking control in a world that felt uncontrollable—and very much is.

The guilt of hearing that he was no better than anyone else and the shame caused by his own low self-esteem created a *monster* who was clutching with his webbed fingers out of the water at anything to keep himself afloat.

Akin to a drug addict, he required more and more dopamine to fire off in his brain in order to function as a man who had a purpose in this world. By latching onto a group of young adults who were in the position of "student," a submissive one, Brother Daniel could take over as "teacher," the dominant one in the relationship, and fulfill all of his needs. Why he thought that doing this experiment for his students would achieve any of his goals remained a mystery for the entire monastery.

But when he was shown how ineffectual he could be in this vast world, his deep-seated feelings of powerlessness lashed out and he could not take it. Instead, he rebelled against his brothers after trying to make them choose a side—the side that works within society and the world at large or the side that works outside.

Most of the monks remained outside in exchange for exploring themselves more deeply. Brother John was among the majority, but now he was wondering what could cause a man to not want to search himself deeply. Brother Daniel, before the monastery, could very well have had demanding parents or ones who neglected him entirely when he was not proving himself to be in control.

He was still running from something—whether that was his own upbringing or a recent relationship or some other cause. This man also had no experience of peace or stability, perhaps the least out of the trio Brother John could think about. That is why his rage had to be shared and smeared over every monk's cell door.

Brother Daniel came like a plague to the monastery and poured his poison into every monk's ear, excluding the abbot's. Only the men with some moral system decided against joining a group to protest violently in favor of starting a new Inquisition. Monks, after all, are not known for their desire to gain power and smite those who refuse to give in. But Brother Daniel always had to be right and there was nothing he could do that could be seen as wrong. The world ran according to his conscious thoughts as if it did not run separately from him.

But when he died in the future, the world would continue to turn. The monks all knew that, but he did not. The world spun because of Brother Daniel, and he would allow no one to forget that. As a teacher, no one could speak back or they would suffer grade-wise. He had the last word and the power to put other people down, but he did this in the name of the Catholic faith so that more of his followers would swallow the sweet-coated pill more easily.

Brother John knew what Brother Daniel was still doing out there since he could do nothing else at this point—he was as fixed in his beliefs as the earth following its orbit around the sun. Brother Daniel was out there teaching a new set of students to feel as out of control of the world as he did—instilling the fear of God in them—and then lighting a match to see what they will do.

CHAPTER III

The bells rang for Terce, and Brother John unwound his cramped legs from their crossed position. As he shimmied off, he nearly fell flat down on his knees because one of his feet had gone numb.

Tumbling forward, he caught himself on his wooden desk, shaking off the pins and needles, waiting for the pain to pass, before walking out his door and toward the great nave.

Brother John's walk was slow and more deliberate than before. He had learned from his meditation time to do better and *be* better as a human being. He wanted to find peace all around him and stability was needed to see it. At least, thus far, he was convinced that such was the case.

Instead of wandering aimlessly or from fear through life, he wanted every single day to be a joy. Even when performing a strenuous exercise of the mind or the body, Brother John was committed to reminding himself of why such struggles were good and made Man stronger. But when chances came for rest, he never took them lightly, rather, he savored them for everything that they could possibly deliver.

So, when he entered the beautiful, spacious nave—still free from the strange vision of phantoms stretching across the aisles—Brother John smiled. The sun had come up now and was shining brightly through the stained glass, covering the nave with the sound of divine color. Even the wood of the pews looked glossier and more refreshed this morning. The world was a lovely, benevolent place for Brother John.

The "Work of God," also called *Opus Dei*, was every time the choir came together to chant. Many of them opened with "Glory be to the Father" or "We praise you, God" or simply an "alleluia" refrain throughout a song. These refrains, however, could only be used on certain days and seasons. The rules dictated by Saint Benedict explicitly laid out the plan year after year. The same rules would be repeated ad infinitum.

With that kind of structure and certainty built into the monastic life, Brother John found so much freedom. His thoughts would nevermore be preoccupied with going hungry, maintaining shelter, getting enough water, deciding what to wear every day, having to sustain a family, or even what to do to fill up his days. The monastery had mapped his entire life out for him.

His mind was free to explore ancient texts in the library or practice calligraphy in the scriptorium or perfect his singing or learn to play a new instrument or play outside in the garden with different kinds of tools or figure out new ways to enjoy tea or meditate.

Brother John's journey could center on bettering himself each and every day. His days may have looked very similar, but every morning that he woke up, Brother John felt new, wiser.

His ability to do something as simple as gargle some water and stretch his mouth out before choir made his vowels more pronounced and his voice crisper. Those minor improvements stacked upon themselves and by the time a new year came around, he was so much further along in his skills than previously.

He dared consider himself a new person after joining the monastery, and the radical changes happening every day exhausted his interest in certain topics quickly too. His tastes changed over time.

The harmonies produced in the early morning Vigils sounded more coarse and sleepy than in the evening when Compline began. His ear used to prefer the morning harmonies, but now he preferred evening. Perhaps there would be a point when he would switch back.

Today, Brother John entered the pew for Terce next to Brother Paul. He was taller than the squat and stout Brother Paul, whose head was still balding, and became shinier with each passing day. The man must have felt quite emasculated standing next to Brother John, so Brother John scooted over a bit to relieve some of the tension.

"Good morning, brother," said Brother John, still smiling from noticing the sunlight dancing around the nave. His voice echoed and got lost shortly after he said his greeting.

Brother Paul was still holding some sort of grudge against Brother John for discovering his whole secret pleasure. But the abbot had not come after him yet, which means Brother John had not ratted him out. So, after a bit of a hidden sigh in his cowl, Brother Paul responded with a "Mornin'." It came out as more of a grunt, but the sentiment was there.

Brother John lost some of his smile, knowing that his only neighbor, for now, was still not pleased with him knowing his secret. "You know I have not told the abbot," he whispered, craning his neck down to Brother Paul's ear.

"Shhh! Keep your voice down," he said. "Yes, I noticed.

Thank you. But I still do not feel comfortable having a fellow monk know," said Brother Paul, a bead of sweat running down his temple.

"You can seek help."

"In confession?" he scoffed. "I think not."

"You can perhaps find your answers in books."

"We are not allowed any books on *my* problems…"

"True, but reading itself or doing work may keep your mind off of it."

Brother Paul pivoted his stout body just a tad to look straight up into Brother John's eyes. "Don't you think I've tried that? Besides, I'm not looking for anyone's advice. I've got it under control, thank you. Now, 'In the presence of the angels I will sing to you.'"

And with that, Brother Paul turned back to face the altar and sang the psalms with all the mind he had left to think about such things. The rest of it was swallowed whole by visions of thick legs and warm caresses.

Brother John realized he should simply learn to mind his own business. He could not control anyone else, only lead by example. So, he was determined to continue living his life the way he was before another had brought him out of the sunshine.

Feeling heavier as he flipped the pages of the Bible in his hands, Brother John tried hard to focus on his own voice. But there was that balding head in his periphery, bobbing up and down with the tempo of the music as Brother Paul rocked from his heels to his toes and back down again.

Once the chants began, Brother Paul felt inclined to pull his hood farther down. Little did he know how distracting he would be to those around him. For there stood Brother John, criticizing every bit of his brother up and down.

He could not help but stare at Brother Paul's tiny hairs that were left on top of his balding head, waving back and forth with the sporadic bits of air that wafted through the drafty nave. To and fro, the little soldiers bent to the will of external forces.

It got to a point where Brother John could only equate the fragility of his individual hairs with his strength as a man. Flashes of him crying in a big-legged woman's arms flashed back at him. Brother Paul lay there limply, being cradled by a false mother figure.

There was not much of a surprise for how a man like that could end up serving in a monastery. He slithered his way here because the world out there was too brutal and resilient. He stood no chance, but here, at least, people had to interact with him—they had to sing with him, eat with him, and generally live with him.

He had a forced band of brothers that had no real say in who could join and who could not—only the abbot, the Voting Committee, and the psychologist had that ability. The brothers here had no choice. Brother John was supposed to get along well with anyone who lived within these limestone walls.

But staring down at his brother's head, he could only cringe. Brother Paul could not survive on his own; he required the help of others constantly. The little hairs flopped about as Brother John glanced at the side of his face with his short and stubby nose and then further down at his growing gut. Even though the monks ate little, somehow Brother Paul was growing a belly like a potbellied pig, which made the monks talk about him possibly sneaking food out of the kitchen somehow.

Perhaps when he was serving the monks during his week in the kitchen, he would eat more than allowed, or maybe it was simply age making him grow wider now rather than taller. Whatever was the cause, his belly began to protrude enough to push out his robes, which made him look even shorter and squatter.

Brother John soon caught himself again getting distracted and the weight he was feeling before was now even heavier. It was astounding to him he could start the morning off so light and full of the sun's glory, but as soon as his thought drifted to others, that light disappeared. As if he had lost his ability to maintain his own happiness, Brother John wanted to slap himself right there in the middle of the psalms.

Trying once again to focus on himself, Brother John angled his body slightly away and even tried closing his eyes at some points. He would not allow himself to glance anywhere near the wiggly soldiers dancing on top of his neighbor's head.

Behind each line of the chant, he kept telling himself, "I cannot change people; I can only lead by example." He repeated this over and over again. The art of focusing was one of the most difficult to achieve while meditating but even more so when interacting with people in daily life.

To go up to the abbot and not think about his status or how he could have handled Brother Daniel better was always at the forefront of Brother John's mind. Or to the garden next to Brother Immanuel when he was alive and wonder how badly his wounds stung. Or to see Brother Paul try to make his way around the church without it being painfully obvious how awkward he was to be around. These generalized judgments plagued Brother John, a sober man who had his own flaws but saw right through most people.

Turning off his mind or his other senses, like sight, was impossible. And it seemed that the more he tried to ignore actively seeing people, the more he thought about them, like Brother Paul today. He made the grave mistake of peering over and seeing his balding head with the hairs still waving back and forth.

At one point, Brother John had to hold in a chuckle after contemplating how much those hairs must tickle up there on top of his head. Hiding behind his cowl, Brother John pretended to sneeze as he let out just a little of the laughter he hid inside.

Focus, I must focus! Brother John swore to himself. A good monk maintains discipline and empathy toward his fellow man. So, standing straighter with his shoulders pulled back, he threw himself back into singing.

With the extra air circulating in his lungs from his posture adjustment, Brother John's voice came out stronger than before. Brother Paul even peered up at him with annoyance since his own voice was getting drowned out.

Closing his eyes, Brother John found strange shapes wiggling on the backs of his eyelids and those further distracted him. However, the longer he kept his eyes closed, the fewer shapes appeared and wiggled in front of him and the more he was able to concentrate. He breathed in and out in a beautiful exchange with the music, where the space for silence was just as important as the sound created by the voice. Brother John relaxed his vocal cords and his other muscles involved in producing sound and then tightened them when in use. By focusing on the movements of his body, Brother John discovered more space for his sound to carry throughout the nave and fill it up to the ceiling, where the sun met his vibrations.

Giving in to the moment, Brother John found a certain sense of weightlessness again—he found the sunshine. A peaceful warmth emanated within his soul and gave him an even greater ability to stay in that focused space, where his heart rate slowed and his body moved to the rhythm of the chants.

Perhaps correlated to his being taller than average, Brother John also had the deepest voice. His crisp bass voice carried the underside of the entire choir, like a basket holding fruit. He wrapped everyone up together in the warmth of his notes.

Without him, the choir would certainly lose its masculine core since most of the men were tenors. Their voices served well for following the tune and enunciating all the words more clearly, but they needed the harmony of the bass singers and the occasional boy sopranos to accompany the tenors.

Usually, though, the monks were split up into first and second tenors and first and second basses. The psalms were meant to be sung as a way to reinforce what the monks were singing about, much like reading out loud. Not only do the monks see and read the words on the page, but then they verbalize them through song. Some of the words are drawn out longer than others to accentuate the point that a particular word is key, such as "holy" or "divine" or "glory." These words are then heard after a line finishes and yet they continue to echo and fill up the entire nave.

The repeated chants are meant to personify the ideals that Saint Benedict taught us of "poverty, chastity, and obedience." The music itself is chaste, simple, and follows specific rules to allow the singer the space to contemplate as they are performing the ritual.

Anyone can participate by just using their own voice, which

is accommodated by the limited range needed to chant. They do not need to bring any instruments besides themselves, nor do they have to know the words, since Bibles are all around the pews. It is in this simplicity that men must discipline themselves to never stray from the harmonies and text even after they know it all by heart. The real training comes from maintaining the routine and not flourishing the notes to entertain the mind.

Brother John knew that this practice was what made the chants universal and beautiful in their sacredness. For each note was made simple in order to highlight the words and not necessarily the music. The words *themselves* were sacred. In an effort to glorify language, the music stays in the background.

Since the ninth century, the Gregorian chant has been used in churches as a way to connect with a higher power than ourselves. With its monophonic style, the nave is filled with such haunting unison. All the monks were suddenly praying for the same thing. Brother John never felt closer to his brothers than when they were singing together.

Even Brother Paul, with his poor habit of rocking on his feet and playing with himself, became understandable through music. They were all human beings with throats to sing praise. Their soaring melody only went so fast, it was between a crawl and a walking pace at all times with a smooth texture to their voices.

Breathing was also a significant part of the chants, as Brother John thought about before. Aside from the fact that the chants allowed enough time and space for breathing, it also included a deliberate group breathing at alternate times from another group to continue the melody with no interruption.

Every man sang the same notes—just in differing octaves to

produce their harmonies. This was part of the way to keep it simple. One of the most famous medieval composers of her time, Hildegard von Bingen, who lived in the twelfth century, created the most beautiful chants on earth. Brother John had first heard her chants coming from the abbot's office, where he was doing some bookkeeping tasks. Brother John paused outside his door while on his way to do some cleaning work in the library.

"Who created such glorious music?"

An old boom box that was donated to the monastery sat there with a CD of her music playing. The abbot smiled. "Ah yes, Hildegard von Bingen, a *wonderful* medieval artist. She composed some terrific music, sometime I should play some during one of our meals if that is not seen as too presumptuous."

"Oh, yes, please. Although I may not feel able to chew while such amazing harmonies are being played."

"Well, perhaps we can find a good time to share such art. It certainly lifts my spirit every time I hear it," said the abbot, while Brother John reluctantly moved away from his door.

There were others that Brother John knew about, like Peter Abelard, whose illicit love story he learned of first, was also a composer of Gregorian chants. But his songs were much darker and all concerning death. It was very difficult to listen to his music for too long without becoming hopelessly melancholy.

With Hildegard von Bingen's music, she lifted up his spirits and gave him hope in this world. Brother John was addicted to messages of hope. He gravitated toward things that made him happy or made him feel inspired to carry on, even when days were tough.

The chants themselves were a part of his journey to finding the peace and stability that he desired out of life. Brother John found while singing that both his mind and his soul were fed. He could express his emotions while thinking about uplifting things. The sunshine grew greater in his soul as he shared such vulnerability among the other monks, who seemed to be shining at least a little too.

Time ceased to be a form of measurement as the men relied solely on the lines of music in front of them to guide their breathing. The day paused in the sunshine and the weight from before evaporated from Brother John's shoulders.

He was whole. Full of breath and life and the anticipation of the next note, Brother John was singing. The simple act of singing gave enough justification and meaning for his existence. But there were other things too that he was cultivating to make his life more and more meaningful. These simple things that others scratched their heads over as to why people even do them at all are exactly what made life meaningful.

Art enriches life by feeding the soul. Brother John desired beauty in his world in order to grow and blossom as a human being. Most of the text was in Latin, a dead language, which allowed him even more space to think about the shape of each vowel in his mouth. Though the language was on display for the modern monk, it was the sounds of the text that were focused on the most.

Holding an O-shape or an A, Brother John could close his eyes and feel the breath leaving his body like a bellows being pressed on by a blacksmith. Once he ran out of breath, only then did he permit himself to breathe in through his nose and refill his lungs. His mouth was used solely for exhaling, while his nose was used solely for inhaling. In their proper exchange, he released the smoothest sound.

Sometimes only one man would sing as the choir waited and his voice flew like one lone bird, twittering up inside the nave and landing for a while upon the rood. But then the rest of the choir would join in like the waves of the sea hitting the shore, especially with the great depth of the basses.

It was incredible how chants made everyone want to remain silent and simply listen. There was no rush or apparent fidgeting, everyone there was present and a part of the music. The beauty of the sounds melding together was *perfection*.

Brother John smiled to himself when he recalled his time as an Observer and the single day that he messed up. It was early in the morning, during Vigils, and Brother John accidentally skipped a line and belted out the improper note, which he quickly corrected. But it was too late. The entire community had heard his mistake, and he knew that, under the rules, punishment was required.

The abbot made him stand apart from the choir and sing on his knees for the rest of Vigils. Although his sentence was light, he made sure to become accustomed to all the chants by repeating them to himself throughout the day. For making mistakes or arriving late to prayer times was considered a grave sin and required strict, quick punishment.

Once Vigils had ended that day, the abbot approached Brother John as he was on his sore knees. "Brother, have you repented for your sin of singing the incorrect line during Vigils?"

"Yes, father. I have repented for my sins in the name of the Lord."

"Very well. Enough."

The abbot's magic word was "Enough" and Brother John was free from his punishment, like a dog trapped in a kennel until his owner releases him. At the sound of the word, Brother John perked up and wagged his imaginary tail around as he lifted himself off his knees and could rejoin the other men for breakfast.

Thankfully, Brother John never made that same mistake again. Although he had witnessed other brothers waking up late and being asked to stand apart from the choir to be shamed by the group for the rest of the prayer time. It was quite embarrassing, as in a boy's schooldays, to be found doing something wrong and for then everyone to know about it.

Since these were a group of grown men, though, tardiness was relatively rare. The only excuse a monk had to be late or miss any part of the ritual was death itself. Only if a reaper-like figure came into your room and held out his skeletal hand to take you away in the middle of the night could you miss the next day's Vigils.

There were plenty of monks throughout the monastery's history that had missed the first prayer service, only to be found stone-cold dead in their bed. The abbot usually was the one to find them and proceed with the monastery's usual procedures.

Brother John felt an immense amount of comfort in knowing that he would never lay dead for days before anyone found him. He would be discovered quickly before his body could start decomposing and becoming unrecognizable. Brother John still wanted his brothers to know who he was, even in the end. He was, after all, a man with a particular face and a particular name, though his monk name was common—his fingerprints were not.

The earth felt very much like Brother John's home after all these years and he tried to suppress any thoughts about his death, generally. To him, leaving such a place is painfully sad. He would have to leave behind the birds and the sky and the grass and even the dirt would be missed. At least he knew that his fate would be much like Brother Immanuel's in that he would get a pine box where his body would lay, the monks would pray, and he would rest among the earth's creatures.

So, in a way, he would never truly leave this home. Now was simply about living his life and filling it with all that was good. Gregorian chants were good, routines meant to better Man was good, working was good, and learning every day was good. And what was good was beautiful to Brother John, who made sure that he finished that day's morning chant strong.

There was no weight or concern about Brother Paul's balding head anymore. Brother John was determined to put on blinders like a horse and commit himself further to that which is good. For the ability to see the Good around one is often harder to find and enjoy for long.

CHAPTER IV

Two years had passed, and there was no sight of Mary helping in the gardens. Her parents came one spring to help, but school friends or homework probably swept Mary away. Brother John thought she must have entered her teenage years by now, while he took his final vows to become a Professed Monk until death took him away.

The abbot gave him a black scapular like the one that Brother Immanuel had donned for so many years before his untimely demise. The world and routine inside the monastery had not changed one bit since Brother John entered it and met his brothers, like Brother Immanuel and Brother Daniel and Brother Paul.

The monastery was like living in a vacuum where the latest celebrities and seemingly urgent news stories went unheard. Some names and stories found their way into the newspapers that came in the door, but most of the monks never paid much attention to them, anyway.

It was the perfect breeding ground for learning how to live life happily as it is—without the social or career climbing that distracted so many people from simply living their lives. The space created by these sacred limestone walls cradled Brother John in them and gave him the solid foundation to stand on his own two feet and relearn how to live again.

After discovering the art of tea and meditation and chanting, he had grown so much in his soul that some days he felt like weeping or jumping with joy.

On the day of his solemn vows, Brother John kneeled before the abbot and declared, as so many monks before him had since the time of St. Benedict:

"I, Brother John, promise my stability, my conversion of life and my obedience until death in accordance with the Rule of St. Benedict, Abbot. I do this before God and all his saints, in this monastery, of the Cistercian Order of the Strict Observance, constructed in honor of the Blessed and ever Virgin Mary, Mother of God, and in the presence of the abbot of this monastery."

Part of the vows was prostrating himself on the ground with his hands at his side and his forehead on the floor in front of the abbot and the altar behind him. While Brother John did this, he felt small and insignificant, which hurt his blooming soul, but what better could he have out there than in here?

Brother John laid there for as long as required before he was allowed to get up and show his face again to the congregation. His final vows were made after his temporary or simple ones, and now he was a part of the landscape forever.

The most important day of his life had come, and yet there was a feeling of loss. He thought about a future lost with his previous lover, or even Mary. He would never have children of his own or a home of his own or, really, anything to call his own. But he would grow like no one else on earth could, as only poets and monks know how to grow and mature within their souls.

Bringing too many people into one's life, Brother John

thought, was debilitating for his growth. There could be no space for healing when a baby screamed for its mother's milk. There could be no meditating when grocery shopping had to be done before picking up the children from school. There could be no time for picking up new hobbies or creating new works when a wife required the full attention of her husband.

Brother John nodded to himself in agreement. This lifestyle was the best for him. He was idealizing a fantasy of family life that was nonexistent. Happiness for him was not to be found there but in the library or the garden.

It just so happened that a few days after Brother John had committed himself, a fellow monk who worked the most in the library—reshelving the books and keeping the ink jars in the scriptorium full and the quills sharpened—gave Brother John a gift of sorts as congratulations.

"I know monks are meant to commit to an impoverished life where they own nothing, but I would like to show you how to use the monastery's calligraphy tools. I have watched you cleaning windows here, making hungry eyes at the books and practically everything within the scriptorium."

Brother John blushed. "Did you notice such things, brother? I am ashamed of myself for being so obvious."

"Well, every monk has to start somewhere if he wants to pick up a new craft or skill. If you can get your work done early enough, then I can teach you all that I have picked up over the years from the time when monks actually served as scribes. It is a *shame* that people have abandoned such a craft for poking like monkeys at keyboards. There is no form in such pokings and proddings."

Brother John chuckled and covered his mouth with his hand to avoid overflowing with excitement. See, he thought, opportunities like this would never appear inside the home of a wife and child who just ate, fed, and slept away their lives. To constantly be learning is the only thing that makes us human, using our conscious minds to discover and think about things. "I would love to learn from you, brother, with all my heart. When shall we begin?"

"You come on down tomorrow during our morning work hours with your cleaning supplies, wipe those dirty library windows clean, and I will spend some time teaching you until the bells ring for Sext. How does that sound?"

"That sounds like I won't get any sleep tonight, brother!"

The men laughed and suddenly the hole he had felt from his final vows was partially filled with a brother's love. Yet, Brother John was no fool. He knew that there would always remain the question of whether he had chosen the correct path. And the only way to handle such a painfully tender question, much like those about death, was to not think about it—to avoid asking the question too much—lest it becomes louder.

Gaining control of the mind was something that Brother John continued to work on since his solemn vows. He had so many thoughts floating through his mind, but only a few of them could he actually act on or properly engage with. He made efforts while meditating to ignore those thoughts that were shrouded in questions and ghosts he could not change or fix or understand or know.

His inability to leave behind the question of his choice gave his face a melancholy undertone. He would probably always have a sense of tragedy about him until he died. Still, Brother John made his decision and he could not change it without severe consequences from the monastery—both mentally and physically. There was no backpedaling at this point.

***

The next morning, at about nine thirty, Brother John entered the library carrying his bucket of soapy water and a rag. Upon entering, he nodded toward his fellow monk who was to teach him the ways of calligraphy. But first, he wiped the windows clean, letting the sunlight shine through the hole he made in the grime. Brother John could never understand how the windows grew so dirty so quickly. Perhaps from the age of the building, things like spiderwebs and crumbling stone were permanent fixtures like crow's feet around a middle-aged person's eyes. They were simply always there by the time the next monk was assigned cleaning duties for certain areas throughout the monastery.

But Brother John found a certain satisfaction in wiping the grimy windows clean again. The very act of cleaning was therapeutic because it was done with the hands. His hands worked to alter the surrounding environment in such a significant way that he began his chores in darkness and exposed himself to the morning sunlight. Being made to clean physically a space represented creating a purer soul in a spiritual way.

Once the job was finished, Brother John carried his bucket with him toward the monk, who was sitting at a desk in front of the library where the entrance was. This desk served as a kind of check-in desk for the library books, which the monk was currently sitting at to sort through them and return them to their proper places on the shelves.

"I have come for my first lesson, brother," said Brother John, with head bowed.

"Good. I saw you come in earlier this morning. Thank you, brother, for bringing more light into this rather dark well of knowledge." The monk's eyes twinkled as he walked out from behind the front desk and toward the scriptorium at the heart of it all. "Most of the books in this library were copied out by *real* scribes before the invention of the printing press. Many of them were monks just like us and we still have a division of dedicated scribes who carry on the tradition. Please, come over here."

Brother John's fingers and toes tingled with excitement. He was unsure whether he would be able to control himself if he was asked to sit down.

"Please, sit if you would like or stand and carefully move to where you can see me best. We must cover a few of the basics before we even touch the quill and ink."

"I will stand, thank you," said Brother John, believing this to be a safer option for his current state.

The monk pulled out a wooden chair quite far from one of the desks. He sat down and began pointing at various parts of his body, like his legs, his back, and his head. "Okay, the first thing we need to discuss is where your body is in order to work for as long as those monks did back in the day. You will be in pain if you do not sit in the proper posture. So, one leg should be bent back, and the toes flexed with the balls of the toes on the ground and the heel up, while the other leg is bent in front and the entire foot is planted firmly on the ground. Since I am right-handed, I usually have my right leg back and my left leg forward. Then, you want to lean forward at the hips toward your desk, while your head is gently crooked to one side, I usually point toward my left. Do not allow your back to curve or your neck, or else you will quickly be sore." The monk then scooted himself in toward the desk and rested his arms on top of it. "Now, your arms, including your elbows, should just touch the desk. Try not to place any bodyweight on them, as you need the ability to move your whole arm when doing things like flourishes." Finally, the monk took out a single sheet of paper and angled it to nearly a ninety-degree angle to his body. "I am a bit strange here when it comes to the angle of the paper. The angle depends on the script you choose to write. The medieval monks were writing in blackletter family or, more specifically, *textura quadrata*. But, if you wanted to get a bit fancier and write in English roundhand, then you may need to angle your paper as I do since the angle is at fifty-five degrees. You will have to practice different angles to see what is most comfortable for your own hand."

"That is *fascinating*. Who knew that the position of one's body could matter so much!" said Brother John.

"Yes, it really does," said the monk, who then rose and signaled for Brother John to take a seat. "I want you now to sit down and find that proper posture with your own body, then do the same with the paper. That is the only lesson we will learn today."

Brother John sat down and felt as if he had never learned to write properly in the first place. He forgot how he held himself normally when he wrote by hand and everything felt foreign to him. He sat up straight and positioned himself in the shapes that his brother advised, but his body was already feeling sore.

"It will take some getting used to, so I advise you for this week to practice sitting in a writing-ready posture and observe how you normally sit when you are just handwriting something, including how you hold your pen. I will see you next week then at the same time, at the same place."

The monk and Brother John shook hands as they both went

off for Sext.

***

Simply learning to sit properly excited Brother John and preoccupied his mind for the rest of the day. He sat during parts of Sext with his back straight up and down and his leg tucked underneath him. He practiced sitting at a bit of an angle to the desk in his room during private prayer times. Then, he wrote out several lines from the Bible with his available pen and paper on the desk in his cell. It was very curious to observe himself from this new perspective.

Spending all of his waking hours thinking about how to sit made him feel like a baby who is just learning how to walk. *Everything* seemed new and scary and frustrating. Relearning how to sit properly and relieve any pressure on the back or neck was something very foreign to Brother John.

So, the next week in the library, Brother John entered with trepidation. He was unsure about whether he was even ready to learn more things about calligraphy. He still felt uncomfortable finding his proper writing position, which is what he expressed to the kindly monk teaching him.

"Well, brother, if things were easy, then who would remain humble to God? Besides, we will not actually start writing until next week. For today, you are to learn about the tools themselves."

The monk led Brother John to the scriptorium and had him sit in his writing position with his paper angled at the ready.

"This piece of paper is simply cheap, modern computer paper. The ink will bleed and feather on this because the paper is too porous and thin. It is simply not made for the heavier layers of ink anymore. When the ink bleeds," the monk asked Brother John to stand up once more as he dipped a quill into the ink and made a line which immediately lost its crispness on the page, "the ink gets absorbed by the paper fibers and reaches the other side—thereby bleeding. Now, feathering is this right here where the ink spreads out from the paper fibers, absorbing it outward like capillary veins in the body. It just sucks all the ink right up into a pooled, inky mess."

Brother John never imagined how much paper reacted to ink before, as if it was alive and thirsty.

"Impressive, huh? Well, all calligraphers strive to produce as crisp and thin of a hairline as possible to create more detail and finesse in their letters. So, you want a hot-pressed piece of thick paper that forces the ink to sit on top and dry rather than soaking it all in. Hot-pressed paper means that it is pressed through metal rollers during its creation, which produces a smooth, thick, and tightly woven texture that is even throughout. Got it?"

All Brother John could do was nod his head up and down, hoping that it would not fall off with all of this information. He was still standing there by the monk's side, watching the simple ink line continue to feather through the paper.

"Now, the ink. The ink cannot be too thick or too thin. If it is too thin, then it will all fall off of the quill tip or metal nib, if you are using those more modern tools, into a blob on your paper. If the ink is too thick, then it will stick to your tool and not come off onto the paper. The consistency of all ink should be about that of 2 percent milk. Very specific, huh?"

Brother John allowed himself a good chuckle at the things that people came up with to define terms. Language itself was such a fascinating area of study, which reminded him that just outside the scriptorium lay even more books filled with the language he loved so much.

"The quill itself is a very old-fashioned tool, though the first was probably the reed, which was used in places like ancient China and Egypt. The reed was used to carve into materials that were softer than the reed, like papyrus. But they were very stiff and soon people began using the feathers from large birds, like turkey and goose. The earliest records for quill-use date all the way back to 100 BC with the Dead Sea Scrolls. Papers like parchment and vellum were popularly used. The medieval monks served as scribes and all used the quill. They had to use a quill knife to sharpen quite frequently the tip, as they were copying out page after page of manuscripts. The metal-tipped quill pen turned into the dip pen with metal nibs only during the mid-nineteenth century. And before we knew it, the fountain pen came out, then the modern ballpoint pen by the end of that century only to be overthrown completely by typewriters and our modern-day computers."

"So most of human history was recorded with quills?"

"Indeed, brother. Quills have ruled for some time, which is why we have them still well-stocked in our scriptorium. If you truly want to connect with the monks before you, then write with a quill. It is much more finicky than our modern ballpoint pens, I can tell you that much," said the monk with a wink.

"Invention sure sped up during the Industrial Revolution then, huh?" said Brother John, mesmerized by the history of writing implements.

"It sure did, but religion suffered enormously from such progress. While people collected shiny, new things, they forgot the quills and the monastic scribes and left them in a dingy corner of their minds somewhere. You see, we are a left-behind item, an after-thought for many people who only circle back around to religion when they are terminally ill nowadays," said the monk as he shook his head.

"But I see guests visit the monastery quite frequently even now. They always eat meals with the abbot."

"The numbers of people we see today are *nothing* compared to what they used to be. It seemed the entire world was at our doorstep before Man learned how to play God." The monk scrunched up his mouth in distaste.

"I have so much to think about today. Thank you as ever, brother. May I come again next week to start writing?"

"Yes, brother. I will see you then."

The following week could not come too soon, for Brother John longed every day to know what a quill to paper actually felt like. He had only observed his brother drawing a single line that bled and feathered out to resemble nothing more than a wiggly blob after their time together. Excitement built up in him to the point of jitteriness that he worked off in the garden.

***

The subsequent week in the library, Brother John already found his teacher in the scriptorium at one of the lovely secretary desks with a quill in his hand.

"Welcome back, brother. Today, we are first learning how to cut a quill, and then we will get down to writing. Okay?"

"Yes, brother," said Brother John, nearly forgetting to breathe.

"So, I have a sharp quill knife here, and the first thing we need is a cured goose feather. Cured meaning that it was left over time or dunked in hot sand to make the end rigid. When you squeeze the end, it should not give at all. First, we cut an incision across the top and then insert the blade into the quill to get the pith out. Next, we will push down and out to scoop out the nib shape. Then, we test the quill in our dominant hand to figure out where the quill sits within it, to figure out where the shoulders and tines need to be. Here, we will pare away at the shoulder to make the tines. And then cut straight down at the tip to make it a left oblique cut quill, and then, finally, insert the knife inward just a bit to create the tines." A slight, satisfying crack was heard as he made the final break during this rather technical procedure.

"That is amazing, but will it write?" said Brother John, smiling.

"Let's have you find out. Here, brother, take this quill."

Brother John took the beautiful specimen in his hands, which felt so light—much lighter than a modern pen made of metal and plastic parts.

Grasping the quill, he allowed it to roll slightly on his index finger until it came to its center point, where he gripped it in a triangle hold with his thumb and index fingers on the front side and his middle finger along the back. His wrist gently rested with a slight tilt up away from the desk, while his pinky supported more generally the entire hand. Once he made his hand connect properly to his pen, he raised it and dipped the quill into the open ink jar that his brother had laid out for him already.

The black ink gently dripped off the tip and landed back into the jar below. The ink rippled like melancholy water. He carefully moved the pen back over the paper which was angled correctly to his body for his own arm and then the quill landed on the page.

A horrifying squeak sounded which made both men jump.

"Goodness! What a frightening sound!" said Brother John.

"Yes, sometimes that happens. See if you have enough ink or if you are properly parallel to the page," said the monk.

Brother John did not want to make such a violent sound again, so he double-checked his ink and position like a pianist stretching out their fingers before a performance.

The sound this time was a more pleasant scratching, which was much milder than the first time.

"Now, just write an *I* in your normal hand, and then I will show you how to write it in *textura quadrata*."

Brother John made his normal handwriting *I* which looked awful. Feeling dismayed by how poorly the letter sat on the page, he looked up at the monk.

"One major lesson to learn is that calligraphy is not the same as handwriting. Calligraphy is the art of beautiful writing and is completed with basic strokes that make up each letter. I started you out with *I* because that is the simplest. In *textura*, you make one vertical stroke down and then add two diamonds—one on the top and one on the bottom of the *I*. And that's it!"

Brother John took the quill out of the monk's hand and tried again, making one single stroke downward and two little diamonds. The *I* looked very similar to the monk's *I*. "I've done it!" Brother John shouted.

Thankfully, the scriptorium was empty apart from them, so he did not disturb anyone else in the vicinity. In his renewed excitement, the monk showed him the rest of the lowercase alphabet and sent him on his way for the rest of the day.

Any private prayer time Brother John had, he practiced. He even looked harder at the scripts in his Bible and started seeing the basic strokes coming out in front of him. He traced the air with letters. A new world had opened up for him, which must not have happened since he was a child learning to speak and read and write.

The most rewarding part of the experience, though, was when he sang with his brothers. During Compline that evening, Brother John could see the Gregorian chants mimicking the exact speed at which *textura quadrata* was written.

The heavy, bold text was just as weighty as the music. The repetition could be felt in both as well. The vertical stroke, followed by the constant diamond shapes, were like a refrain to a song or the ending to each line.

Brother John lost himself in the rhythm of *textura quadrata*. He entered an even more powerful meditative state when he could combine the chants that sometimes reached his cell from the abbot's bookkeeping room with his writing.

At first, he wrote the alphabet repeatedly and then he linked them all together with one repeated letter, like an *N*, until he felt comfortable moving on to words and sentences. The letters flowed out of his hands in a deliberate, determined way, which his own body began to recognize. He used his breath as in singing to write smoothly, where every breath was part of the spacing between each letter.

CHAPTER V

Calligraphy quickly became one of Brother John's favorite hobbies, and every chance he got, he thought about it. But his excitement was soon distracted by yet another of his loves: gardening.

Brother John had learned to help plant and care for the monastery's garden when he initially arrived. But with the heat of the spring and all the fresh growth, Brother John desired to spend more time outside. He took a break from the library meetings with his teacher and took to the gardens to soothe his soul.

The monastery's garden included a section for organic vegetables and herbs, and then the rest of the walkways were surrounded by gorgeous flowers. His favorite place to tend was the rose garden.

One of the senior monks taught him when he initially arrived. He explained that most of the plants need about six to eight hours of full sun a day to grow. There were some shade plants, like the huge hostas, that did not require direct sunlight, and those were planted elsewhere in the garden.

Then, he showed Brother John a new flat area of ground, freshly cleared of weeds, in which he was about to plant baptisia.

"You've got to slice under the sod to get to the good, mineral-nutrient soil. We add organic matter to our soil before planting new seeds each season. Then, we loosen the soil with our hands just enough that the plants will get the water and nutrients they need more easily. It should fall apart when you drop some of the soil. It should not be too dry or too wet.

"Now, the fun part is to get your seeds out and plant them! The beautiful baptisia plants have purple flower petals and their seeds come in these dark pods that look a whole lot like bad pea pods. Inside, the seeds look like brown, little beads. A *beautiful* reminder of the complexity of God's creation, I'd say," the senior monk said.

Brother John smiled at the senior monk, who let him feel the seeds in the palm of his hand. Then, the two of them dropped a few seeds into the prepared hole.

"We can cover this plant up now with the soil. These are wild perennial plants that are pretty easy to grow for a beginner. They love the sun, are resistant to pests, and are tolerant to periods of drought. They are tough plants, although it takes about a year for their flowers to initially appear. Hopefully, you will stay with us long enough to witness its amazing purple flowers," he chuckled.

"In fact, the American colonists gave it the name *Baptisia* because the Greek term *bapto* means 'to dye,' which they used to dye their fabrics an indigo shade. Fascinating, right?" asked the senior monk.

Brother John was in awe of how innovative the early American settlers were. They had to live off of the land and, yet, they still desired to color their clothes in the latest European fashion. All that he could muster to say in response was, "That is pretty interesting."

If only he could have expressed his deep, overflowing excitement bubbling up inside. But then again, he did not want to appear childish in front of a senior monk, whose face resembled a bulldog's more than a human's.

"It sure is. God supplies *everything* for those who look for it properly. Now, seeds should never dry out, so we must water these new ones daily. If you are unsure whether they are too wet or too dry, stick your finger down in the soil for about three inches to feel. If it is too dry, then you need to pour the water over the seeds slowly so that it has time to soak in and not just run right off, which is another reason that we plant most of our garden on a flat surface to prevent water runoff.

"And the earlier in the morning you can water them, the better. The sun will not have enough time to evaporate all the water in the early hours.

"Then, we keep an eye out on the weed situation, plucking up the naughty roots as needed. But we can also add mulch to the top layer of soil to prevent it from drying out and new weeds from growing as quickly. The mulch can be made of shredded bark or compost or straw—things that will eventually completely decompose over a few months' time.

"And finally, every monk is made to tend to the garden at least once a day. A garden is just as living and breathing as you or I. God wants his garden to grow and thrive. We are his servants and must abide by His will. So, we are always out here pulling weeds, plucking fresh vegetables and herbs for the kitchen, pruning dead or diseased parts off of plants, getting rid of pests with water or special soaps, and supporting taller plants with stakes.

"The beauty of a garden is that every day you walk outside and something is different. New plants are sprouting out of the ground or buds have opened to the sun or tiny vegetables are growing larger and heavier on their vines. There is a surprise packed away in the garden for everyone who enters it to enjoy, but especially for the monks who tend to it every day and can watch the changes happening in real time.

"Monks and poets are about the only people I know who can truly appreciate a good garden. Don't you agree, young man?" asked the senior monk.

"Yes, I have heard that idea floating around before. I think it takes the quietest types, those that enjoy their silence, like monks and poets, who actually take the time to watch the world breathe," said Brother John.

"Yes," smiled the senior monk. "I thought you would understand. I can see it in your eyes that this monastic lifestyle is perfectly suitable for you."

***

Looking back, Brother John did feel like he had moved rapidly in his progression toward making his solemn vows. In a way, time moved both more quickly and more slowly in the confines of the monastery. The individual days quickly sped from sunrise to sunset, but the individual hours of prayer ticked by painfully slowly, followed again by the years which squished together to become one finite point of time in the mind. The elasticity of time to Man worked in such strange ways, thought Brother John.

He was focused today on plucking more weeds from the garden. One by one, he stuck his hand deep into the soil to make sure that he plucked out the entire root. He became a destroyer in this capacity, which he did not particularly enjoy. Why did weeds get treated differently from the plants that the monks chose, anyway? he wondered.

As he felt his way around the ground, another monk approached. This monk entered the monastery only a couple of years before Brother John did, so he was still considered one of the younger monks.

He had long, gangly arms and no matter how much he was allowed to eat, no fat would stay on his skinny frame. The only piece of information Brother John knew about him was that before joining the monastery, he had worked as a horticulturist for some wealthy family nearby.

"Need any help, brother?" the young monk asked.

"Sure. Hey, I was just wondering too about something that you must know about," said Brother John.

"Which is what?"

"Do you know why weeds are so bad and must be plucked like this from the garden?"

The young monk smiled as he said: "Boy, you know I could go on about this subject forever. But today, I will spare you. Firstly, weeds are competing with the plants we planted for the same sun, water, soil, and air."

"They can't all just share?"

The two men laughed.

"No, unfortunately, plants do not know how to share," said the younger monk. "But, secondly, if they cover the ground, then they may also make it more difficult for you to see where your plants need watering or hide pests from being eradicated."

"I see," said Brother John, starting to check underneath the leaves for bugs. "Look! I found a worm crawling around in the dirt."

"Well, he's not exactly the kind of pest I'm referring to. He's actually good at breaking down organic matter the plants can use as nutrients. I mean little critters like mealybugs and aphids and scale insects. They look like white mold on the underbelly of plants, but they are really tiny bugs sucking away at the leaves' sap. And, thirdly, weeds are not nice to look at and they provide no food or nutrients for us. So, they are weeds. They also tend to spread quickly and are hard to get rid of completely."

"I suppose that makes sense, but is it the monks who chose what is valuable?"

"Yes, the monks did choose what to plant here. And perhaps you think that is playing God a bit, for why would God create these plants if they were only to end up destroyed by us? I can only say that no one has been struck by lightning yet for plucking out any weeds."

The two monks kept working side by side in silence. They each must have been contemplating the question of how they could choose. Brother John certainly wondered why it was that he had such a funny, abstract thing as free will.

He stared down at the weed sticking up right under his nose, a bright, yellow dandelion, which could have been of use to someone who wanted some dandelion tea or to blow away a puffball when it was done blooming. It could even be considered pretty to look at and not at all esthetically unpleasing. Brother John could choose to pull out this plant, thereby killing it, or allow it to continue to grow and thrive in its environment, continuing to live. The only reason he decided to take any action at all was that the monks were told by the abbot to "weed the garden" every day, and dandelions were considered weeds.

It took this long process of actions on behalf of people to point their energies on addressing this particular dandelion right in front of Brother John. As an exercise of his free will, at that moment, he chose to leave the dandelion there—though he knew another monk would come along and, without a second thought, pluck the dandelion from its roots.

Still, whoever came along to do the deed and end its life, they would have less of an awareness of what they were doing than Brother John did. Killing things, he thought, should never be taken lightly or without serious consideration of the consequences. Though the consequence of pulling that dandelion was really moot.

Yet, Brother John, having chosen to spare that yellow flower, felt more empowered as he moved along his path in the garden. Nothing external to him turned him around like a disobedient dog to shove his face in the weed that he missed. No one barked at him to go back and do it right. There was no supernatural event knocking him over or pushing him about for making a choice on his own.

The sense of *freedom* this realization brought him was intoxicating. He could choose to treat things in the ways he found appropriate. Brother John weighed his pros and cons, the benefits and the consequences, and then *acted* on those decisions. Perhaps the idea floated into his mind from his subconscious to his conscious mind, then he thought about a particular one of those ideas, and then he acted appropriately. This is what made Man different from plants and animals. That he had a conscious mind he could use to survive. The process that Brother John had taken advantage of so often was the very thing that allowed him to live another day.

Brother John dug his hand deep into the soil. He decided it was necessary to pull his mind out of the abstract hole he found himself in. Sure enough, a worm rubbed up against his left pinky finger and he was snapped right back into his task at hand—tending to the garden. Spending the time to think through every process he performed in his daily life was part of growing as a human being. Being self-conscious about all the things that Man does automatically reminds us to be grateful, thought Brother John, and he was grateful.

How wonderful it was to spare the dandelion for another moment, how special it was to know it, and how right it felt to do so. The world could not be so scary as long as cause and effect were the laws of nature. Brother John could pick up his weeding knife at will and then set it back down. If he chose to dig into the soil, then there would be a hole left there. In a giddy moment of joy, Brother John did just that. He was movement and he could move the things around him at will too—what a *wonderful* world, he thought.

The familiar sun warmed his back while the birds chirped freely and the light breeze refreshed him. The bells pealed for scripture reading or private prayers. It was mid-afternoon and Brother John was loath to go inside the dark corridors again on such a lovely day.

But he knew that the routine was sacred. So, he immediately put away his gardening tools and headed with a swift step toward his cell, only to run into the elderly monk who served as a porter at the main door of the monastery.

"Hello, brother," said the hunchbacked old man.

The porter had never looked up into his face before. It seemed that he was longing to say something. "Hello, is something wrong?" asked Brother John.

The old monk approached a bit closer so that he could whisper in Brother John's ear. "I have heard that Brother Paul is being looked at as a potential prior to this monastery. But my goodness, after what he took part in with Brother Daniel—why, his hands are red with sin!" The old man shook all over, expressing out loud such a horrible word.

Brother John was admittedly shocked for "those who sin should be reprimanded in the presence of all, that the rest may fear" and, yet, instead this man was being upheld as an example? It made no sense. The abbot must not know of the depth of his sins. Clearing his throat, he said, "That is surprising, I must say."

"Yes, indeed. I felt the need to express myself to someone who knows his neighbor well. You *must* understand that this is a grave mistake and must be challenged. Could you put in a word to the abbot?" asked the porter. "I am afraid that I have no sway over the abbot's heart like the more youthful monks of the monastery."

"Of course," said Brother John, "I will do so right now on my way to my cell."

"Bless you, brother," said the old monk.

The abbot allowed Brother John into his own cell and heard his warnings, but it seemed to not affect the abbot. He appeared neither shocked nor appalled at the sins Brother John relayed to him.

"Father, are you not reconsidering placing him at your right hand, just a step beneath you? Can such a man yield more power?"

The abbot cleared his throat before suggesting that Brother John "go back to his cell and pray on it."

That was the end of their conversation on the subject, and Brother John suddenly felt bereft of his sway over the abbot's decision-making powers. The cause did not lead to the proper effect in this situation where free will had a choice and it chose incorrectly, according to Brother John. A welling sense of resentment rose to his lips and nearly escaped before he reached his own cell.

Collapsing into his pillow, Brother John yelled out of frustration. There was nothing he could do to make this wrong right; he held no such power to choose the new prior. Yet, he knew that if Brother Paul were to gain more power, then there was no justice in this move.

Over the next few days, Brother John grew more isolated from the other monks. During the few times where an occasional passing word was allowed amidst the silence, he stopped responding or reaching out. Perhaps as an experiment, he latched onto his routine and his work and his chanting—focusing solely on these tasks to fill his soul. After all, he felt that his work could never revolt against the Truth as Man could.

Throwing a unique kind of tantrum, Brother John ignored any of his brothers' eye contact. He completely shut himself off from every other human being but himself as a way to protect his soul from betrayal. They all stood there as Judases, waiting for the next moment when they could turn away from reality.

In hindsight, only Brother Paul was the true offender, but Brother John knew other monks said nothing about this potential scandal to the abbot. If he became a prior, Brother John may never speak to the other monks again.

In a week's time, Brother Paul became prior to the monastery, one position below the abbot—being groomed to perhaps one day take over the monastery as its next abbot. Brother John felt ill. He shunned his brothers and shared his soul with no one else but his work and his dreams.

There was a general malaise hanging over the monastery, which made the gargoyles look extra menacing and the environment ripe for returning phantoms. It rained every day for a week after Brother Paul was selected as prior. Most of the monks believed it to be a sign from God, but the abbot said nothing.

***

In the gloom of the monastery, Brother John's world grew smaller, while his soul experienced some kind of expansion. For over the course of that stormy week, Brother John watched his roses bloom and his newly planted baptisias begin to poke their heads out of the soil. He grew more technically skilled at calligraphy as he spent whatever time he had to spare in the scriptorium. Brother John sunk deeper and deeper into more meditative states while in his cell and during his chants. The minor tasks throughout the day of cleaning his teeth or his habit or preparing meals in the kitchen or making his bed were all highlighted by the self-awareness Brother John had in performing each task.

Like a child, he relearned the reasons for brushing his teeth and making his bed and cleaning his clothes. Feeling a powerful pull toward his mother during these days, he wished he could thank her for showing him all of life's most important skills from the very beginning. Everything she taught him was in line with the *Rule*, which served as a basis for beginning his path on the way to perfection. Monastic life only served to quicken his path toward such an ambitious goal.

These days Brother John felt closer than ever before to tasting perfection. Everything he set himself to work on was done with the utmost care and skill. It was clear that this pursuit would take his entire lifetime to reach, but that was what he wanted more than *anything* else. He did not care to be pestered by screaming children of his own or a wife who required his attention to flourish or a job that sucked out the marrow of his soul. The only way to live for him now was the monastic way—the way of silence.

Brother John was not built to be a fighter. He was thin and pale of skin with a cherubic face. His blue eyes were lit with the fires of intelligence and passion and ambition. The dark hair stood out on his pale skin and his hands were too soft for more hard labor than gardening, and his soul was even softer. He was an ethereal man, a man of the spirit, a man of silence.

There was nothing that could dissuade him from leaving these lovely limestone walls. He had made his solemn vows. He had dug his own grave in the monastic fields on the day of his vows. One day, he would lie in that sacred ground, next to his brothers. The maggots would have their picnic on his flesh and the soil would grow all the richer for it. But Brother John would die peacefully, knowing that he did everything in his power to perfect himself as a human being. His own hero's journey was to prove that he was indeed a man worthy of breath—a chosen one in his own right. He knew the fact that he even existed at all was a miracle, but then to respect himself and all the living things that had also made it into existence seemed a requirement. The deal was to live and breathe and create and only then to die.

Death's bony fingers were not to touch him, though, until he reached old age. Part of the reason for entering a monastery for Brother John was also to avoid the risks of the outside world—driving accidents, drug overdoses, gun assaults, being hit by a car as a pedestrian, airplane crashes, drowning in a boating accident, dog attacks. There were so many things out there that could cause an untimely demise that being kept within the bounds of a monastery felt much safer. His risks decreased on the day he entered and he could feel more confident about surviving until old age.

Brother John needed to survive as long as possible to figure out life's many mysteries. He was a man who could read endlessly in search of answers. His deep hunger to know probably made his brothers worry a bit.

In his cell, Brother John read books from the library—some of which were snuck out of the banned section of books with a little help from his calligraphy teacher. Since monastic life suited him, though, Brother John was never late for any of the regularly scheduled duties. So, essentially, nothing could be said about his ambitious behavior, though the abbot did sometimes tell him to pay more attention to his scriptural prayers and readings.

Without bringing more attention to himself, Brother John knew he needed to survive for long enough because he was only allowed to read and learn so much in a day. The rest of the time, he labored hard physically in the garden and sang fully from the diaphragm in the choir. He was a monk who lived in extremes—he pushed his mind and his body to their limits each day in the hope of finding the Truth.

To Brother John, life was wonderful. But others on the outside, he had heard as guests visiting the monastery, made comments about how trivial their lives were or could not make sense of exactly what they did all day or how they could repeat the same things over and over again until death. The monastic life to most outsiders felt small and insignificant. But if only they knew, if only they could see the inside of Brother John's soul—how light and shiny it felt, how expansive and empathetic it felt, just how *whole* it felt for the first time.

He had no more worries or fears, there was no race to win in life, and everything had been sorted out for him. The monastery was his haven, a place for him to hide and bloom without some unthoughtful child traipsing over and plucking him raw from the ground. He could grow without other stresses competing for his time and energy. Now, Brother John was free to develop his soul.

CHAPTER VI

The monastery was made from limestone and weighed hundreds of thousands of tons. It took over thirty years to build on what were very sporadic, small funds. But the men who built it over time were passionate about this perfect space housing monks for the rest of time.

And as Brother John stood there looking up at his magnificent home, he thought: Someone constructed you, bathed you in their precious time. You were molded, crafted, and shaped by Man's fingers. And yet you tower over us in power and might. Oh, you unchanging monastery—what a testament you are to the divinity of Man.

In his years working under this roof, Brother John learned to grow more sensitive after having become desensitized to so much in the outside world just to survive. But slowly, the layers peeled off, and the world appeared less dull and cold. He looked around himself and remained open to new experiences. Suddenly, gardening became a much more enjoyable task and singing became such ecstasy to partake in and hear. His tea tasted finer and his rituals all felt more cohesive, as if he was dancing through each day.

Today, he entered the monastery and walked up to the front altar, took a few more steps, and sat down on the creaky old pews to his right. He was beside the organ Brother Immanuel used to play very often, its enormous pipes heading toward Heaven itself. The loud, pristine sound of angels being squeezed to death by the omnipotent hand of God. The musky smell of the dead sitting amongst the living in the main pews. The musk laid itself deep beneath the pages of the Bible, in between the abbot and his holy attire, underneath the very foundation of the monastery itself. It even covered him and his brothers if they sat too long and breathed in too deeply. Mostly at the beginning of his journey as an Observer, Brother John remained light-headed throughout his day from the secondhanded musk he had inhaled. He even had the silly thought that everyone in the monastery, both the living and the dead, should be made to wear doctor's masks. Can you imagine? he thought. The whole monastery would be full of those blue-colored masks. Heck, even the tombstones would have one. Sure, they may muffle a few songs about Christ, but none of us would feel light-headed afterward, he often thought as an Observer, except even if we did do that I have a feeling that my reaction would remain the same.

But as the years went on and he became accustomed to the musty smell of age, he rarely ever noticed it at all. It was as if he had become a part of the monastery and all of its dirt and grime and dust. His habit must carry with it all the musty smells and odors of the furthest corners of the monastery where he had cleaned or hurried past or sung by. His entire identity, as he went through this process of relearning sensitivity, became intertwined like a weedy vine wrapped around the statues of the bowels of the monastery.

The thought even struck him that perhaps the statues in the monastery were really just monks who were covered

248

over with soot and grime over the years from the monastery until they were weighed down and trapped by it. They were frozen in time while the fresh batch of monks came in to work until the monastery preserved its workers. If that was true, then Brother John could look forward to living forever entombed inside his home or outside in its fields. Either way, he was trapped there for good. Smiling gleefully, almost madly, Brother John felt so safe and comfortable being tied down in this fashion that he never wished to leave.

Even though he still had passing thoughts about Mary or his past lover and what they could have created together, a maddening rush of images of children and the blaring sound of their screaming shut off all thoughts of women for Brother John. He could not take their desire to have a household filled with children. For being a man of silence meant no room for those still learning how to live; for being a man of silence meant no room for women who constantly needed to feel love and attention when there was no more of him to give; for being a man of silence meant having the freedom to bury oneself up with books and things and not be disturbed by other people for days.

Now that Brother John was a Professed Monk, he had certain privileges that he could not have before. The largest perk was the nearby space for a sort of hermitage. The tearoom was the main space, but off to the side, a shed was built with a running sink and toilet and fridge so that all human needs were fulfilled apart from the monastery. This new place was open to monks who wanted to see no one for about a week at a time. Now, Brother John could take his books from the library and for an entire week make himself tea, chant on his own, eat alone, and sleep by himself. During this time, he could join the others in the garden during work times or else spend those times doing extra private prayer for the sinners of the outside world, for that was also considered God's work.

He took that time to read and think. Sitting on the tatami mats of the tearoom, Brother John meditated, searching deeper in his mind for hidden pieces of the Truth. The hours soon turned into days of endless thinking and reevaluating and weighing certain things he had consumed from his books. Scribbling his thoughts down on bits of leftover paper that the abbot had spared him, Brother John wrote. Within that single week of living as a true hermit, the most extreme type of monk, he felt his soul *explode*. He grew more sensitive and everything in the world grew with him.

The trees looked greener, brighter, more alive than ever before; the tiny sounds that his brothers made could disturb him now; the mechanics behind all the man-made mechanisms became visible to his conscious mind. When he rejoined his brothers after a week, it almost felt like their way of life was too fast-paced, too full, too exciting. A brother cooking for all the monks in the kitchen made Brother John lose his breath just watching him. A monk feeling unwell, on bed rest, whom Brother John had to spoon-feed, made him weep and feel like he, too, was ill. A man visiting the monastery looked like a complete alien to Brother John with his pants and shirt from the outside.

Nothing appeared the same way to Brother John, and he grew overwhelmed. There were times when the moment became too much for him and he had to run away to a place outside, normally in the garden, where he could close his eyes and take deep breaths. A plate clattering on the floor in the kitchen could make his heart race. Brother John grew tired more easily, but still, he persevered in striving to become more sensitive to his surroundings, and he continued to learn more about how everything around him worked.

***

One spring morning, when the freeze of another winter began to thaw, Brother John saw Mary. She was in the garden, between her parents, when he was just about to plant some of the new turnips. The monks planted many of their organic vegetables in the early spring to harvest many of them by the early summer. Then, they could sell their produce to guests, use it in the kitchen for meals straight away, or pickle and can other produce for the long winter months. Brother John had turned his head to spot her, blinking hard to make sure that it was not a teasing phantom in his midst, but there she stood— even after just a few years' time, Mary had developed so much. She must be a teenager now, he thought, with dreams about boys and menstrual cycles and breasts and new hair growth in strange places. How vulnerable she must feel! He suffered for her plight into the world of young adulthood. However, that glow, that something special that only she possessed when she first visited the monastery, the spark that he worried she would abandon with age, was still there.

He saw her smile and his hands shook, spilling all the turnip seeds onto one patch of the freshly tilled ground. Clumsily trying to find each brown, round seed turned into an impossible task, especially when his heart was racing so. In a violent moment of frustration, he threw the rest of the seeds down into the dirt, abandoning his duties to stand upright.

The blood rushed down from his head too quickly and he saw black spots in his vision, which blocked out her face. Curses! he thought. He had never even thought about curses or swears since the fiasco with Brother Daniel, but now all of his emotions were in disarray. His insides knotted up tightly, especially when she looked over and seemed to recognize him—a monk dressed like everyone else, and yet, she could pick out his face from the sea of other men. His heart ached. Brother John loved her without even knowing all that much about her. But he had made his choice. He had taken his solemn vows.

Besides, he rationalized, he would never be able to do anything else with her around constantly. She would distract him from finding the Truth. Or what would be worse is if he grew bored with her, or if his love for her was just lust...but he knew such a thing to be untrue, for he loved her for her innocence and that ambition to know.

Mary ran over to Brother John, careful to avoid any of the freshly planted bits of land. Her smile drew tears to Brother John's eyes, which forced him to hide his face momentarily behind his cowl to re-collect himself. God, he wanted her so violently! Why must women remind men of the outside world? They bring nothing but trouble with their kind of love! The only love that could be tolerated was brotherly love. But a woman's love? Flashes of Brother Paul weeping in his thick-legged woman's arms made him cringe.

"Hello, Brother John!"

He suffocated, hearing her voice again, a voice he had forgotten over the course of years. She still sounded so young. He would do anything right now, *anything*, to hold her in his arms. He imagined how small her frame was and how delicately she would hold him back.

With weak knees and an even fainter voice, Brother John mimicked back: "Hello, Mary Baptisia."

She popped up onto her toes for a moment in delight that he even remembered her name. "I thought you may have forgotten me!"

Oh, Mary! he thought. How little do you know about a world inside a vacuum, where all the people you have ever met and will ever meet greet you in your dreams nearly every night and follow you around at your daily tasks. The people we monks know are never wholly forgotten. With a short, belated chuckle, Brother John said: "Of course, I remember you."

"Well, I figured that you monks greet so many visitors over the year that I must have been just one in many!"

"No, you are special. There are not many young girls who help their parents in our monastic garden."

"Yeah, well, I didn't for the first two years…sorry. I had dance classes and other things going on at school. But this year I thought I should give gardening a try! I'm very excited," she said, beaming.

"I'm glad to see you are so excited about gardening," said Brother John. His heart felt like it was pounding blood into his throat so hard that he could no longer speak. Instead, to buy himself some time, he reached down and picked up one of the many little, round, brown turnip seeds from the dumped pile.

"Do you see this?" he asked.

"Yeah, barely." Mary squinted to see if she could get closer to the seed, like with a camera lens.

"This is a turnip seed. We are planting these today so that we may harvest them in the early summer. It is just the right temperature outside nowadays—not too hot, not too cold. They should make it through some of the nippier nights now."

Mary dove down, snatching up one of the turnip seeds like a seagull to a fish. She was so quick that it startled Brother John, who, when surrounded usually by much older men, thought himself the spriest, suddenly made him feel old. He could not move his back down in the way she did, like a wobbly rubber band. After springing up with her find, she brought the seed up close to her little face.

Brother John let her take all the time she needed with the seed. He wished she would inspect him with such curiosity and interest. But there she was, really in front of him, turning it round and round in between her fingers.

"I really think it's cute!" she said.

That was her assessment after five minutes of staring at it—that it was cute. Brother John could only smile at such innocence. He said: "It is cute, indeed, but it will one day grow into a large turnip that could feed at least one very hungry monk!"

Brother John placed his seed down in the proper individually dug hole for the one seed and, again, tried to collect the other ones in the palm of his nervous hands.

"You dropped them, silly!" said Mary, as she squatted down without one thought about her knees or where her opened legs were aimed as she helped him. Brother John tried with all of his might to keep his head down, in fact, he wanted to thrust his head right into the soil like an ostrich. But the temptation was too strong, and he kept peeking up at her now and then— her legs swung to and fro, with her bottom swiping the tips of the grass as she rocked. Her beautiful hair teased the plants around her as she shook it off her face. And her thin, pale wrists conducted how her little fingers would wag.

She was much more efficient at picking up the turnip seeds

than Brother John was. He kept trying to keep his arms down in his habit to hide the smell of sweat from her delicate nose. In his embarrassment, he rose quickly, taking the seeds and properly dropping them in their holes as if he was burying the journey that he could have gone on with Mary bit by precious bit.

In his agony, he kept letting the seeds fall, while she watched him doing so. Then, getting the gist of what he was doing, Mary skittered over to the end of the line of holes and started from the opposite side.

They bent over, Brother John with a hunched back and Mary with a perfectly straight one. She moved like water and he like mud. Mary made her way up to Brother John much faster and when they met each other, he lost the ability to stand.

Getting down on his knees, awkwardly facing her with nothing that he could possibly say, he just turned to face the holes and started to fill them back up with his hands. He could say nothing to her. His grave had been dug and now he must stand by it. There was no other storyline, no other plot to his life. He was a monk from now until death. He would stay planting new turnips every spring in the same clothes, while Mary finished school, chose her career, married, and had babies, and then she would take care of her children's children. Her life was going to change and evolve so rapidly that no two days would be similar, while Brother John would think of her as he lay in the same bed at night to get up and perform the same chants in the morning.

But this is what he *wanted*. He needed time to discover the Truth, to find himself, to prove himself, to enjoy every little thing that life gave to him—even when it arrived in the softest of whispers. He would be there to learn and grow. None of his days were truly the same when a person could become sensitive enough to the world as he was, and yet, he would always *wonder*.

Brother John would forever wonder about life on the outside, just like with death on the other. Mary was *terrible* for him. He could feel it in the way his heart yearned as it beat. He touched his chest for one moment only to hear: "What's wrong?" from Mary's sweet lips.

"Nothing, nothing," he choked. Only he could feel the knots tightening still. She caused him *so* much pain and such sorrow. In order to regain control, he hid his face in his cowl again and breathed deeply. Closing his eyes for a few seconds, he felt the soil beneath his hands as he patted down the earth that he had become so familiar with.

This is the soil that I am wedded to, thought Brother John. I shall *never* marry a woman. I am a servant of the Lord and a slave to making myself a worthy man of the Good Book. I am to make myself into a wealth of knowledge and a pure seeker of Truth. Life is too short to have family *and* become an enlightened being—that was the *real* tragedy, he thought.

Mary had several holes filled with dirt by the time Brother John reopened his eyes. They finished the task shortly thereafter, and Brother John could stand up again. He grabbed the monastery's hose from nearby and showed her just how much water each seeded spot needed before handing it over to her.

She reached out much too greedily for a monk's taste, but Brother John felt it light a fire in his soul. Her desire was palpable, and it nearly burned him as he handed her the hose.

Mary took it and did just as he showed her—trying to avoid carefully drowning the seeds and rotting them before they even had a chance to grow. Her eyes were wide and bright as she watched the soil magically absorb the water. The soil grew dark and looked as if it shriveled up when the water hit it. Her actions made the very ground she stood on move. Mary held all the power now.

Serving as his Eve, Brother John watched as she gave life to those seeds below. She had the ability to drown them or, by the same token, give them the life-producing water they needed to survive. But the serpent in this story came in the form of a single baptisia plant, poking its head out from the ground.

She noticed the plant growing awfully close to where she was watering, so she avoided the spot completely and looked over at Brother John, asking, "Was this already watered? I don't want to kill it. What is it?"

"It is the plant that bears your last name, Mary. Remember?" Brother John winced with pain at witnessing the two most innocent creatures on earth meeting in front of his sole gaze.

Mary begged him to turn the water off so that she could further inspect her plant. "Oh, I had never seen a baby me before!" she giggled, as his heart bled.

The dam finally broke. Brother John could no longer keep his emotions checked and instead a flood of tears ran down his cheeks.

He remained quiet through his tears until Mary looked up at him. "Oh, what's wrong? Did I say something?" She stood up and backed away a bit.

"No, no. I'm...I'm so sorry, but I can't bear to see you anymore. You...you are too perfect. You belong in a nunnery and not here in a monastery where watching you makes my soul *scream*. I shouldn't be saying anything...I'm sorry. Just please tell me you will never come back to this monastery? For my sake…"

Mary stared at him without comprehending a thing that he said. Blankly blinking, she tried to take hold of his hand since she knew he was probably not allowed to hug a girl, but he pulled away as if she would brand him. He recoiled so far back into his habit that she could barely see him. Brother John appeared like the infamous grim reaper in his hooded habit. For a moment, Mary believed a skeletal hand or head might pop back out of the darkness.

Her lower lip trembled, still fearing that she had done something vulgar in front of the holy man.

"Brother John…," she whispered.

There was no response.

"Brother John, I'm sorry. I did not mean to upset you in any way. Please don't get me in trouble with my parents. They're right over there." She pointed out into the field where her parents were picking weeds together and talking to the other monks.

Brother John sniffled before saying: "You have done absolutely nothing wrong, my child."

Mary began carving circles into the soil with one of her shoes. "Are you really happy here?" she asked.

It shocked Brother John that such a young girl could ask such a profound question. He hesitated for a while until he said: "Yes, I am happy here. I chose this life. It suits me. Here I can discover the Truth and create things to the best of my ability. I can learn as much as I can in a lifetime without delay… But when you are here…I seem to feel an ache that is so overwhelming that I become unhappy."

"I make you unhappy. Why?"

"You are more perfect than I. That's why."

Mary still did not understand the answer, but wanting to appear more mature, she nodded as if she did. Then, "But how can you stay here without feeling stuck or life becoming dull? Do the other monks do as well here?"

"No. Many of the monks are not happy. They think they can survive better here than in the outside world or they are trying to fight themselves and their urges here without burdening others. I would say that very few monks are happy, Mary. But, then again, very few people, in general, are happy. Everyone has a choice to make and many of them are even good choices, but the monastic life is a particularly extreme choice for many people.

"I, myself, believe that the monastic lifestyle suited me best and I enjoy it because it seems to bring me the most happiness out of all the other choices I had open to me. And now, as a man, I have made my choice, and it is a final one. I shall live and die in this monastery."

Mary stood there looking sad when he declared he was mortal in front of her. It seems that she had always imagined that he would be there—working out among the fields, awaiting her whenever she visited. But now she was reminded that people die and that choices will await her one day.

A tear ran down her cheek and Brother John wanted to kiss the tear away, holding her, and pretending that Man could be immortal, but all that he could do at that moment was present her with an amaranth flower from the garden. "This is called an amaranth flower," said Brother John. "It has come to represent immortality and immortal love. You can take this to remember the monastery by, and me, if you would like. But please, Mary, please, I beg you never to return."

Mary took the beautiful flower in her slender hands, still looking hurt. But his smile reassured her of his well-meaning and kind gesture. She gave a slight curtsy and with one last question on her lips, she asked: "Brother John, how do you *really* stay happy in such a place?"

He smiled, deciding to reveal his soul to another person for the first time since entering the monastery: "Mary, I do not believe in god."

THE END

About the Author

Kaitlyn Bankson (born Kaitlyn Marie Quis in New York, January 3, 1994) is an American writer. She studied literature and philosophy throughout her education, which shaped her creative voice. She is the author of the novels *The Paper Pusher* and *The Dormant Age*. Kaitlyn's unique perspective and raw prose bring light to matters that are often left untouched. She lives in Dubuque, Iowa, with her husband. Readers can see more of Kaitlyn's work at www.kaitlynbankson.com.

You can connect with me on:

- https://kaitlynbankson.com
- https://x.com/kaitlynbankson
- https://linkedin.com/in/kaitlynbankson

Subscribe to my newsletter:

- http://eepurl.com/glJhKf

www.ingramcontent.com/pod-product-compliance
Lightning Source LLC
Chambersburg PA
CBHW052040240626
47153CB00006B/2173